# When the Lion Roars

# When the Lion Roars

## DiAnn Mills

**RIVEROAK**®

*Good News in Fiction*

COOK COMMUNICATIONS MINISTRIES
Colorado Springs, Colorado • Paris, Ontario
KINGSWAY COMMUNICATIONS LTD
Eastbourne, England

RiverOak® is an imprint of
Cook Communications Ministries, Colorado Springs, CO 80918
Cook Communications, Paris, Ontario
Kingsway Communications, Eastbourne, England

WHEN THE LION ROARS

This story is a work of fiction. All characters and events are the product of the author's imagination. Any resemblance to any person, living or dead, is coincidental.

**Published in association with the literary agency of Winsun Literary, 3706 NE Shady Lane Dr., Gladstone, MO 64119.**

First Printing, 2005
Printed in the United States of America
1 2 3 4 5 6 7 8 9 10 Printing/Year 09 08 07 06 05

Publisher-owned map by dlp Studios, Colorado

Library of Congress Cataloging-in-Publication Data

Mills, DiAnn.
  When the lion roars / DiAnn Mills.
    p. cm.
  ISBN 1-58919-030-0 (pbk.)
  1. Sudan--History--Civil War, 1983---Fiction. 2. Kidnapping--Fiction. 3. Slavery--Fiction. I. Title.
  PS3613.I567W48 2005
  813'.54--dc22
                2004028301

# Acknowledgments

I would like to thank the many people who made this book possible, those who prayed for me and provided insight into the decades-long civil war in Sudan:

Frank Blackwood, director of Aid Sudan, for his knowledge of and love for the Sudanese; Jack Casey, who "showed" me how to fly a MU2; Abraham Nhial, for revealing his life as a Lost Boy of Sudan and rising victoriously above it; James Okuk Solomon, who shared the tragedy of his murdered family; my critique group, which kept me from straying from the story; Eric Reeves, for his commitment to Sudan; Beau Egert, for his unique perspective on the civil war; Jeff Dunn, my editor at RiverOak who believed in me; Mark Littleton, for his support; and my dear husband, Dean, for his love, prayers, and encouragement.

Most of all, I thank my Savior and Lord Jesus Christ, who gave His life for me—and you.

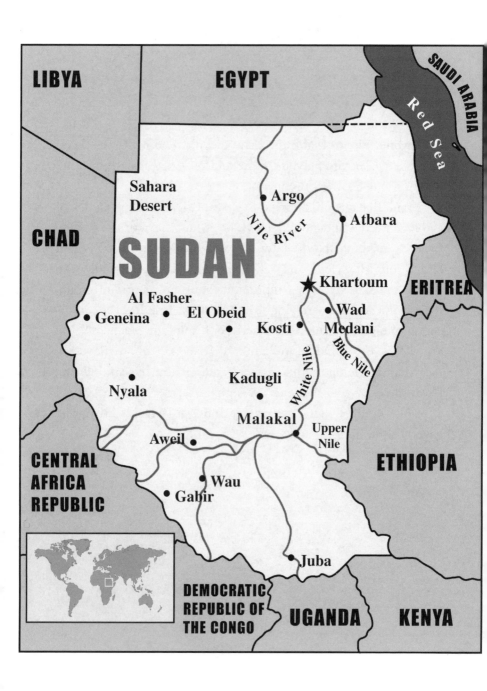

We are hard pressed on every side, but not crushed; perplexed, but not in despair; persecuted, but not abandoned; struck down, but not destroyed.

—2 Corinthians 4:8–9

# 1

Paul Farid drew in a breath and held it, the magnificence of the unfolding springtime terrain filling his senses. Captivated by the lush earth below him, he scanned the area for signs of government soldiers who might have his plane in their sights. He could see for miles across the vast southern Sudan. Herds of gazelle, antelope, and zebra, along with an occasional lion, dotted the plain—some finding shelter from the scorching sun beneath a lone tree while others raced aimlessly about. Birds scattered in a rush of flapping wings, rising above the tall grass into a cloud and soaring gracefully across the sky until they found another spot to roost. A tingling fluttered in Paul's stomach. The sensation greeted him every time he flew over Sudan. The mystery and splendor lured him in, like an intoxicating spell that refused to let him go. He was the intruder, the only one who had not dwelt among the southern Sudanese for centuries.

Paul did not intend to lose his Mitsubishi MU2—a twin-engine, turboprop aircraft, the missionary cream of the crop—to any Muslim bent on destroying or confiscating food and medical supplies targeted for the needy civilians. Sometimes Feed the

World (FTW) had Khartoum's permission to deliver provisions to the starving masses caught in the civil war strife, but not today. Despite the danger, Paul brought aid to the village of Warkou in the province of Bahr Al Ghazal, district of Aweil. It lay along the Lol River in a setting so breathtaking that it rivaled man's thoughts of paradise. He had committed to help those affected by the government's genocide in this beautiful but turbulent land.

The countryside looked peaceful, serene, as though untouched by the forces that could erupt at any moment into an explosion of violence and mayhem aimed at the innocent. Not far to the east, the White Nile snaked through Sudan. Some called the river the lifeblood of the country; others claimed the waterway as the entrance to Eden. To the inhabitants, it served as a symbol of hope.

Just to the west of the plane a worn path would serve as Paul's landing strip. A few cows and goats ambled in the middle until the jet-sounding engine seized their attention. At the sound of the aircraft's high-pitched screams, the animals scrambled.

Paul focused his attention beyond the makeshift landing strip and noted the grass huts of Warkou, which means "bend of the river." There he planned to deliver the much-needed supplies. Paul peered closer to view the several craters below. How many had been killed or wounded in the latest bombing? Not a single person roamed beneath him. When the distinct hum of a plane alerted the villagers, they ran for bomb shelters. He did not blame them. They had learned to keep their mouths open so as not to damage their ears from the concussion of the bombs and to run for shelter when the bombing and shooting started, but many still became casualties. Nothing saved their churches, schools, and medical clinics. The bombs were crude—metal drums filled with explosives and metal—designed to inflict maximum death and destruction.

With the area cleared before him, Paul put down the flaps to add to the wing area and cruised over the rough landing strip. He studied the area in all directions for debris and ruts along the dirt path, taking special note of blowing dust to calculate the direction of the wind. He laughed at three cows headed in different directions from the incoming plane. In the following moments, he circled the area and repeated his inspection.

Certain of flying into the wind, he snatched up his landing checklist with his left hand and gripped the control wheel. With both feet on the rudders, Paul used his right hand to quickly maneuver across the cockpit and flip switches and levers in a steady, organized flow. Once completed, he ran through the checklist, then replaced it in a tight, upper-left-hand corner until needed again. No matter how experienced the pilot, one little mistake could make the difference between a safe landing and tragedy.

"Here we go." Adrenaline raced through Paul's veins. He loved flying, but he loved his mission and the God who had called him to serve the southern Sudanese more. The cost did not matter, only the purpose.

At the beginning of the runway, he placed the landing gear switch in the down position. The speed of his plane decreased and created tremendous wind noise inside the aircraft. He lowered the airspeed to 130 knots, then down to 110, using the precision necessary for a smooth, safe landing. When the wheels touched down, dirt and dust flew everywhere, alerting the countryside of his presence. If the Government of Sudan (GOS) soldiers were in the area, they now had no doubt of his location.

Once the engine ceased its earsplitting hum, Paul double-checked his procedures before climbing from the cockpit and taking shelter under one of the wings. He wiped his forehead, already beaded with sweat.

"Hello," he called to the still unseen villagers. He knew they understood Arabic. "I have food and medical supplies from Feed the World." His gaze swept over every hut and tree in the area, knowing that those who hid among them heard every word but were afraid to show their faces. He would be fearful too. "I need to speak to Dr. Larson Kerr."

From behind a hut an elderly man appeared, then three more men and two women. Slowly more people crept forward with mothers and children lagging behind.

"Greetings from Feed the World." He waved, grinning. "Is Dr. Kerr available?"

"Yes, I'm here." A woman stepped from the group. Shorter than the towering Dinkas, her ruddy complexion and thick mass of sandy-colored hair, worn in a ponytail, immediately set her apart from the ebony-skinned, dark-haired villagers native to this land.

*Larson Kerr is a woman?*

He had heard tales about the doctor's tenacious ability to work incredibly long hours and travel to remote areas in the name of healing. Dr. Kerr also ventured into the oil-rich regions to aid the injured and help the victims reach safety. He had skimmed documentaries of how the doctor was the first to climb from the bomb shelters to seek out the wounded. The words flooded his memory. Peering into her impassive face, respect and admiration sealed his thoughts.

She walked toward him in long, purposeful strides. In the States he would have been amused at her pace, but not here. Here he understood what motivated her. She moved toward him, dressed in khaki shorts, a faded T-shirt with the logo of Ohio State, and hiking boots. Her callused hand reached to grab his.

"Paul Farid?" she asked in an American accent. "You have the supplies?" Her striking blue eyes bore into his. They were not the least bit friendly—instead, suspicious, challenging.

"Yes." He had seen and felt the animosity before. In this part of Sudan, his Arab nationality and surname labeled him the enemy before he opened his mouth.

"You're an American?"

He nodded.

"Then you speak English?"

"Yes," he replied in the requested language. He experienced a mixture of awe and curiosity about the noted Dr. Kerr.

"Your accent is heavy," she remarked. One of the children, a small, naked boy, crept closer and wrapped his arms around her leg. "Move back, Mangok," Her gentle tone reverted to the language Paul believed to be Dinka. The child slipped into the small crowd, and a young girl lifted him onto her hip.

"I'm a naturalized citizen." Paul breathed friendship into every word.

"Many Arabs are American citizens."

He clenched his fist. Since September 11 and the free world's war on terrorism, he had met a stream of hostility everywhere he went. "Do you want to see my résumé?"

"I might." A thin-lipped smile was pasted on her face.

He bit back a remark. "While you contact Feed the World for my personal credentials, I'd like to get these supplies unloaded."

"Of course." She turned to those behind her and motioned for them to join her. "What do we have?"

"A few thousand pounds of grain and medical supplies."

She focused on him for a moment as though attempting to read deceit. "Thank you."

Paul set out to make small talk about the heat, the cloudless sky, and the villagers, but Dr. Kerr chose not to reply. He stopped the questioning and idle remarks. Whirling around, he opened the plane's hatch to where packed grain lay inside several large bags. They were tied to wooden pallets in case the village did not have a cleared landing path or the GOS threatened the pilot's safety. If not for the precious medicine, he would have released the load from the air, and the bags and wooden pallets would have separated once they hit the ground. The people wasted nothing. The villagers would have snatched up the pieces of wood to construct furniture and the packing straps for whatever purpose the finders deemed fit. Even the cloth bags would be sewn into clothing or stretched over poles for shelter.

The sound of shouting women stole Paul's attention. Two women who wanted the same bag of grain tugged with one hand and slugged with the other.

"There's enough." Dr. Kerr stepped between the women and nearly took a blow to the chin. She yanked on the bag. The struggle ceased. Larson Kerr could definitely hold her own.

Paul had seen this type of interference before. A woman needing food for her family was a formidable opponent. He couldn't blame them; they were most likely mothers who only wanted their children to survive. The villagers' emaciated bodies needed more than grain for proper nourishment, but this food offered the difference between life and death.

Once the last bag of grain was dragged away, Dr. Kerr lingered with a young woman and a tall boy as Paul unloaded the medical supplies.

Dr. Kerr scooped up a box of sterile gauze squares and gauze wraps. "I really need these," she said. "I've been using my old shirts as bandages." She peered into the storage compartment. "Look, Rachel, antibiotics to treat malaria." She laughed. "And lidocaine. And sutures. And plenty of Betadine!"

The tall, thin young woman smiled and held out her arms for a box. "God has blessed us."

Paul handed Rachel a case of sterile gloves and took a glimpse at her. "Indeed He has," he said.

She couldn't be much more than sixteen: high cheekbones, flawless skin, and huge eyes. She would no doubt bring a high bride-price to her family.

"You're Christian?" Rachel asked. "I didn't expect …"

Paul waved away her anxiety with his free hand. "I understand your reservations, but I do serve Jesus Christ."

"I will pray for your dangerous missions," Rachel said. She stood erect, determined.

"Thank you. I'm always in need of prayer."

The boy stepped forward, his arms outstretched. "I want a heavy one."

"Oh, you do?" Paul chuckled. "What's your name?"

"Nyok, and I'm twelve."

Paul saw the v-shaped lines etched across his forehead. The boy had gone through the rites of manhood. "And I see you're a warrior."

Nyok thrust back his shoulders, accenting his nearly six-foot height. "I protect Dr. Kerr."

"I'm sure you do a fine job." Paul doubted if the doctor needed much protection, but he knew well the boy's role. From the looks of Warkou, there were not many cattle for Nyok to tend—a shame for a culture that had revered its cows for hundreds of years. He piled two heavy boxes on Nyok's muscular arms.

Paul gathered up two cases containing prescription medicine and headed after the small troop. Dr. Kerr turned around. "You stay here. I don't want those supplies disappearing."

"All right." He glanced about him and saw no one, but that didn't mean a thief didn't lurk nearby. "One more load will do it." He grabbed a bottle of water from inside the cockpit and again waited beneath the wing. The temperature felt around 43 degrees Celsius—almost 110 degrees Fahrenheit—noticeably hotter in the sun. It matched the upheaval in the area and in Paul himself.

Men in camouflage carrying Kalashnikov rifles suddenly captured his attention. *Guerilla soldiers.* Their Russian-purchased weapons made him inwardly squirm. He hadn't heard a shot fired or the sound of resistance. Paul carried a handgun inside the plane, but it was useless against these weapons. Although the soldiers fought for the south, they didn't always have the best interests of the civilians in mind—at least in Paul's opinion.

A few moments later, Rachel and Nyok hurried back. Paul filled their arms with the remaining boxes and pulled the last two into his own. "Why are the soldiers here?" he asked Nyok.

"They're watching you," the boy replied. "They don't trust anybody."

*Least of all an Arab.* Fortunately, he had all of his papers with him, and they could peruse his flawless record. He had nothing to hide.

He trailed behind Rachel and Nyok. This wouldn't be the first time he had been the object of debate, and he certainly didn't want to risk the lives of the two young people in front of him.

"You there, stop," a soldier said in Arabic. "We want to see your papers." He raised his rifle and pointed it at Paul's chest.

"Some are inside my shirt, and the rest are in the plane. Can I put down these boxes?"

The soldier nodded, but his weapon didn't sway.

"Rachel, Nyok, take your load on to Dr. Kerr," Paul said. He lowered the two boxes to the ground, making sure none of the contents would break. Holding out both hands, he turned his attention to the soldier.

"Go ahead, take them from me."

The soldier reached inside Paul's buttoned shirt and pulled out the papers. He scanned them before calling for another soldier to take the FTW verification to their colonel. Paul wondered if the man read English. Meanwhile, he waited once more in the torrid sun with sweat streaming down his face and neck and a familiar churning in his stomach. The longer he lingered, the more frustration at the situation ate at his heart.

"He's all right." Another soldier strode toward Paul, his Arabic rough. "Colonel Alier wants to talk to him."

Paul inwardly sighed. Colonel Ben Alier of the Sudanese People's Liberation Army (SPLA) had a reputation for his clever tactics, courage, and ruthlessness. His guerilla soldiers offered him undeniable allegiance. Under otherwise more pleasant conditions, Paul might have welcomed an opportunity to speak with the rebel leader. Plenty of media sources in the States clamored for such interviews. The SPLA had interrogated Paul a few times, and none of them had been enjoyable. The forces held a common distrust and accused him of spying. He would probably do the same, if his people had been persecuted by the Islamic-controlled government. How did the SPLA successfully manage the southern war front when it refused to recognize Paul's name and the humanitarian organization that fed and administered medical aid to the suffering civilians? Of course, who could be trusted when the different rebel factions warred against each other while fighting the GOS?

"Move ahead," the soldier said, sticking the rifle in Paul's ribs.

"Can I take these supplies?"

"If you hurry."

Paul had no idea where he was going, but he plodded ahead in the direction he had seen Dr. Kerr, Rachel, and Nyok venture. A circling of soldiers appeared to have the villagers a bit tense. They spoke in Dinka, and Paul didn't understand the dialect. He could only surmise the meaning of the conversations from the rise and fall of the voices and the facial expressions of those speaking. From Paul's observation, the soldiers seemed more intimidating than hostile.

"To the right," said the soldier behind him, and Paul picked up his pace toward a far hut.

Dr. Kerr stood outside a dwelling that must have served as a clinic. Some of the bags of grain were stacked outside the door along with the medical supplies. Nyok was at her side like a sentinel, and a soldier had his arm around Rachel. The young woman smiled, and the soldier planted a kiss on her forehead. Suspicions mounted in Paul's mind at the gray woven through the soldier's hair. He looked old enough to be her father. He had to be Colonel Ben Alier.

"Ah, Paul Farid," the man said, releasing his hold on Rachel. A wide smile prefaced his words. "I've heard much about you."

*From information inside Khartoum?* "I've flown several missions throughout Sudan."

"Yes, and you are noted for your food drops in dangerous areas—Nubia one of them." The smile did not leave his face while he extended his hand. "Ben Alier."

Paul responded and noted the firm handshake. "It's a pleasure, sir."

"Your planes have never been shot down." The colonel stuck his thumbs inside his belt loop. "How lucky you are when others face enemy fire constantly."

"For the record, I have been fired on and nearly lost a plane. God is with me."

"Not Allah, I presume." Alier's tone deadened, the pleasantness erased.

"I am a Christian, Colonel, and I believe you are too."

"Rare for an Arab to follow Christianity, don't you think?"

Paul refused to cower to the man. "There are many Arab Christians in this world."

"Wealthy ones?"

"Sir, I don't believe our Lord chose only the poor to follow Him. Those who have monetary means to aid the less fortunate are a blessing to those they serve."

Alier chuckled. "I've been told as much. Would you like to contribute to the SPLA's cause? We are in need of food, tents, weapons, uniforms, medical supplies. The list is endless."

"My ministry is to the civilians suffering in this war. I'm sure there are others who would consider financing your army's equipment."

"But not you?"

"No, sir." Paul stared into the colonel's eyes. He would not waver from his cause or his purpose.

"Most men are afraid of me, Mr. Farid. And you are not?" Alier paused. A wry grin met Paul's gaze. "Do you know the power I have? I could have you killed on the spot, tortured for suspected spying."

"I am very well aware of your capabilities."

Alier studied him a moment longer. A hush had crept over the village. He sensed the villagers and soldiers were captivated by the friction between the two men. "Give me one reason not to kill you."

Paul nodded slowly. He felt an amazing peace, a sense of calm that flowed through his veins, warm and comforting. "If you kill me, then thousands of people will not receive the benefit of the food and provisions my money buys. They'll still get the aid of the many humanitarian organizations dedicated to Sudan, but their assistance is not enough, and you know it. If you kill me, how many Sudanese villages will harbor your men knowing you destroyed their chance for survival?"

Alier's eyes narrowed. He clenched his fists and swallowed hard. "I asked for a reason, and you gave it to me. For now, you live. But I don't trust you. I'll be watching for you to make a mistake."

"I don't doubt your words, Colonel." Paul forced a smile. "Now, may I take my plane and fly out of here?"

"I won't delay you a moment longer."

Paul turned to Dr. Kerr. He had felt her scrutiny during the interrogation. Curiosity was evident on her face, that and a mixture of something else he couldn't quite discern.

"Thank you, Mr. Farid. I am most grateful for the provisions and your willingness to deliver them."

The lines around her eyes softened, and for the first time he saw her beauty. Even there, in the wilds of Africa, without the aid of those things women use to make themselves more attractive, she was a rarity.

"Good luck to you." Dr. Kerr crossed her arms over her chest.

"May God bless your work here." Paul turned and walked toward his plane. He had no doubt Colonel Ben Alier would have enjoyed nothing better than to blow a hole right through him. Sometimes when Paul contemplated his vile past, he wished someone would put him out of his living nightmare.

A small gathering of children played around his plane, most likely inquisitive as to how the flying machine worked, if they had ever seen one up close at all. Any other time, he would have played with them. Since most of his work was from the air, Paul seldom received an opportunity to mingle with the villagers.

"I have to leave," he said to the children and hoped they were old enough to understand Arabic. "Make way for me. Perhaps we'll play another day."

The children scattered; their laughter gave him the lift he needed. He opened the door and spied a small, fragile container meant for Dr. Kerr. The item, a wound staple gun, had been an afterthought from a medical adviser for FTW. *Alier may have the opportunity to shoot me after all.* Snatching up the box, Paul retraced his steps to the clinic where the rebel leader and Dr. Kerr stood talking.

"Put the bag down," Dr. Kerr said.

Paul glanced to the side of him where the doctor faced Alier. The colonel had hoisted a bag of grain to his shoulder.

"My men need the grain. You can contact Farid for more."

"I said put it down, Ben." Anger rose in Dr. Kerr's voice, not loud but emphatic. "These people are starving."

Alier laughed. "What can you do, Larson? And how can my men defend them if they are hungry? It's not as if we can put down our weapons and plant a garden."

Dr. Kerr stepped inside her hut while the colonel continued to laugh. Before Paul had an opportunity to tell her about the additional box, she pushed back through, rifle first.

"So help me, I'll blow your head off before I let you take that grain."

# 2

*L*arson Kerr aimed the rifle at Colonel Ben Alier's chest, just above the left pocket underlining his heart. She trembled, not from fear but from fury. Her villagers needed the grain to survive—the bag he so easily lifted to his shoulders. No one would take it from them. All of her people bordered on malnutrition; many were near perishing. Pregnant and lactating mothers needed proper nourishment, and the children ... well, she would gladly give her life—or take Ben's—for one of those precious little ones.

"Larson, Larson, what is one bag of grain?" Ben said.

His singsong teasing moved her finger within a hair span of the trigger. "Don't push me. My finger is itching to let you have it."

"Now you sound like a character from some bad movie." Ben chuckled—his irritating, sarcastic, obnoxious laugh that made her even more furious. "You know you aren't going to do a thing. Besides, if you shoot me, then you'll have to patch me up."

"Not if you're dead. Then all I'll have to do is roll you into the nearest crater and pile on the dirt." Larson meant every word.

Ever since she had met the man seven years ago, he had strutted his arrogance in her face. He had tried to bully her, and when that didn't work, he had intimidated the villagers. This time would be the last.

"What about your oath to preserve life?" Ben raised a brow.

"I'm a doctor, not a vet," she said. "I mean what I say. You're not taking the food intended for my people." From the corner of her eye, she saw Paul Farid. *I thought he'd left.* The man hadn't said a word, just stood there with his mouth agape. With his small features, he looked like a boy. Where was a real man when she needed one? Nyok would be of more help than this so-called brave pilot.

Nyok stepped beside her. "Dr. Kerr, this is dangerous. You could be hurt. Why not let Colonel Alier take the grain?"

"Because it's not his." Larson refused to cast aside the weapon. "And he's a thief."

"Put down the gun," Ben said. "I have things to do."

"Not until you leave the bag."

"Dr. Kerr—" Rachel began.

"Stay out of this. I know he's your brother, but remember that when your stomach's empty or when a child begs you for food."

Larson steadied her attention on Ben's face. Rachel always took Ben's position, no matter what her power-hungry brother did. She loved him regardless—and there were a lot of unlovable things about this guy.

"All right." Ben pressed his lips into a thin line. "I'll get it later." He dropped the grain with a thud.

"Thank you," Larson said. "Farid's still here. Talk to him about getting your supplies." Her muscles relaxed. For a moment she had thought she would have to back up her threat, but Ben knew he had angered her beyond reason. Slowly she lowered the rifle. She had never used one on a human and really didn't intend to do so now unless Ben goaded her.

"Sometimes you push the limits of our friendship." Ben pushed back his cap and wiped the sweat with the back of his hand. "You know one of the villagers will give me their grain."

"Not while I'm looking." Larson swallowed down a dry throat. "And as far as the friendship goes, friends don't steal from friends."

He leaned on one leg and paused. She recognized his stubborn, know-it-all stance.

"Wouldn't you steal from me if the villagers needed something I had?" he asked.

Larson moistened her lips. Once again he had got the last word. "My people don't spend their energies killing innocent civilians."

Ben blinked. "We're fighting to stop genocide, Larson. We're fighting so the southern Sudanese can govern themselves without Khartoum's Islamic mandates." His voice grew louder. "We're fighting so the south can utilize its own oil and not have the government's profits used against us. And we're fighting so *your* villagers can once more grow their own grain and not have to worry about land mines!"

The still air thundered.

Larson knew that the circumstances surrounding southern Sudan were true. It was the SPLA's methods that she criticized, the often selfish motives behind Ben's and too many other southern rebels' self-proclaimed martyrdom. The reminder made her weary, for there were no easy solutions or pat answers, just problems upon problems.

"I know a source of provisions that could provide supplies," Paul said.

Ben's attention whipped to the pilot. "What are you still doing here?"

Paul held out a box. "I left this in the plane. It's for Dr. Kerr." He set the wound staple gun down next to the hut's entrance.

"You two will not settle Sudan's problems this afternoon."

"Shut up," Larson said. "No one asked for your opinion." Instantly she regretted her crass remark, aimed toward the man who had flown over hostile territory to bring food and supplies. She had hardened in this African sun, just as she had vowed would never happen. "Look, I'm sorry. I do appreciate everything you've done."

"No problem." Paul held up his palms. "I shouldn't have interfered. Looks like both of you are capable of taking care of yourselves." He glanced about him. "I'll be going."

Larson watched Paul walk away, his shoulders erect as though he were part of a military brigade. A glance at Nyok revealed the boy's longing.

"Go ahead and take another look at his plane," she said to the boy.

"I need to stay here with you."

"Nonsense. Ben and I are finished with our discussion. Run along, and take Rachel with you. It may be a long time before either of you sees another aircraft this close."

Nyok hesitated. "Only if you are sure."

"I am." Larson forced herself to laugh. Such a serious protector she had. Rachel grabbed Nyok's arm, and off they ran.

Paul turned to greet Nyok and Rachel. Strange, an Arab-born American flying dangerous missions over Sudan for a Christian organization. Ben must know a good bit about him. Larson decided she would ask him about Paul later, after the two of them had cooled down.

"Don't you have things to do?" she asked. Ben's penetrating gaze unnerved her. "I have patients to see, and they won't come near the clinic as long as you're here."

He scowled. "You need to respect me and my position." In the heat of the late morning, his black skin fairly glistened.

She glanced at the weapon in her hand and carefully formed

her words. He would take out his anger on someone else if she didn't make a move toward making amends. "I do respect you, and I do value your protection." His sable gaze bore into hers. "But I love these people, and they will always come first. I'd do anything for them ... anything."

The lines in his face softened. "I understand, Larson. We are much alike, which is why we put up with each other."

Larson took the rifle back inside the hut and paused while her vision adjusted to the shadows. Seven years ago, she wouldn't have considered pulling the trigger for a statement like Ben just made, but now she knew his words were true. Too many sickened people, too many starving children, and too many mutilated and tortured bodies had calloused her toward polite, canned responses. What would people like herself and Ben do without a cause?

Ben Alier had honestly earned his reputation as one of the most valuable leaders of the SPLA. He and his men were often involved in actions that critics slapped across the newspapers, but most guerilla armies fell under worldwide scrutiny. Ben fought with one purpose in mind: to free the southern Sudanese from a Muslim government that murdered those who refused the mandates of the *sharia*, the code of law based on Islamic tradition.

Unfortunately, Ben had put together his own law of ethics, and he had set himself up as prosecutor, judge, and executor. Earlier, Paul Farid had almost tasted the colonel's wrath. If not for his mission of mercy, the pilot would be lying in a pool of blood.

Tossing aside her deliberations, Larson sorted through the medicinal supplies. Relief lifted her spirits. Scores of the ill would now have hope. She selected a few of the bottles and stored them inside a small, generator-powered refrigerator, her only vestige of civilization. Pulling out a key chain from her pocket, she locked up the remainder before her patients lined up for care.

On the outside, her *tukul*—hut—looked like all the others,

except that she had asked for an exhaust hole at the top. Without ventilation, all the cooking odors, medicinal smells, and the spicy aroma of accumulated bodies created an unpleasant environment. In other huts, the only source of light and air came from a small door. Animals roamed in and out freely, and combined with their manure and other odors, the air inside soon grew rank.

Larson saw the doorway darken and knew that Ben had followed her inside. Exasperated, she wanted to pick up something and throw it at him. At the moment, utter silence seemed to be her best defense, but she doubted if she could hold her tongue for very long.

"Why are you so angry?" His tone clearly depicted his frustration.

Larson hesitated. She had patients to see. "I think that's obvious."

"It's more than the grain. What's bothering you?"

She expelled a heavy sigh and whirled around to face him. In the dim hut, he appeared larger, more ominous than in the open. "I heard a rumor."

"And what this time?"

"That you shot two men from a village west of here for no apparent reason."

"They were suspected spies, and I don't have to explain my military procedures to you."

She saw his clenched fists and realized she had probably pushed him to his limit, again. At the moment, she didn't care; reason didn't overrule her anger. "Suspected! For heaven's sake, they had families."

"Do I tell you how to practice medicine?"

"No, but you try to tell me who should get treatment, and I'm telling you that I'm not patching up your ragtag men if you're going to kill innocent citizens. Makes me wonder who are the real enemies." She rammed her finger into his chest.

"Woman, when you walk in my shoes, then you can tell me how best to win this war."

"Is that what the professors taught you in the States?"

Before Ben had an opportunity to speak, the distinct hum of engines alerted them to enemy aircraft. Larson turned and flung open the refrigerator door. She grabbed as many valuable medicines as she could and dumped them into an empty box. Her mind sped with what to snatch up next before she raced to the shelter. The clinic wasn't marked, which meant her hut had a chance to survive the bombing. The engines grew closer. She had heard Ben leave without a word. He had his agenda, and she had hers.

Normally Rachel and Nyok would be right beside her. Surely Ben had pulled them from the plane and shoved them toward a shelter.

Larson filled a huge basket with dressings and whatever else she could put her hands on in a frantic attempt to save every priceless item from the shipment. Engines roared above her. *No casualties. Please, no casualties.* She cringed at a bomb's whistle and explosion; a moment later screams pierced the air. Visions of other bombings played across her weary mind. The innocent were always killed and maimed. Another bomb fell, then another. She would never make it to a shelter now. Plopping down in the middle of her hut, she protected her treasures with her body.

Another sound whipped around her ears. The whirling of helicopter gunships. She had seen them too many times. Snipers leaned from their choppers and picked off civilians with their machine guns. The soldiers laughed as they shot men, women, and children scurrying to safety. The practice became a vicious game.

Helicopters like these also brought another fear. The soldiers often landed and chased down women and children for slaves. Not if Ben had a say in it. She wondered if the GOS knew the SPLA was there. No matter, the southern rebels would give Khartoum's finest a beating. For the first time today, she was grateful for the camouflaged men firing shot after shot in retaliation.

Her mind drifted back to the reason she stayed in southern Sudan. At the moment it made no sense. In the beginning she had thought her presence in this third-world country would make a difference, especially after the mistake she had made. Now she no longer deliberated the matter. Each time she thought the situation could grow no worse, it did.

Her attention shifted to the hut opening. She saw the gray swirl of smoke and felt the earth beneath her quiver. One of Ben's men raced across an open stretch, firing as he ran. Could the enemy be that close? She would never get used to this, never. If not for sheltering the medicine and bandages, she would have covered her ears. Her focus captured the rifle leaning against the hut wall. A dead doctor couldn't take care of anyone. She loosened her hold on the treasured supplies and wrapped her fingers around the weapon, drawing it into her arms. She had never wanted to kill anyone before—a hyena once—but for the sake of her beloved villagers she would blow a GOS soldier into the next world.

No sooner had she secured the rifle and rested her finger on the trigger than a representative of the demon world stepped inside. The soldier lifted his weapon. He looked to be only a bit older than Nyok. His victorious smirk provided ample time for her to send a bullet through his chest before the soldier could send a bullet through hers. He fell backward, the river of life flowing from his body.

Ben's words echoed. *When you walk in my shoes, then you can tell me how best to win this war.*

Sickened by the sight, not that she hadn't seen her share of blood-soaked flesh, she shuddered at the realization of taking a life.

"Larson."

She glanced up to see Ben in the doorway. "Are you all right?"

She nodded. Their gazes met, and in those dark pools she saw understanding and compassion.

"We have them on the run." He pointed to the body. "I'll be back to remove this. Stay inside until I give the shout."

Larson silently refused to obey him, and she knew Ben didn't really expect her to. The moment the shots ceased, she would be looking for those who hadn't escaped the bombs and bullets. She averted her attention from the dead man and realized that her grip on the rifle had turned her knuckles white. She laid the weapon aside and grabbed another basket to gather up the supplies she would need for treating the wounded.

She anticipated Rachel joining her first, and together they would work quickly. Larson adored the young woman. She quickly caught on to Larson's instructions and didn't have a squeamish stomach. Ben had brought her to Warkou five years ago when their parents had been killed in a village raid. He had neither the time nor the patience to care for his sister. Since then, Larson had taken Rachel into her heart and mind, teaching the young woman all she could about medicine and loving her as fiercely as if she had been Larson's own flesh.

Rachel held one flaw: religion. She believed in God and refused to consider any other answer to the ways and purposes of man. Larson had no use for such weakness. She believed in science and the use of modern technology. Anything else was speculation. If a God truly existed, then why did He allow this continual genocide among a people content to live their lives as their ancestors?

Larson hadn't heard a rifle crack for the past few seconds. Securing her basket, she stepped into the sunlight to view the damage. If given the sentiments of most women, she would have cried at the carnage. A man lying face down to the left of her hut didn't move. She knew his family well. She had delivered all four of his children ... two boys, two girls. How would his woman get along without her husband? Worse yet, how would his children fare in the plight of so many other Sudanese children?

Larson often wished she hadn't formed bonds with the villagers, but they had become her friends, her family. She hoped most had escaped the bombings and shootings. Once Rachel surfaced from the shelter, she would report on the casualties. The two had a system whenever they entered the aftermath of a war zone. Rachel checked the vitals, and Larson worked on the wounded. Nyok assisted by handing Larson dressings and instruments. The boy had been with her four years—another war orphan. It hadn't taken long for her to draw the boy into her motherly instincts. She had taught him to read English and instructed him in every aspect of learning.

The villagers emerged from the bomb shelters. Neither Rachel nor Nyok was among them. Fear raced through Larson's body. She remembered Rachel and Nyok had followed Paul Farid back to his plane before the bombing. *The plane was in the open.* Larson stood and straightened. Her mind screamed for signs of the slender beauty and her boy-warrior. She left her medical basket beside the dead man and ran to the landing strip. "Rachel. Nyok." The sound of her voice struck terror to her heart. "Rachel. Nyok."

Up ahead she saw the plane riddled with bullets. No bodies lay nearby. They had to be safe. They simply had to be. Larson stopped and whirled completely around, trying to find the two young people she loved the most.

From somewhere in the village, Ben raced to her side. "I heard you call for Rachel and Nyok. Where are they?"

"I'm ... I'm not sure. They were with the pilot." She stared into his face, hoping to find reassurance.

Ben called to two of his men. "Have you seen my sister and the boy? The pilot?"

One man pointed to the right, beyond a clump of huts. There, Nyok clung to Paul's arm draped over the boy's shoulder. Blood oozed down the pilot's left thigh, stark red against his khaki pants. Larson couldn't get to them fast enough. She froze at the sight of Nyok. Panic registered across his young features.

"What is it?" Larson asked. Every nerve tensed at the sight. "Are there more wounded at the hut? Are you hurt? Wasn't Rachel with you?" The words fell from Larson's lips, while her eyes raked the boy for signs of injury.

Ben reached for Farid, relieving the boy of the burden "Where is Rachel?"

The boy shook his head, barely able to speak.

The pilot lifted his face. He had been hit by a blunt object, for already his eye and cheek were swollen and darkening. "Rachel," he said through a ragged breath. "I tried to stop them, but they took her."

# 3

Alarm rang through Ben's mind. *Not Rachel.* Not his beautiful little sister. The atrocities done to women slaves assaulted his thoughts. Savage beatings, brutal rapes, denial of food and water, forced labor, unwanted children fathered by Arab owners. So many horrible circumstances, and he ached thinking about it.

"No." He allowed Farid's body to drop to the ground. The mere idea of aiding an Arab—even a member of FTW—repulsed him, especially one who had once been a part of the Khartoum government, the ones who advocated the inhumane treatment of his people.

Fury raced through his veins. He knelt and grabbed Farid's throat. "You did this. Where did they take her? I'll kill you. I'll kill you with my bare hands."

"I had no part in those soldiers' activities," Farid said through a labored breath. "I'm their enemy too."

Ben tightened his hold around the wounded man's throat. Farid could no longer talk, his face a mass of blue, his lips purple.

Nyok attempted to pry Ben's hands from Farid. "He tried to stop them, Colonel. That's why he's shot." The boy's action only incited Ben more, and he shoved Nyok backward. "Get out of my way before you get hurt."

"Stop it." Larson pulled on Ben's arms. "This isn't his fault. Look at him, Ben. He was shot trying to help Rachel. Killing him won't bring her back."

Ben didn't care what Larson said. His sister had been abducted by the GOS, and he had a representative of them in his grasp. He elbowed Larson and heard her cry out. She lunged at him, tugging on his shoulders and shouting like a wild animal.

"Listen to me. Stop this now. Talk to your men. Make contact with the slave traders, but don't kill this man. It won't solve a thing." She hammered her fists into his back, screaming for him to come to his senses. This time, he whirled around and with his fingers still wrapped around Farid's throat, he slammed his shoulder into her body and sent her sprawling backward onto the hard ground. When he lifted a hand to strike her, the fear in her eyes stopped him cold.

*What have I done?* With his breath in short spurts, Ben lowered his hand and loosened his fingers from around Farid's throat. A moment more, and the pilot would have been dead. Ben scooted back on his heels and stood. This wouldn't be the first time he had killed a man in anger. Although he detested his volatile temper, sometimes in the heat of battle the extra adrenaline spurred him on. This wasn't a battle or a reason to kill a man in front of Larson, but he wanted to do so. His fingers itched to end the Arab's life.

"Step away, Ben. Let me tend to him," Larson said, and he obeyed.

Staring up at the sky, his gaze followed the direction of the aircrafts' departure: northeast. The farther they went, the less the likelihood of having his sister returned.

*Rachel, don't tell anyone who you are.*

He tore off his cap and threw it to the ground, grief weaving a path through his body. Rachel's last words to him now pierced his soul. *Ben, I'm praying for you. I know God is looking to do a mighty work in you, my brother. He's going to bring peace to Sudan and peace to your heart.*

Curses against God fell from his lips and echoed around him. How could God have done this to an innocent girl? She loved Him, served Him, and this was her reward? Rachel's huge eyes and innocent face pierced his heart. So naïve. So unaware of what evil men could really do. His Rachel....

Forcing himself to gain control and to think rationally, Ben took two long breaths. He glanced behind him at his men, the bombed village, and the fallen civilians and soldiers. All required his attention. He had to force himself to handle his present responsibilities before seeking out help for Rachel. He focused on Larson, who had immobilized the pilot. She and Nyok dragged and carried him back to the clinic.

Suddenly, Ben heard the wails of those who had lost loved ones and the cries of the injured. He had been too absorbed in his own distress to notice anyone else. Three of his men were hunkered over a fallen soldier. It worried him. The thrill of war soon lost its appeal when his men's blood soaked the ground.

He motioned to a pair of soldiers. "Take the wounded to Dr. Kerr, and get me a list of the casualties."

The two responded and left him alone to his tormented world. As he walked, thoughts of Rachel consumed him. He should have arranged schooling for her in the States long before this. Ben had obtained his education there, and Rachel could have studied anything she wanted. Truthfully, he wanted his last living family member near him. He knew Larson cared about her and looked after her in his absence. Love and laughter walked with her. Everyone loved Rachel.

The danger had crossed his mind on occasion, but he had always thought Rachel had some natural immunity to the horrors of war. How stupid he had been. Now he doubted whether she would make it to the final destination without facing rape by the government soldiers. Hadn't he known about the same things being done by his own men? Hadn't he closed his eyes and ears, knowing they had taken advantage of some young girl when he should have intervened? He was their leader. What kind of an example had he set for those who looked up to him? Although the SPLA had never had any rules of proper military conduct, the leaders had an obligation to represent a moral army, an obligation they had failed repeatedly. Now it was payback time.

Ben smacked his fist into his palm. In the beginning, being a SPLA leader had challenged his mind and spirit. He hated the GOS and its oppressive regime. This warfare against the oppressors had seemed to be the answer to his restless, rebel mind, and he had quickly risen to champion the rights of the southern people. Since Sudan had gained its independence in 1956, internal conflict had escalated, and two civil wars had not produced a way to negotiate the problems between the north and south. Every day the death toll rose, and the list of wounded grew. Ben turned toward the village. He was tired of fighting and dealing with all the aspects of the war: religion, politics, and oil. Each one wove into the web of the other, and for the Muslims, all three called for the blood of the "infidels," the innocent southern Sudanese.

*Dirty, Arab Muslims, death to them all. Farid included.*

"Sir," said a soldier.

Ben shook his thoughts.

"James has been injured."

Ben's pulse quickened, and he searched the soldier's face. "How bad? Where is he?"

The man moistened his lips.

"Tell me, soldier." His voice rose.

"He's unconscious. Dr. Kerr is treating him."

Ben barely nodded an acknowledgment before taking off in

the direction of Larson's clinic. His sister had been kidnapped. His best friend was wounded. Could things get any worse?

The mournful drone of those struck down during the attack met him at Larson's hut. Grief-stricken families and friends nursed the injured the best they could until Larson doctored them or they died. Ben ignored their frightened sobs and stepped inside. Dr. Kerr neither looked up nor hesitated from her ministrations to the patient. Ben expected her to be working on Paul Farid, not James.

His longtime friend had been shot in the lower stomach, leaving a gaping hole that exposed his intestines. Some spilled out onto his flesh. Ben wanted to scoop them back inside, make it right somehow. James failed to move or cry out. Glancing from his friend's face to Larson, Ben attempted to read her prognosis. As he expected, she worked diligently without a sign of emotion. Nyok acted as Larson's assistant, taking Rachel's place. He attached an IV bottle to a pole and dabbed at the blood.

"Don't stand in my light, Ben," Larson said, not once glancing up or pausing.

He moved from under the overhanging light bulb strung by wire to the generator. "How is he?"

She swallowed hard, and Ben had known Larson long enough to know what that meant. The anger he had felt earlier over Rachel's situation attempted to resurface, but he refused to give in to its fervor. James was a fighter; he could pull through. Ben needed his friend now—for more reasons than he could count.

"Don't quit on me now, James," Larson said through a heavy breath. Immediately, she sprang into action and began pumping on his chest. "Come on. Stay with me."

James' body convulsed as Larson worked to restart his heart. Ben watched, wanting someone to tell him what to do. Finally she stopped and peered up at him. "He's gone. I'm sorry. I did all I could."

For the first time that day Ben had nothing to say. He ached from the losses of this war, stripped of his emotions as though others around him expected him to feel nothing. His dear Rachel was now the property of the GOS. James had died defending the cause of the southern Sudanese. And if Rachel had been here, she would have watched James breathe his last. Larson detached the IV, and Ben lifted the body into his arms and carried it outside. Somewhere on the outer perimeters of the village, he and his men would dig a grave for each one who had perished.

While he carried James to the lineup of the dead, he remembered all their boyhood games, their dreams, and their goals for Sudan. Inseparable since childhood, James and Ben had been closer than brothers. They had joined the SPLA at the same time.

An old, toothless woman stepped into his path. "Bishop Malou will come and say prayers," she said. "We'll send word, and he'll come."

"I'm sure he can help you," Ben said. He realized they were the first decent words he had spoken all day.

Ben knew the Episcopalian bishop's reputation. Malou's family lived in a refugee camp in Kakuma, Kenya. The man traveled mostly through the northern Bahr Al Ghazal region, evangelizing and establishing churches. Many times he had narrowly escaped with his life. The government had raided his churches, killing members and snatching up the women and young girls for slaves. Malou claimed his good fortune was the hand of God. Ben accepted just enough about God to blame Him for all the suffering in Sudan.

Dusk swept across Warkou, and mothers hurried their children inside before the lions started to roam. Ben had gone through the motions of fulfilling his responsibilities for hours. Now, he made his way back to Larson's hut. He had given her a rough time today, and she might want a little help. Besides, he needed to talk.

Inside the clinic she stitched up Farid's thigh. "I thought you finished with him long ago," Ben said, a little more gruffly than intended.

Larson responded without a hint of emotion. "He insisted I take care of the others who had worse injuries."

Instead of building a sense of trust in the man, her statement fueled Ben's anger. "Why's that? Feeling guilty?"

Farid lifted his head and stared directly into Ben's eyes. "Some could wait. Others could not. The ones who haven't received treatment have surface wounds."

Ben tapped his foot against the earthen floor. "Before I leave, I want to know everything that happened out there with Rachel."

Every muscle on the Arab's face tensed. His face had swollen until the entire right side was purplish black. "It all happened so fast. Once we saw the helicopters, we ran for the village. Bullets flew everywhere, hemming us in. One hit my thigh. A chopper landed, and two soldiers jumped out and headed toward us. One grabbed Rachel, and the other tried to take Nyok, but I positioned the boy behind me." Farid took a deep breath. "They made off with Rachel before one of your soldiers opened fire. That man fell." Farid paused. "Rachel called him James."

Ben glanced at Nyok. "It happened just like he said," the boy said. "Except for the part where the soldier hit him in the face with the butt end of his rifle."

Exhaustion swept over Ben. He crouched in the middle of the floor and attempted to make sense of the day. This encounter with the north was like so many others, but none of those had involved his sister or his childhood friend. A tear slipped from his eye, and he swiped at it with the back of his hand. He should apologize to Larson, but the words refused to come.

"Why do you think they targeted us today?" she asked, dabbing Farid's wound with Betadine. "Were they expecting you?"

"My visit today was a decision made this morning." Ben cursed. "Does Khartoum really need a reason? Could be they found out about the clinic."

"It's not marked. How could they?"

Ben shrugged. "A woman said Bishop Malou has a congregation here." When Larson nodded, he continued. "That might be the answer. Maybe not. But I know it wasn't my men here in the village. No one had any idea about our arrival."

Silence prevailed, and the darkness drew its heavy cloak around them.

"I'm sorry about your friend," Farid said. "Rachel called to him when he tried to stop the soldiers from taking her."

"They were in love," Larson said. "James planned to speak with Ben, but there was a problem with the bride-price."

Ben remembered the conversation from the evening before. "We'd worked that out." James' words echoed in his mind.

"I love Rachel, and I want to marry her," James had said. "You know I don't have any cattle—all are gone. But if you will grant permission, I'll give you sixty cows for her once the war is over and we can restore our way of life."

"And what kind of a life will my sister have with you away fighting?" Ben had asked. The idea of his little sister considering marriage had shaken him more than he wanted to admit.

"No worse than she has now. I will be with her whenever I can, and Dr. Kerr needs her at the clinic."

Ben had taken only a moment to consider James' request. "I think of you as a brother. The age difference between you and Rachel bothers me some, but … I can't think of any man who is more deserving of my sister. My answer is yes, although seventy cows is the bride-price." Ben had chuckled and slapped James' shoulder. Another matter had snaked through his mind. "Don't get yourself killed. I don't want my sister to become just one more Sudanese widow."

James had shaken his head, then laughed. "I have no intention of filling an early grave. I want many sons and daughters."

Now James lay beneath the dirt, and Rachel knew a living death.

Larson interrupted his thoughts. "How do you plan to get her back?"

"I've already sent a runner to the slave traders—to let them know a family wants a kidnapped girl," Ben said. "I hope she doesn't tell them who she is."

"She's a smart girl. I don't think she'd jeopardize her life or your position." Larson laid her hand on his arm. Her touch soothed his weary mind.

"If there's anything I can do, I'll be glad to help," Farid said.

Ben whipped his attention to the Arab-American. "Filthy Arabs like you are the ones who took her. I don't need your help—except to offer you in trade."

# 4

Paul chose not to respond to Alier; no reaction was better than taking the defensive. He knew his actions spoke volumes about what he believed, and what others said about him didn't really matter. After all, Jesus kept silent in front of His accusers.

"What's wrong with you, Ben?" Dr. Kerr adjusted the light above Paul's wound, and Nyok held it steady for her.

"He's one of them. That's all I need to know. I should have killed him when I had the chance." Alier stood from the floor and brushed past her. The hut shook. He stomped into the night, leaving an air of hatred in his wake.

"Guess I can't blame him," Paul said, breaking the thick silence.

Larson peered into his face. "It's not your fault. He loves Rachel very much." She picked up a box of the medicine that Paul had delivered. Pulling a knife from her pants pocket, she deftly slit it on three sides. "She's all Ben has left of his family, and he feels responsible."

"I understand."

She studied him curiously. "You're a strange man."

"Not really, Dr. Kerr—"

"Larson, please."

"Okay, Larson, and I'm Paul." He watched her sort through the bottles. "I'm not so unusual. You have a purpose and a commitment to these people, Colonel Alier has his, and I have mine."

"My opinion of Ben leaves room for improvement. Of course, I believe this genocide of the southern Sudanese could be stopped if both sides were willing to give instead of take." She lifted a small bottle to the light.

"If that's pain killer, I don't want it," Paul said. "Save it for someone who is really suffering. I'm pretty tough."

"I don't think so. I need to dig in there a bit to yank out the bullet, and it will take quite a few stitches."

Paul closed his eyes as a stab of pain seared his thigh. "Don't waste it on me. Nyok can help hold me down if need be."

"Forget it. Save your heroism for another time. If you don't heal properly, I won't have anyone to bring the village supplies."

"I … I don't look at it the same way."

She wiped an antiseptic-soaked cotton ball over his thigh and quickly administered the pain medication. "That's why I'm the doctor and you're the pilot."

He nodded. His thigh throbbed, not unbearably but getting worse. Even with the medication, Paul felt Larson's probing. The soldier's bullet had sunk deeper than he thought. Perspiration streamed down his face.

"You know," Larson said. "When I was a kid and the family piled into the car for a long trip, my dad had this philosophy. He believed the car didn't stop until we ran out of gas or we reached our destination."

Paul forced a smile, thankful for any conversation.

"The problem was when one of us had to use the bathroom; we were out of luck. We learned it did no good to cry or complain, because Daddy had his philosophy. Once, I had to go so badly that

I couldn't stand it. Mama knew and tried to get him to stop, but he wouldn't hear of it."

"What happened?" Paul swallowed hard and clenched his fists.

"I asked every half mile, 'Are we there yet?' until he turned into a gas station."

"What's the reason for telling me this?"

"To tell you we're almost there."

Paul wanted to smile, but the pain soaked up his efforts. "Thank you, I guess."

She lifted her gaze to meet his and smiled genuinely. "My nonpaying patients are forced to hear my stories. Isn't that right, Nyok?"

Nyok nodded. "Some are very bad stories, Mr. Farid."

"I can pay."

"Naw." She reached for the gauze. "This one's on the house."

He watched her bandage up his leg, noting Nyok observed her closely. No doubt with Rachel gone, he would be assisting the doctor. Blood stained everything around Paul, although not all of it belonged to him. The sight spoke volumes about Larson. Most U.S. doctors wouldn't last a day under these conditions. The smell of sweat and dirty bodies in the cramped quarters tugged at his stomach. "How long before I can get around? I need to take a look at my plane and get out of here before Alier decides to finish what the GOS started."

"Not for a few days. It's going to take a while for your leg to mend, and your face is rather pathetic." She glanced about the hut. "You can stay here for now. I have a few patients in the other room, but they've filled the cots."

He realized his eyes were nearly swollen shut. Luckily he could still see. "Thanks. I do remember seeing this listed as a five-star property."

"Wait until you taste the cooking." She began to clean up

around him, and Nyok helped. "Actually, I like your sense of humor."

Paul fought to keep his eyes open, weariness taking its toll. "It's kept me alive."

She turned to Nyok. "Check on the other patients for me. I'll be there in just a moment." Nyok disappeared, taking orders from Larson as though she were a colonel. "Paul, what did Ben mean by offering you in trade?"

"Bad joke." Blackness engulfed his senses. He fought to stay awake, but his body knew its limitations. As he slowly gave in to the overwhelming sleep, he thought he heard the sound of gunfire.

Larson noted Paul's blood pressure and pulse before adjusting the mosquito netting around him. She would check on him in a few hours along with her other patients. With his strength, he would recuperate much faster than most of the patients in her care.

Death, maimed bodies, disease, the cries of the wounded. If she allowed herself, she would go crazy with the devastating job before her. Most days she felt more like a Band-Aid lady than a real doctor.

With everything completed for the night, exhaustion swirled around her body, which begged for relief. Suddenly a surge of realization attacked her. A lump formed in her throat, one she could not swallow.

Rachel is gone. James is dead.

How could life be so unfair? Just when she thought the GOS couldn't hurt her or the southern Sudanese anymore, they had unleashed another banner of fury. Hot stinging tears flooded her eyes, the grief piercing her heart as though a knife twisted inside. Larson slipped to her knees on the dirt floor. She buried her face in her hands and wept. For how long she didn't know, only that time ceased while memories of Rachel played like a movie reel across her mind—the young woman she loved as her own.

She remembered when Ben first brought her to the village, a frightened little girl who, like so many Sudanese children, had seen far too much for any child. Nightmares plagued Rachel's sleeping hours, and fear stalked her waking ones. She refused to leave Larson's side for even a moment. The insecurity is what led the girl to observe and ask questions about Larson's work. She learned what instruments were needed and how to sterilize them. Later on, she assisted in medical procedures—inserting an IV with the touch of an angel or administering injections under Larson's critical eye. Rachel soothed the patients and kept them comfortable. She sang to them and read to them from the Bible.

Larson urged Ben to send his sister to England or the States where she could study medicine, but he repeatedly refused. Even Rachel begged him. For some reason he wanted her in Sudan. Larson attributed it to Ben's selfish and controlling nature.

Larson's stomach lurched at the thought of Rachel among the GOS. Only a fool ignored the fate of a beautiful young woman thrown among ruthless captors. Rachel would fight them, and they would torture her. No exceptions. They had no respect for women and even less for Christians. Better she had died in the heat of battle. Where was God in the midst of such a hell?

Poor James. An image of the tall man standing before the clinic with a broad smile and asking to speak to Rachel flashed before her. All he had wanted was a chance to love Rachel and to build a hope for the future. Why did so many believe they were invincible? She blamed Ben for today. He could have sent Rachel away; he could have insisted James not join the SPLA. Did it really matter that Ben would pay any price to have Rachel returned? The damage had already been done. Even as Larson sobbed, those animals were using her for their own pleasure.

She drew her knees to her chest as another series of tearful sobs racked her body. Rocking back and forth, Larson tried to gain control before she awakened her patients.

She despised war. How could the free world continue to ignore the weeping of the Sudanese people? The sky dripped with their tears. September 11 had shocked many to their senses about the atrocities going on around the world, but many others had turned their eyes from the suffering of southern Sudan's black Africa to the safety of their own soil. How quickly they would change their mind if their children were born into a country bathed in the blood of civil war.

"Dr. Kerr?" Nyok knelt beside her. "Are you all right? Can I do something for you?"

Larson wiped her eyes and nose with a tissue that he offered, one of the precious items in Paul's cargo. "I'll be fine. Today's been difficult."

Nyok nodded, age and wisdom beyond his years evident in his young face. "I failed Rachel today. I'm a warrior, not a boy. I should have died defending her."

"You did everything you could. You helped save Paul's life." Larson bit back her liquid emotion, and Nyok helped her stand.

"It was not enough."

They stood eye to eye: grown woman and man-child. *Nyok should be in junior high, playing sports, discovering girls ... not here enduring this horror.* Larson hugged his shoulders. He was Dinka, a warrior among a proud people. He wouldn't want the traditions of his people changed, but he did want the government's soldiers to leave his country alone.

"Go on to bed; I'm right behind you." He shook his head, and she added, "I need some time alone."

Nyok disappeared into the hut adjacent to the clinic. Larson knew he would lie awake until she had settled down in the hut beside his. A family had once lived in these three huts she called her own: one for the parents, the second for the son, and the third for the two daughters. They were killed during an attack before she arrived.

Taking a deep breath, she slowly released it. She dared not allow the villagers to see her in such despair. They thought she had the market on strength and courage. What a joke. So many times she wanted to quit—to leave Sudan and never return—but something always stopped her. Sometimes it was a child's smile; other times the cry of a newborn infant; often it was a patient regaining his health. The truth was, she no longer fit in the States, and she had never quite fit here either, like a square peg in a round hole. The weight of that truth smacked her in the face. She had no place to go, and loneliness stalked her night and day. Nothing else remained but to continue tending to the sick and wounded. Clenching her jaw, Larson wished away the remaining tears.

She had come to Sudan when a missionary's child died in her care, a darling little boy only four years old. The parents had brought him to University Hospital in Columbus, Ohio, in the vain hope their son could be cured of an aggressive cancer. Because of his death, Larson had committed four years to helping the people of Sudan, one for each year of the child's age. She never dreamed her commitment would turn into a love and move her to stay for as long as she was needed.

With a deep sigh, she checked on her patients. Peter, an elderly man, didn't look like he would make it beyond the morning. The others slept. Sometimes she slept on the floor beside the critically ill. Gazing at Paul, she wondered again what Ben meant when he suggested trading him to the Arabs. Trade him for what? SPLA soldiers held by Khartoum? Other slaves? Why would the GOS want Paul, except that he flew supplies into the south? He represented a highly respected Christian humanitarian organization, often compared to the International Red Cross. What value would Paul be to those in Khartoum?

Anxiety swelled in Larson's chest. She hated this feeling, the tremendous urge to run until her legs refused to carry her a moment longer. She had to get out of the clinic, away from the stench of death and the reminders of today's carnage. Snatching up her rifle, she stepped out into the starlit night.

Ben had posted guards around the village; even so, she stayed in the shadows and strode just beyond the cluster of huts. They saw her, and so did the warriors who guarded the village with them. None would approach her unless she asked for assistance.

Larson longed for solitude to ease her heartache and push the chaos of today into some remote part of her mind. Somehow she must erase the memory of the cries and the sights of her beloved people being picked off like flies at a picnic. When the enemy had finally finished its eradication, it would feast on the spoils. Her thoughts served to remind her of the oil-rich areas where a scorched-earth policy ensured who controlled the land. It was just part of the government's method of making sure the southern Sudanese had nothing to return to. The GOS destroyed every home, animal, and blade of vegetation to pave the way for drilling.

Lights from the village fires flickered, reminding her of tiny torches. Normally the shoots of waving light represented warmth and friendship to a people she loved. Tonight numbness and fatigue overshadowed those feelings. When she had finally worked through her grief and pain, the firelight would guide the way back to the clinic.

Glancing up at the sky, she momentarily forgot her sorrow and noted the various star formations. Rachel enjoyed doing the same, something else the two had in common. Larson quickly choked back the tears. She needed reason now, not sentiment.

*If only I could open my eyes and discover this has been a horrible dream. Rachel and Nyok would be asleep, and Ben and I would be debating some issue about war tactics while drinking bitter coffee.*

On she walked, swinging the rifle as if she carried it every day instead of a medical bag. She must gather her wits and find a way to make it through tomorrow and the next day.

A rustling in the tall grass alerted her. She instantly glanced behind her to see how far she had come. The guards and warriors knew where she had ventured, but were they close enough to reach her if she was in real danger?

A shiver snaked up Larson's back and settled at her nape. She felt a sinister presence. *Stupid. Stupid. How many years have I lived here?* She stopped and took a step back. Now the rustling was behind her. Fear held her in its clutches. A predator pursued her, one she would not see until it clamped its knifelike paws into her flesh, and she smelled its hot breath on her neck.

The rifle. She lifted the weapon into her trembling arms. The sound might scare off the animal. In any event, when the crack split the air, soldiers and warriors alike would rush to bring her to safety.

"Dr. Kerr."

She heard the even voice of Nyok. "Yes."

"A lion is before you, a lioness to your rear."

# 5

Nyok's heart pounded hard against his chest, so loud it sounded like beating drums. Adrenaline flowed through his veins and strengthened his body and mind. He understood his role as a warrior-protector. He had undergone the rites of manhood and endured the pain of mutilation when a warrior slashed his forehead with the markings of the Dinka tribe. With his head held high, Nyok had proudly recited the ancestry of his father while blood dripped in his eyes and mouth.

With God's help he would kill the lions. If he lost, he would be under the shelter of all those who had gone before him. Sometimes Nyok had no faith at all, except to exist by his own wits. Right now, he needed more than the confines of his body.

His destiny had arrived, and it filled him with challenge, excitement, and terror.

"I have my rifle," Dr. Kerr said. The tremor in her voice increased his alarm. She might attempt something unwise.

"You have no bullets." Nyok gripped the thick wooden club in his hands. "Colonel Alier removed them when you were tending to patients."

She seldom wept, except tonight, yet he heard the grief in her words. The grass rustled, as though foreshadowing the terror to come. The lions were circling in on their prey. He had seen two, but more could be lurking in the shadows. Lions traveled together when they hunted.

"Why would he do that?" she asked.

"He thought you might hurt yourself." He inched closer. "Don't be afraid. I'm here to protect you."

"You have a gun?"

The male lion moved closer to her. Nyok had mere moments before the huge cat attacked. The soldiers would hear the fighting once it started. "I have a weapon."

"Can you see to shoot? The lion's closer. He's so big, Nyok."

"I can see." Nyok couldn't wait any longer. He crouched and ran toward the animal, shouting and praying with all his might.

Dr. Kerr screamed. The soldiers and village guards must have heard, but for Nyok the time had passed for his rescue. He slammed his club onto the lion's head. The crack gave Nyok little comfort. Dazed, the animal hesitated, then angrily roared. Nyok trembled. Sickness swept over him. *Watch his paws. Be ready for his teeth. Stay crouched.* Instructions from warriors who had fought lions raced across his mind. The club struck the lion again across the back, finding its mark with a dull thud. The beast's back legs buckled. It roared and whipped around, ready to pounce, but Nyok laid a blow to its face. He swung again, this time into the animal's mouth. Light from somewhere kept the animal in full view. Power filled Nyok's arms, and determination ruled his heart. Nyok saw its every move, anticipated each twist before the lion leaped forward. He felt the animal's breath full of hate and yearning for blood.

Gunshots split the air, then another and others. Help had come. Dr. Kerr would be safe. The lion charged, and Nyok met its angry assault with another strike to the head. The animal hesitated, and

Nyok seized the opportunity to pound the animal's body—the back, the head, the mammoth face. When it fell, he rushed forward and clubbed the lion until it no longer moved. Blood wove through its mane and drained from its mouth.

With sweat streaming down his face, Nyok whirled to direct his attention to the lioness. What had happened to the female? The females were the fiercest in battle. In the darkness he attempted to make out the other lion. The light had vanished. Confusion edged his mind.

"Dr. Kerr," he said. "Are you all right? The lion is dead."

"Yes," she said, barely above a whimper. "Are you—"

"I'm fine, unharmed. Where is the lioness?" His breathing came in short gasps.

"Dead," Colonel Alier said.

A torch lit up the colonel's face. *The gunfire.* Nyok saw other soldiers and men from the village. One held a flaming torch.

In the next instant, Dr. Kerr stood at his side. He could smell her, the unique scent of a woman and medicine, life and healing. She grasped his arm, and he felt her shaking like a lost child.

"You killed it," she said with the same tremor he had heard earlier. "You killed the lion with a club."

"God was with me," he said. Dr. Kerr didn't believe in God, but Nyok dared not take the glory for destroying the animal. Suddenly, he realized where the light had come from. *Thank You, Holy Father. I am grateful.*

A firm hand rested on his shoulder. "You're a brave warrior," the colonel said. "You should be pleased with your heroism. I know of no man who has killed a lion in the dark without a gun."

"God Almighty lit up the night for me. He gave me strength and courage to kill the animal."

Colonel Alier deepened his hold. "Dr. Kerr is most fortunate to have you as her protector."

Nyok wanted to say he should have done more for Rachel, but

the words refused to come. Perhaps the colonel already knew his thoughts.

"I know you tried to stop the soldiers today. Don't blame yourself," he said.

Those were the kindest words the colonel had ever spoken to him. Nyok believed the man could not have uttered them in the daylight; darkness concealed his emotion. He also knew Colonel Alier wrestled with insurmountable guilt. His sister had been kidnapped, and he had removed the bullets from Dr. Kerr's rifle. Inward struggles were always the most difficult to bear.

"Back to the village," the colonel said. He took Dr. Kerr's rifle. She snatched it back, then relinquished her hold.

Nyok stayed by her side. Tonight he had earned the right as her warrior-protector. No longer would the others make fun of his devotion to her, mocking him as though he were a boy clinging to his mother. He had earned their respect. Satisfaction settled on him like a cool evening. They would make up songs about him and sing them around the fires while tending to the cows. At last he had become a man.

Larson felt Nyok's arm around her waist. She wanted to cry and draw him to her as though he were a little boy again, cradle him in her arms and beg him never to do anything so foolish. Or maybe she needed his strength. Later she would sort out her muddled thoughts and work through the happenings tonight.

Larson had never experienced the privilege of giving birth, but if motherhood had graced her, she would have wanted her children to be exactly like Rachel and Nyok. Today she had nearly lost both of them. How did so many African mothers face the death of their children? How did they bear the pain? Children were supposed to bury their parents, not the other way around. She remembered a woman who had been brought to her for treatment when government soldiers raided her village. One of the soldiers saw she had a newborn baby and sliced off her breasts, so both mother and infant would die. Larson had been able to save the woman by closing the wounds and administering antibiotics to prevent infection. Other mothers in the village nursed the baby, and today the child was nearly three years old.

Why did she stay in this forsaken part of the world? The government destroyed its own people because of their resistance to Islam and because it wanted the oil flowing richly like the waters of the great Nile.

Where had their faith in God got them?

She trembled, and Nyok tightened his hold. Larson despised weakness, and tonight she had clearly displayed it, first in succumbing to tears in the clinic and now by giving in to fear of the lion. Glancing up, she saw women in the doorways of their huts anxiously searching the crowd for husbands, brothers, and sons. Some held children, but in the firelight Larson observed incredible strength. She envied and feared this enigma. Such a proud people, these Dinka, so committed to their pastoral way of life that they would rather die than give it up. Some fled to other places, like Kakuma, the refugee camp in Kenya, where thousands of African refugees lived. The people there had not given up either; they simply were waiting and contemplating how to win back their homeland.

Fury washed through Larson's quivering body at the thought of the near tragedy. "Ben, why did you unload my rifle? Nyok and I could have been killed." She stepped from Nyok's touch, no longer needing the young man to give her courage.

Ben exhaled slowly, and silence prevailed.

"Why?" She wanted to sound more forceful. They stood near a fire. The guards and villagers filed by. Some returned to their posts, while others made their way to their homes.

"You were angry, irrational. I didn't want you doing something stupid."

"I guess not. You handled that department quite well all by yourself."

"I did what I thought was best at the time."

"Like not sending Rachel away from this horrible life?"

"That's not fair." Ben's words echoed around them.

She hugged her shoulders. "And what about today? Sudan doesn't operate under equality or justice. You of all people should know that." Rage and grief left her head spinning. "You refused to let her leave, and now she's in the hands of some dirty Muslim who's using her for whatever he wants!"

"Shut up, Larson. I've had enough."

"I really don't care what you've had. Isn't the issue about how you will look to your comrades? I mean, you command a battalion of southern guerillas and can't even protect your own sister."

Ben swore. Flickers of light danced off his rigid features. "I remember you enjoyed having Rachel here with you."

"Enjoying someone's company and risking their life for selfish reasons are two different things." She stared into the flames as if looking for a spark to burn him.

"Who are you to blame me?" Ben asked. "You don't even have a country to call home. How would you know how any of us feel?"

"What's that supposed to mean?" She attempted to gain control of her emotions and the conversation. Why did she and Ben always end up this way? They needed to be civil for the sake of the village and all those who needed protection and medical attention.

"You're a white woman in a black man's country. You head back to the United States, and you're not wanted there either."

Hadn't she considered the same thing? "I believe you went there to school."

"I have a country." He stole a glimpse of Nyok. "Go on home. I'll escort Larson to the clinic."

Nyok looked to her for instruction.

"I'm fine," she said. No longer could Larson stand not being able to touch the dear young man before her. She wrapped her arms around Nyok's neck. "Thank you. Words cannot express my gratitude for tonight. I love you, Nyok, as though you were my own son."

He smiled before walking back to the clinic, carrying the club stained in lion's blood. Weariness tugged at Larson's bones, and she saw no relief in tomorrow. Patients still needed her care, and new ones would be standing outside her door at dawn. Like so many nights in the past, she craved sleep. She stared into Ben's face, his towering frame and black skin blending in the night shadows. Fury creased his brow. If they had been standing in sunlight, she would see the coldness there as well. For certain, any ceasefire between the two must come from her.

"Ben, please, let's stop this arguing." When he didn't respond, she ventured on. "Today has been a nightmare, and we're grieving over Rachel. I know I did something really crazy by walking out of the village and endangering Nyok's life."

"Why did you go?" Ben anchored his massive hands on his hips.

Hot tears sprang to her eyes. "I was upset about Rachel. You and I had quarreled. I needed time alone."

He nodded slowly. "I won't ever unload your rifle again."

Ben's words were the closest he would ever come to an apology. She would have to bury them in her heart for the future when he angered her again—and he would. *Calm yourself. Be rational.*

"Can we not argue?" she asked.

"It's better for the villagers and my men if we get along."

"I will do my best to hold my tongue." She breathed a sigh of relief. "I hope this also means you will leave Farid alone."

"Maybe so, maybe not."

She elected not to push him, and for a moment she considered asking him why Khartoum would want the pilot. "What are you going to do about Rachel?"

"I'm leaving in the morning with my men. I'll see a few slave traders and offer them a good price for her."

"Will you keep me informed?"

"As much as I can. We both know the dangers of the government learning her identity."

"I don't believe she'll tell."

Ben clenched his fists. "I'll kill any man who touches her."

She considered Rachel's innocence, now likely lost forever. Was it just a week ago the two had talked about saving herself for James?

"I want James to know me for the first time," Rachel had said. They had been sitting outside in the early morning, watching the sunrise in shades of bright orange and yellow. "I believe my virginity is a sacred gift to be given to my husband. God promises many blessings for those who are obedient to purity."

"I'm glad you feel that way." Larson's thoughts were different on the matter, but she respected Rachel's beliefs.

Larson ushered in the present with a shudder. "I believe I'd help you kill him. I love her so much."

"I know you do. She has a charm about her. She makes my life full of hope." He paused. "You're right. I should have sent her away. I'm to blame."

"This war has caused enough tragedy. We should concentrate on getting her back and keep fighting, so other young women will not have to face the same situation."

"Which is why I must continue waging war against Khartoum. They will be defeated."

Larson stretched her neck muscles. "Don't you believe in the peace talks?"

Ben spat at the fire. "Not when the bombing still goes on." He peered into the darkness to where the lions lay dead. "Nyok is very brave. He'd make a good soldier."

# 6

Paul battled the haziness from sleep to reality. He swam through a sea of pain hoping his agony stemmed from a nightmare and not foggy remembrances from the day before. Every time his heart beat, the torture in his upper leg increased, building momentum as he struggled to awaken. Yesterday's events flooded his mind: delivering medicinal and food supplies to the village, the attack, Rachel's kidnapping, the bullet in his thigh, Alier's hatred, and Larson's coming to his aid. Too much to consider with a mind dulled by a bullet wound.

He forced his eyes open, and when he could focus his attention on an object that didn't spin, he glanced about him. Although the inside of the medical clinic looked dim with only a stream of sunlight from the door, he wanted to tear back the bandages and take a look at the wound. Too weak to consider such a feat, he slipped his left hand down his leg to gauge the amount of swelling. His entire upper leg felt large, and the skin was stretched tighter than the bark on a tree. The idea of infection entered his mind, but he pushed away the image with the realization that Larson had given him excellent care. Besides, he needed to get on his feet. His plane's bullet-ridden condition loomed over him, and he had to find a way to inspect the damage.

Feed the World must be notified of what happened yesterday, or it would be sending out a search plane. The area was too dangerous for his pilot friends to risk getting shot out of the sky for the likes of him.

Attempting to ignore the white-hot throbbing, Paul fumbled around looking for his global satellite phone. He wanted to call Tom back in California and let him know he was still alive—or at least that his heart was still beating.

"Is the pain causing you to thrash around like that, or are you looking for something?" Larson asked.

He glanced up to see the doctor carrying a basket full of cups, a few mangos, and a pottery pitcher full of milk. "Both." She looked tired, but Paul imagined that was her trademark expression.

"I thought so." She set the basket on the dirt floor and unlocked her medicine cabinet, which looked more like an oversized safe. "Would you have asked for pain medication, or suffered through it?"

Paul forced a smile. "I think you already know the answer."

"Bravery belongs to the healthy," she said. He spied the needle and alcohol-saturated cotton ball briefly before she stabbed his arm. "As soon as the pain subsides, I want to take a look at your leg."

Nyok stepped into the room. Sleep etched his face like that of a tired little boy.

"How's my warrior today?" Larson's hand caressed Nyok's face. "Any nightmares?"

"I'm doing fine." His attention spanned the small room, and he reached for the food-laden basket. "I don't have bad dreams."

"I guess not," she said. "You live them."

Paul studied the worry lines on Larson's forehead. She was strong and determined. Of course, here she would have to be. Having lost Rachel yesterday, Larson most likely wouldn't let Nyok out of her sight anytime soon.

"I'll take the patients their breakfast." Nyok lifted the basket from the ground. "Mr. Farid, have you eaten?"

"I'm not hungry. I don't suppose you have any coffee?"

Larson selected a mango from the basket and handed it to Paul. "Eat this, doctor's orders. I can make a pot of coffee. Go ahead, Nyok, and give the others their breakfasts." A thin-lipped smile met Paul's scrutiny. "I'm a tea drinker myself, but I always have it for Ben," Larson said.

Paul said nothing at the mention of the colonel's name. He didn't intend to say a word that might be construed as controversial. This morning, living sounded a whole lot better than dying, even with his wounded leg. "Don't bother with the coffee. I'll make it later."

Larson tossed him a warning look. "You aren't going anywhere today, least of all around a fire where you might fall." From inside a makeshift cupboard she pulled an aluminum pot, stained nearly black, and proceeded to measure out coffee.

Contacting Tom pressed against Paul's brain. "Have you seen my phone?"

Larson nodded and stepped over to pick it up from the ground near his cot.

"Thanks, I need to call headquarters and let them know I'm alive."

He leaned back on the cot, frustrated at how a simple conversation exhausted him, and he had yet to punch in Tom's number. Closing his eyes, he elected to rest a moment longer. In the cloudy portals of his drugged mind, he vaguely remembered Larson examining his leg.

Sometime later, Paul woke. He heard people talking in Dinka

outside the clinic and glanced at his watch. Moaning softly, he realized it was the noon hour. His fingers felt for the phone at his side, and once more he picked it up. He must have powered it off. Unusual, since he always kept it on. With a shrug, he punched in Tom's number.

"Hey, Tom." His attempt to project enthusiasm sounded weak at best.

"Where are you? I've been trying to contact you but couldn't get through."

"In Warkou, where I flew in food and medical supplies." From the noise in the background, Paul envisioned his friend scurrying through FTW's warehouse making sure there were enough supplies to fill an order.

"Why? Does Dr. Kerr need your assistance?"

"Uh, more like I need hers."

Tom chuckled. "Oh, so the doctor is a woman?"

"Right, you knew that."

"Heard she was pretty. Say, are you all right? You don't sound like yourself."

"I've been better, but I'll be okay."

"How about telling me what's going on?" Tom asked.

Paul recapped the events of the previous day, telling Tom everything. His friend had a habit of asking about every minute detail, and Paul learned a long time ago to hold nothing back.

"So you don't know the extent of the plane's damage?"

"Not yet. I wanted to hobble out there today, but I don't think it's going to happen," Paul said.

"Take care of yourself first, but keep me informed. I think it would be a good idea to send someone after you."

The concern in Tom's voice warmed Paul. "No, thanks. I have a good doctor. As soon as I find out what I need to repair the plane, I'll call back. Besides, Khartoum's forces know I'm here and might return."

"All the more reason to get you out of there," Tom said.

"Too risky. No one else needs to be in my shoes."

"Do you think any of them recognized you?"

Roasting alive over an open fire was more appealing to Paul than being captured by enemies he had once called his friends.

"No. Not in the least."

Ben tramped down the dusty path with his men. They all carried rifles and grenades; their attention was tuned to every sound and movement. The noises of nature often deceived the best soldier. Ben's battalion, part of the Rhino division, had a fierce reputation, and his men deserved the credit. They followed him without question, no matter where he led them. All but two were members of the Dinka tribe. The other soldiers were Nuer tribesmen.

He gripped his rifle tighter and clenched his jaw. Thoughts of Rachel drove him crazy. His sister in the hands of government soldiers twisted at his heart. Every time the image of what those Arabs did to women bolted across his mind, he breathed vengeance. He wanted the blood of every loyal Khartoum man, woman, and child he could find.

Yesterday afternoon he had buried a comrade. At least James had died for his country. Nothing nobler existed on this earth. Ben had given him a Christian burial by quoting a few memorized pieces of Scripture and ended it with the Twenty-third Psalm. As a Christian, Ben's reputation preceded him, but murder ruled his heart, and today that characteristic dominated him.

Paul Farid deserved to die. Ben no more believed the man tried to save Rachel than he believed the GOS wanted peace. The reports from FTW and Christian publications were merely propaganda to disguise the real man. Those who trusted Farid were fools and deserved whatever fate befell them for believing a Muslim could convert to Christianity. Farid had been a member of the royal family in Khartoum until he "found the Lord" and escaped the country with the GOS hot on his heels. Of course, the man had managed to transfer his wealth to a safe account. How convenient. Now, Farid had access to all the humanitarian organizations in the world committed to aiding the innocent victims of Sudan. His actions looked like sophisticated terrorism to Ben. One day those poor, duped idiots would learn the truth and wish they had listened to Ben Alier.

Farid's wound yesterday was only an accident, or even intentional, possibly staged to prove the Arab's credibility. Even Larson believed the pilot's story.

A dormant emotion tugged at Ben's senses, one he often denied except in the early hours of dawn. Bracing his shoulders, he shoved the inclination aside. No one knew; no one would ever learn the truth.

Ben had sent word about Rachel yesterday and again early this morning by way of a villager to every slave trader he knew. No point in sending one of his men to raise suspicions about his sister. The message was simple: A young woman from a village near Warkou had been taken in a government raid, and the family wanted her back. No one would suspect the missing young woman had a notorious brother. Perhaps the message would get through to the government, and Rachel could be returned safely and without having endured too much suffering. Yet in this war it was always the innocent who suffered—the defenseless ones.

Up ahead three trucks with mounted machine guns ground across the rutted road, paving a way for the Rhino division. Reports revealed that GOS forces had bombed a second village yesterday and seized five women. Ben intended to make sure no more enemy lurked in the brush. He also needed to obtain a full report from the villagers. Maybe Khartoum had followed a pattern.

Khartoum spent a million dollars a day on this civil war, the same amount it earned from the oil reserves. Ben had heard that one of the larger international humanitarian organizations spent about that much a day on relief aid to the southern Sudanese. Innocent blood was being spilled for the sake of the rich reserves of oil situated under the southern soil. Ben cursed just thinking about the genocide in his beloved country. The GOS bombed the villages in the oil-rich regions, while helicopter snipers killed many of the people and chased the remaining few from the area. As a result, widespread famine attacked the displaced people. Even if the refugees wanted to return home, their villages were destroyed and their fields burned. Khartoum's scorched-earth policy continued, while the free world seemingly displayed its indifference.

Sudan's government didn't have the money to invest in drilling for oil, so it had contracted with international oil companies to do the work, allowing them to take the majority of the profits. China, Malaysia, the Netherlands, and Canada were among the worst offenders, having constructed a thousand-mile crude oil pipeline from the south to Port Sudan on the Red Sea. Sudan National Petroleum Corporation (Sudapet), the government-controlled oil company, held only 5 percent of the oil shares. *Look what the government is doing with it. To blazes with them all. Oh, for the day when the southern Sudanese seize control of what is rightfully theirs.*

Rifle fire sounded to the right of Ben. Fully alert, deserting all thoughts but the war storming around him, he spun into action. After years of combat in the wilds of southern Sudan, his every nerve and muscle were ready to respond without hesitation. A grenade exploded near one of the trucks; it was followed by the screams of the injured. Ben signaled for a band of men to follow him into the brush. Up ahead he saw GOS soldiers, some on foot and some on horseback. Ben was determined that Khartoum forces would meet another bad day at the hands of the rebels.

When all else disappeared, when all else around him collapsed, this is what Ben lived for.

# 7

The second night after the GOS attack on the village found Paul unable to sleep. His leg cried out every time his heart beat, and the pain seemed to grow worse instead of better. The thought of infection once more crossed his mind, but he refused to dwell on it. Besides, he had the best doctor in the area. Tonight, he had turned down Tylenol with codeine despite Larson's insistence. The sacrifice wasn't much, but to Paul, the small dose of pain reliever might help a suffering man, woman, or child.

While enduring the blackness of night, his thoughts played back over the years spent in Khartoum when he agreed with those who hunted down the "infidels." Although Paul never signed any death warrants, he supported the government that murdered many innocent civilians and forced hundreds of others into camps that offered no water, food, medical assistance, sanitation, or housing. Their crimes were their faith, either Christianity or one of the tribal religions. More atrocities than Paul cared to remember stemmed from Muslim beliefs, and he had been in the middle of it all. He hated himself for those actions and values. Nighttime traumas plagued him.

Paul knew the Truth. He had told himself repeatedly that he had been washed clean in the blood of Jesus. Still guilt whispered accusations that he would never be good enough; his sin was too great for the Creator of the universe to pardon: *Fly over the enemy twenty-four seven. Drop food and medical supplies until Sudan soil is littered with them. Give away all of your money. But you are still an animal. Nothing will ever change what you did.*

At times, Paul shoved the haunting aside. But on nights like this one, combined with the agony in his upper leg, the voice magnified until he thought his head might explode.

But then there came a different voice: *Pray, My son. I am here for you.*

Sweat streamed down Paul's face, not from his physical pain but from the inner war threatening to obliterate his faith. Staring into the blackness, he reached into the coils of time and remembered the man who showed him the Way. *Are you with Jesus, Abraham? Must I wait until heaven to see you again?*

Abraham would be in his sixties by now, and Paul doubted whether the man still lived. The GOS had cut off one of his hands when he lifted it to praise God. The barbarity hadn't stopped the utterances from Abraham's lips and heart. The man found more strength to endure beatings and deprivation of the necessities of life.

"See what you can find out," Paul's father had said. "Then dispose of him."

Paul was prepared to follow through with the commands, but when the time came, he discovered that he couldn't do it. The look Abraham gave him and the love generating from his eyes stopped Paul from inflicting any harm on him. Instead he nursed Abraham the best he could and found a way for the prisoner to escape.

Abraham refused to leave the prison compound until he had explained the Gospel to Paul. After listening to what had been done for him in the name of love, Paul accepted Jesus Christ as

Savior and Master of his life, and he hadn't been the same since.

Now, lying there in the confines of the clinic, Paul whispered prayers until dawn burst over the horizon. Exhausted, yet encouraged in faith, he renewed his commitment to make a difference in Sudan. His nightmares always ended the same way—with a rejuvenation of his commitment to God's plan for his life. He prayed for Rachel and her family and friends. He prayed for Ben Alier and the guerilla bands seeking to free Sudan. Many times captured Muslim soldiers heard the Gospel and accepted Christ as their Savior. Paul didn't know if they did so out of fear for their lives or because the Holy Spirit had actually spoken to them. He prayed it was the latter reason; after all, God had found him. He prayed for those kept in bondage for their faith. He prayed for the free world to finally see the suffering in southern Sudan and take action.

"Did you sleep well?" Larson asked when she entered the hut with the breakfast basket. How she managed a smile with the schedule she kept baffled him. Her eyes were red and swollen, and the sense of guilt pierced him again.

"As compared to what?" Paul asked.

She raised a brow. "That means if you'd taken the pain medication, you'd have slept like a baby."

"But someone's baby might have needed it."

She studied him, tilting her head and trying to look beyond the exterior to the inside of the man entrusted to her care. "You're a strange one," she said, and he caught the tone of appreciation in her voice.

Humbled, he shook his head. "It's my purpose."

She set the basket aside, taking out a mango for him and placing it beside the coffeepot. "I want to take a look at your thigh. Knowing you, the idea of running back to the States for more supplies has entered your mind."

He forced a chuckle. For a moment he thought someone had lit a match to his leg. "All I want to do is check on the damage to my plane. I must maneuver from this hut and find out what's ailing it."

"So you're a plane doctor too?"

Paul flipped back the thin blanket for her to examine his leg. "I'm an apprentice mechanic, nothing more. If my aircraft has extensive damage, I'm at your mercy."

She tossed him a feigned sympathetic look. "I could always train you in the fine art of assisting the doctor."

"Then what would I do?" Nyok asked from the doorway. "I'm doing a good job for both Rachel and myself."

Larson kissed the boy's cheek, despite his scowl. "Of course you are."

While Larson redressed Paul's thigh, he observed the wound. To him, it looked redder than it should. "Is infection setting in?" he asked.

"I'm applying an antibiotic ointment, and you're taking antibiotics orally."

She hadn't addressed his question, which gave him the answer he sought. Paul had to trust Larson and get on with what he needed to do. He seized the opportunity to speak with Nyok. "Are you free later on this morning to help a cripple?"

"As soon as I finish some chores for Dr. Kerr," Nyok said. "I need to store the extra medical supplies in the bomb shelter—the food too."

"Good. I need a walking stick and help to check out my plane."

"It has holes in the side." Nyok leaned against the doorway of the hut.

"I remember." He hesitated. "My fear is whether the fuel tanks or the engines are destroyed. If they are, you may have a new resident."

Nyok shrugged. "Sudan is not so bad, but it will be better when the SPLA frees the south."

If only peace in Sudan could be won that easily.

The hours after breakfast sped by as Paul observed Larson examining and treating patients. She had a special bedside manner that he admired and appreciated. Each patient was her most important one, and her touch was gentle, loving. No wonder the villagers were so loyal to her.

At midmorning, Nyok entered the clinic with a long, thick stick. Just right for a crutch.

"I took a look at your plane," the boy said.

"Yeah? What did you see?"

"Fuel is spilled on the ground beneath the wings."

Paul cringed and reached for the makeshift crutch. Nyok eased up beside him and slipped Paul's arm around his shoulder as he had done when he was first injured. The slightest pressure sent liquid hot coals up and down Paul's leg.

"You choose," Nyok said. "Stay here and heal, or hurt like crazy while taking a look at your plane."

Gritting his teeth, Paul took a step. "You have my answer."

Once outside, Paul blinked in the bright sunlight. The villagers were going about their business as though nothing had occurred two days earlier. Children danced around him wanting attention. One accidentally bumped against his leg, causing excruciating pain that stung his eyes. Nyok shouted at them in Dinka, and they scattered. From the sound of Nyok's voice, it seemed evident that the children would not be bothering him soon. Paul regretted sending them away; he would make it up to them as soon as he felt better.

"Let's go," Paul said. If not for his stubbornness, he would have turned around and headed back inside the clinic. Every step sent perspiration streaming down his face. He craved water but refused to ask for a drink. Glancing in the near distance, he saw the plane emerge like a fixture on the plains.

"We're almost there," Nyok said, as though reading Paul's thoughts. "Just a little farther."

Paul nodded.

"Am I going to have to carry you back?" the boy asked. His teasing tone bordered on a hint of alarm.

"Naw, I'll race you." Paul moistened his lips. "Do I have my phone in my hip pocket?"

Nyok paused and glanced behind him. "You do."

Paul expelled a labored sigh. "I hated the thought of going back for it."

As they neared the twin-engine aircraft, Paul focused on the bullet holes.

"Is it bad?" Nyok asked.

"Not sure yet. Help me take a look."

Nyok helped him limp to the back where bullet holes riddled the tail. Paul wasn't surprised. He expected the GOS to hit the biggest target on the plane. A good amount of rudder damage captured his attention, but metal patching would take care of that. Further inspection showed damage in the fuselage.

"What about the holes there?" Nyok asked, as Paul scrutinized the cabin.

He sighed. "Some metal patching will stop any leaks, so that pressurizing the cabin won't be a problem." Paul glanced up at the wingtips, then down to the ground where a puddle of fuel had accumulated below the wings. "Looks like there are a few holes in the tip tanks."

"Some of what you say I don't understand," Nyok said, his voice iced with a little irritation.

Paul patted him on the shoulder. "Looks like I'll have plenty of time to explain all this to you." He reached inside the cabin and pulled out his backpack containing his Bible and journal.

"So is the plane destroyed?"

"Not at all. In fact, I have a roll of 300-knot tape that will patch it just fine and get me out of here," Paul said. He patted the cabin and examined a bullet hole. "I've got a lot of miles from this

plane, and I'll get a lot more. Guess I'd better report in to FTW."
He pulled out his cell phone and entered Tom's number. His
friend answered on the second ring.

"Hey, how is sunny California?" Paul asked with more enthusiasm than he felt.

"You sound better."

*Good disguise.* "I'm working on it. Right now I'm standing
beneath the wing of my plane."

"How bad is it?"

Paul recapped his assessment. "The plane can still fly, but not
too high or fast. I can patch a few places with tape and get out of
here in a few days."

"Why don't you let me send in a little help?"

Paul didn't know why he wasn't ready for FTW to risk
another pilot and plane, except that danger lurked in the
shadows, and he suspected the GOS might drop more bombs.
"Let's wait a day or so. I don't feel comfortable about losing
another plane."

"What else is going on, Paul? Something with Dr. Kerr?"

Paul hesitated, uncertain how to answer Tom's questions. "I
don't know why I feel I'm supposed to be here."

"Are you in a hostage situation?"

Paul glanced at Nyok, who appeared to be memorizing every
inch of the plane. "Not exactly. These people are wonderful. You
know that."

"Just checking."

"I need some time to let my leg heal a bit more, and I want to
see if there is anything else FTW can do to assist these civilians,
other than what we are already doing."

"Now I get it," Tom said, obviously exasperated. "Guilt
has you over there. I thought you'd settled all of that. Those
nasty feelings rearing their venomous heads come from Satan,
not God."

Hadn't he just had this conversation with God? How could he make Tom understand when Paul himself didn't fully comprehend the power of God's love? "Tom," Paul said, "I can't expect you to see things the same as I do. For some reason, I need to stay. God will tell me why in His time."

"I don't want you killed," Tom said. "Be careful."

Larson crossed her arms and stared at Nyok and Paul. Even from where she stood, she could see how the man struggled with every move. She recognized his commitment to FTW. Like hers, she knew that only death would cease his dedication.

Raw memories from the day preyed on her heart. Paul and his plane should have flown away after the provisions were delivered. Rachel should be beside her, speaking words of encouragement, shining love to those around her. *Where are you, my precious daughter? What have they done to you?*

Ben would find her. Larson had to believe in him. Aside from his crude mannerisms and sometimes savage treatment of others, he had good intentions and a passion for Sudan and its future. That future held his dreams for Rachel. The plight of the southern Sudanese kept him awake at night and moved him on to the next battle. He planned and schemed, cleverly outthinking the enemy. For certain, Ben cast fear into the hearts of the GOS. Larson disapproved of many of his methods, but she agreed with his purpose. The war had to end before millions more died.

Larson massaged her shoulders. She would give her soul to have Rachel returned unharmed.

If she had a soul.

# 8

Nyok watched the women scoop up buckets of water from the stream amid the cattle and goats. Some laughed. Others merely went through the motions of living. After the bombing, he had committed himself not only to protect Dr. Kerr, but also to spend every spare moment keeping guard on the village with the other warriors. With the added responsibility, he had little time for serious thought.

He pledged that no enemy soldier would kill their few cattle or seize their women. Colonel Alier had given him a rifle and taught him how to use it. Nyok would not hesitate to use the weapon. In fact, he welcomed the opportunity to kill the *mujahadeen*—the so-called holy warriors. He would never forget what the GOS had done. The memories rained terror on him: the screams woke him at night, and the gruesome sights would horrify the worst of evil spirits. Nyok shivered while his face dripped in sweat. He longed to join the SPLA and avenge his village's murders, but always Dr. Kerr interfered and Colonel Alier stopped Nyok.

"Dr. Kerr and Rachel need you as their warrior and protector," the colonel had said. "You know how to use the rifle. Don't let any harm come to them. You are a soldier, Nyok. They are your charge. Soon we will talk of other things. Remember, this is your training ground."

The words still weighed in his mind, as though a giant accuser stood over him. He had failed with Rachel, and he blamed himself for her abduction. If he forced himself to admit the truth, he should have been the one the colonel attacked, not Paul Farid.

Nyok understood the SPLA leader all too well. If Nyok hadn't been at the plane with Paul and Rachel and seen the pilot's bravery, he would have held the man down while the colonel wrapped his fingers around his throat and choked him to death. Nyok clenched his jaw. So many things to consider, and he had no answers. Farid was a Christian, like Rachel, always ready to help anyone in need—almost to the point of foolishness.

Nyok pondered on the thought of God giving him light and strength when he faced the lion. At times he didn't want to believe it, that some mystical, ancestral Deity had shown him the way. Confusion about God picked at his mind. Maybe he believed his single act of bravery was insignificant because he had never been given the opportunity to seek revenge. Even killing the lion hadn't fulfilled the deep craving that roared in his soul and thirsted for blood.

"You'll make a good soldier for the SPLA," Colonel Alier had told him.

The words bit into Nyok's thoughts, prodding and building until he ached to abandon his pledge to Dr. Kerr. Sometimes the hate welled inside him until he thought he couldn't stand it a moment longer. The unrest. The nightmares. The memories. The clawing at his throat. When he didn't remember, he believed in God. But at moments like this, his faith trickled away.

In the next breath, Nyok slipped back in time to a peaceful village. He was one of six children, and he remembered laughter and love. Even now he could hear his mother calling him. She had a sweet voice and a lingering smile. Nyok didn't have a hungry belly then; no one wanted for anything. The garden he tended held plenty of vegetables, and the forests provided an abundance of fruits and nuts. Back then, Nyok inwardly grumbled about pulling weeds, because childhood chores lessened his play hours. His father had many cows, and this wealth brought respect among the villagers. Nyok smiled, remembering his greatest happiness came when he tended his father's herd.

For a moment he thought he could taste *ghee*. His mother made it from the liquid remaining from churned butter. She cooked it until it looked like tiny lumps of brown sugar. Then she placed the ghee on top of porridge with milk and sugar. Nothing could replace the flavor, though it wasn't necessarily the taste he missed but rather his mother's love.

He attended school in the village and started to learn Arabic and English. Math was taught by using sticks for numbers and marking in the dirt. And he always had Bible lessons. Nyok memorized countless verses and recited them for his family. In turn, his parents talked about Jesus and His love to all the villagers who would listen.

Bile rose in Nyok's throat. What had God done for his family? They were all dead, tortured … slaughtered.

Nyok swallowed hard and swiped at his eyes before glancing about to see if any of the women or other warriors had viewed his emotion. He dared not defile his position as a warrior by shedding tears.

Before the soldiers came to his village, his family had nothing to fear but wild animals. Sometimes, he could still hear the birds singing and remember his younger brothers and sisters roaming about with no thought of terror.

"Play with us, Nyok," they would say until he gave in. "We'll hide, and you find us."

The day, four years ago, inched unbidden into his mind. He didn't want to relive the horror, but he couldn't stop the demons from marching forward.

Nyok had been in the fields tending his father's cows when he heard thunder. He glanced into the cloudless sky and pondered the strange sound. Again the countryside echoed with more of the same sounds. He looked about him at his friends who were just as confused as he was.

Nyok ran toward his home. His heart pounded until he thought it would burst through his chest. Bloodcurdling screams mixed with rapid cracks filled his ears—a woman's high-pitched shriek and a child's shrill cry.

"Stop, Nyok," one of his friends said. "Soldiers are killing the people."

Nyok refused to listen. He raced ahead. From behind his hut, he peered at his mother and father. Their bodies lay in a bloody heap. His tribe didn't allow children to see bodies. The horror left him paralyzed. His two sisters lay alongside their mother. The sight sickened him, yet he could not tear his eyes from the sight.

One of the soldiers threw his baby brother into the air and shot him before he hit the ground. The *mujahadeen* laughed and continued their murdering and pillaging.

Nyok crept to his family, believing one of them must still be alive. He held each one close and paid no attention to the blood covering his body. The voices of soldiers echoed over the sound of muffled screams and the crackle of flames devouring homes. The enemy had returned to Nyok's hut. He slung a leg over his mother in hopes the soldiers would think he too was dead. For at least two more hours, the soldiers tortured and killed the innocent. They severed the arms and legs of some of the villagers and let them lie there unaided until they died from loss of blood. The soldiers celebrated and sang praises to Allah for bringing the infidels to their death.

Even after the soldiers had left, Nyok could not move. He thought that surely the day had just been a nightmare and that soon he would awake. When he awoke and the nightmare continued, he thought he must be dead. Then dusk swept across the village, and the hyenas arrived and began to eat the bodies. The will to live spurred Nyok to his feet, and he ran through the forests. He would stop for only a breath, but the snarl of preying animals or the sound of searching soldiers behind him pushed him on. All night he thrashed through the darkness, crying, reliving the sight of murder and treachery.

The following morning, Colonel Alier found him wandering through the forest. At first the guerilla leader thought Nyok had been wounded, but only Nyok's feet had been pierced and cut from the forest floor. Through his tears, Nyok told the colonel what had happened.

"Every enemy soldier from Khartoum deserves to die for what they have done to your family and village," Colonel Alier said. His features were like rock, casting fear as vivid as the enemy. The big man suddenly softened and placed a hand on Nyok's shoulder. A comforting hand … like Nyok's father's.

He urged Nyok to eat, but the images of the massacre choked any thought of food. Colonel Alier promised to take him to a village where a doctor would tend to his feet.

"When you're healed, come join us. My army needs soldiers."

"I will fight," Nyok said. "Show me how to fire a gun, and I will kill every Muslim soldier I can find."

A few days later, Nyok met Dr. Kerr. He had seen a white man once, a missionary who had visited his village. He had smiled a lot and talked about a God who loved them. Lies, all lies. Nyok wasn't sure he wanted this woman to touch him, but in the end he allowed the kindly, fair-haired doctor to treat his infected feet. When he refused to eat, she fed him as though he were a child. Sometimes she held him, but he refused to cry. He was finished with childish ways, including the juvenile belief in God. He didn't think Dr. Kerr believed in such stories because she never mentioned Him. The girl who lived with the doctor felt differently. Rachel believed strongly in God and encouraged Nyok to rekindle his faith.

"God did not bring this evil," Rachel said, her face peaceful and shining. "Those soldiers chose to murder your family. Would your parents want you to turn your heart against the God of their faith?"

Nyok did not reply. He knew the truth, and Rachel had been deceived. Even now he wrestled with God and the anger swelling inside him.

He believed he must have gone insane during those first few weeks following the massacre of his village. He slept constantly but was plagued by recurring nightmares, and he feared the waking hours because he was certain that death awaited him any day.

When Nyok's feet had healed and his body had recovered its strength, Colonel Alier urged him to join the SPLA.

"Boys your age are a great asset," the colonel had said. "You can avenge your family by killing the enemy."

"I'm not trained," Nyok said. "I need to know more than how to shoot a gun."

"I have men to instruct you. Don't worry. There are others who require training too."

Dr. Kerr heard the conversation and grew angry. "How dare you take this child—or any other child—for your bloody purpose! They will be nothing but decoys! No, I won't let you pull him into a death trap. He's in my care now."

Colonel Alier and Dr. Kerr argued; their voices grew louder over the peaceful afternoon. Nyok feared one would kill the other.

"If you take Nyok, I will never treat your soldiers again." She pointed a finger in the colonel's chest.

"You are bound by your oath to care for every person who needs it," the colonel said. He looked fierce, but the woman did not show fear.

"Please, Ben, leave him here with me."

"No!" Nyok protested. All the hatred swelling inside him exploded at the thought of being left behind. "I can learn. I can fight and kill the enemy."

Dr. Kerr took him by the shoulders. "You have not gone through your manhood rites. How can you be a soldier in the SPLA? Stay here with me, and be my protector."

"I am ready for my rites," Nyok said, shaking away her hold.

Dr. Kerr focused on Colonel Alier. "Rachel and I need a protector. If this boy is able to fight in your army, then he is able to watch over us."

The colonel peered into the doctor's face. For the second time, Nyok saw the lines soften around his eyes. Long moments followed. Finally the colonel spoke. "The boy can stay with you and Rachel until after his manhood rites. Then he is mine."

Dr. Kerr raised her chin. "If the war still rages, he will choose whether to fight or remain with me."

"We will see," the colonel said and walked away.

Dr. Kerr postponed Nyok's manhood rites until last year when he turned eleven, still young in some villagers' eyes, but he was ready. Finally he had come of age, but Dr. Kerr possessed a certain power over the colonel. Eventually, she had her way, no matter what the argument. Nyok used to wonder about this invisible hold, until he saw the truth in Colonel Alier's eyes.

Ushering his thoughts back to the present, Nyok shifted his weight to view the surroundings. He had devised a plan. Another boy in the village showed courage and a willingness to live with Dr. Kerr. He could be her protector, and Nyok could join the SPLA. He would kill ten men for every one of his family and friends who had been slaughtered. Surely God understood.

# 9

"It's infected."

Paul suspected Larson's diagnosis before she spoke the words. The possibility had occurred to him the previous morning when his leg took on a red cast. He had caught a glimpse of what looked like pus, but she was the doctor, and she had said nothing. Larson had given him an injection in addition to the antibiotic he took twice a day. She had frowned all the time she was redressing the wound. He should have guessed the truth or at least had the sense to question her treatment.

"So fix it," Paul said.

Larson pressed her lips together. "You don't have to stay here. You have a way out. Call FTW and have someone pick you up."

"Are you saying you can't treat it?"

"Look at this." She waved her arms around the hut. Her eyes blazed. "Does this look like a state-of-the-art medical facility to you? Infection here is as common as breathing. Are you ready to die in this third-world country?"

At times Paul was ready to die anywhere, but it had to be God's timing, not his.

When he didn't reply, Larson continued. "Get out of Sudan while you still have your leg and your life."

He wasn't ready to leave. Of that Paul had no doubt, but what good could he accomplish dead? "If I leave, I'm coming back."

She startled. "With more supplies?"

"Yes, and I want to do something here."

"What's that? Get yourself killed? Die a martyr? I'm sure there are enough GOS around to take care of those aspirations." She crossed her arms over her chest. "For that matter, Ben would oblige."

Paul studied her for several long moments. How long before her smooth features hardened in the Sudan and the bleak outlook for tomorrow cemented her heart? "I want to do what I can to get Rachel back. Have you forgotten she was with me when she was abducted?"

"Chivalry died in the Victorian era, Paul. You took a bullet attempting to help her. Fly your missions. That's more than most of the world would do."

A stab of pain caused him to grit his teeth. Larson snatched up his phone and handed it to him. "Make the call, or I will."

He punched in Tom's number. He fumed all the while, but he realized she was right. His leg needed attention.

"Tom, I need a favor."

"Sure. You name it."

"This leg of mine needs more medical treatment than Dr. Kerr can provide here."

"Okay. I'm on my way. And I'll see if I can't get Hank to come along. Your plane's flyable, right?"

"I think so. At least enough to get to an airport for repairs."

"Sounds like it's in the same shape you are."

Paul lifted a brow. "Very funny."


Larson heard the rumble of the FTW plane as it circled overhead checking out the landing strip. As soon as the plane made contact with the ground, the pilots would pick up Paul and transport him to Nairobi, Kenya, where he would receive proper medical attention. A feeling of incompetence snaked its way through her body. This wasn't the first time she had been unable to help a patient. She lived with the inability to heal all those who sought her out. If she admitted the truth, her fight against those feelings was what kept her among the Sudanese. Here if someone died, all anyone had to do was look at what she had to work with, not at her credentials. Even so, she blamed her own lack of ability.

"I admire your commitment to these people," Paul said from his cot.

Why did that man always seem to say the right things? "Don't put me on a pedestal." She flipped her ponytail over her shoulder. "You'll be very disappointed."

"I don't think so. You have no idea the respect and admiration that humanitarian organizations all over the world have for your work here."

"Yeah, yeah, I have the letters, plaques, and articles to prove it." She wished he would change the subject.

"You must love these people very much."

The statement twisted in her heart, and she turned away.

"I didn't mean to upset you." Paul's words were gentle, as though he spoke them to a lover and not to a doctor in the middle of a war zone. "I simply wanted to congratulate you, and for what it's worth, I'm honored to have met you."

*Maybe if I keep hoping, I'll make a difference.* "I'm sorry. I know you mean well, and I do appreciate what others say about my work, but I feel very inadequate." She pointed to his leg. "Like now."

He smiled, not so much from his lips but from his eyes. "Thank you for all you've done for me."

Before she could respond, before she could state he had been the one to bring food and medicine, before she could say how much his companionship over the past few days had meant to her, Nyok entered the clinic. "I came to help," he said to Paul. "You need a shoulder to lean on."

"That I do. And thanks for helping this crippled old man get about. When I return, I'll teach you all I can about the plane."

The boy grinned. "You're coming back?"

"Yes, as soon as I can get this leg on the mend and my plane patched up." Paul reached for Nyok's hand and shook it vigorously. "You're a fine young man, Nyok. I wish I had you protecting me. And thanks for helping me tape up the holes in my plane."

Nyok's face brightened in the shadows of the clinic. Paul had a friend with this one; the boy didn't warm up to many people. He had a difficult time trusting, but rightfully so. With an inward shrug, Larson scolded herself for referring to Nyok as a boy. He had long since been a man—a very old man with a troubled mind.

If she possessed the funds, she would send him somewhere to seek psychiatric help and then to get a fine education. A few times, she considered taking him to Kakuma, Kenya, where more than 80,000 refugees from Sudan, Uganda, Somalia, Ethiopia, and other war-torn areas had fled to escape persecuting governments. Although the camp faced serious food shortages, and the authorities there fought to keep peace and offer the refugees some dignity, Nyok could have received counseling and a sound education. Every time she mentioned the possibility, Nyok balked. If she didn't need him to protect her, he said, he would join the SPLA.

A few hours later, Larson watched both planes ascend into the African sky and fly south toward Nairobi. There a medical team would take her findings and administer treatment to Paul's infected leg. His friend Tom had urged him to return to the States, but Paul refused to consider it. He wanted his leg taken care of and his plane repaired in Kenya. As soon as the two were working normally again, he would return to Warkou.

Larson scrubbed the clinic with Nyok's assistance. Neither spoke. She was too absorbed in her own thoughts, and he appeared to be consumed with something. All around her, the work at the clinic mounted, and those requiring care continued to come. Friends and families knew no limits or boundaries when it came to seeking medical aid for their own. Many times they carried the sick and wounded from other villages in hopes she could heal their diseased and broken bodies. Their dedication made perfect sense to Larson. When one loses everything, precious life is all that remains.

She felt that Paul understood why she stayed—the complex, often ineffable reasons she kept her feet planted on Sudanese soil. Deep in his dark eyes, she had read the same longing and searching. Their different roles represented more than a compelling compassion for Sudan, more than a dauntless sense of urgency, and by far more than mere humans could communicate in their finite ways. Larson believed she understood this portion about Paul more than his friend Tom or the many humanitarian organizations that shook their heads at his fearless dedication. In a brief moment in time, a man had touched her in a way she had never imagined possible, and maybe she had touched him too.

"Do you think he'll be back?" Nyok asked.

She wanted to say no and not build up his hopes, but her heart echoed the truth. "He said so. He's not like most men."

"Why, when he has everything he could ever want?" Nyok lifted a pan of boiling instruments from the single electric burner.

"If you had the world in the palm of your hands, if you could buy anything and everyone at a mere whim, would you be satisfied?" She stared into his eyes. *When had his shoulders broadened and his voice deepened?*

Nyok glanced away, his gaze beyond the edge of his world—

his eyes fixed on the place where he refused to allow her inside. "No, neither would I be happy. Life has to mean more than wealth and power."

"Therein lies your answer," she said. "Some say religion provides stability to the faltering spirit."

"But you don't."

She shook her head. "Many believe science explains man's role in the universe. I have no answers for you other than we are all on a quest. Perhaps we'll find our peace before we die."

"You are in a strange mood today, Dr. Kerr."

She sighed and battled the heaviness in her heart. "I'm missing Rachel, and my mind races with fear for her." She hesitated to say more about her bewildering thoughts. "I want to know that her life has meant something in the realm of things."

"Her ways have helped me," Nyok said. "There are many who come to the clinic who look for Rachel. She has made a difference."

"We have to hold on to that belief."

"You saw something different in Paul." Nyok's words were not spoken as a question, but rather as an answer to the day's unrest.

Because Larson dared not audibly admit the truth, she hugged him close. "Without you, I am lost. Together we'll carry on whatever needs to be done."

"I wish you'd reconsider." Tom raked his fingers through his thinning red hair then rubbed his jutting jaw.

Paul couldn't focus on anything with the pain in his thigh, but he did know where he stood on returning to Warkou. "I'm not changing my mind, and my leg hurts too much to argue." He closed his eyes. Larson had given him a heavy dose of Tylenol with codeine, but it hadn't taken the edge off the pain yet.

"Okay. We'll talk when you're feeling better. Right now rest.

We'll be in Nairobi soon."

"Yeah, if I could sleep, I'd get my mind off my—" The sound
of a firing aircraft jolted Paul alert. He shot a glance at Tom, who
reinforced his fears. "GOS," he said.

"They're right on Hank's tail." Tom pounded his palm on the
side of his leg. "He can't climb or outrun them."

"Dear God, no," Paul said. "Bind the enemy. Put Your angels
around him. Get Hank out of there."

The sound of machine-gun fire continued. "I'm going to get
between them," Tom said. "We can take a few hits."

*But Hank can't.*

Tom picked up his radio. "Hank, I know you're in trouble.
I'm going to do what I can." He paused. "Hank, come in." He
turned to Paul. "I'm not getting anything. Didn't we check your
plane's radio before leaving?"

"The signals were fine." Paul watched the damaged plane
continue to fly despite the attack.

A stream of fire knocked off the pressurized tip fuel tank.

"He's hit." Paul's cries echoed throughout the fuselage.

The MU2 took a snap turn toward the damaged area followed
by a mixture of gray and black smoke. The plane circled once,
then began a fatal spin downward.

"No!" Paul watched the plane smash into the treetops and
burst into flames. "He's in God's hands now," he whispered.

# 10

Ben gazed up and down the river for a spot to cross that didn't have rocks or ledges. He needed a slow-moving current where his men could pass through the waters easily without thrashing. A couple of new recruits traveled with him, and most likely they weren't used to fording or swimming crocodile-infested waters. The first few times a soldier treaded into their territory usually determined how he would react in a firefight. It was a great training ground as far as Ben was concerned. He signaled for one of the men to head his way.

"Yes, sir," the soldier said.

Ben pointed down the river. "The best place to cross is just beyond that ridge. Take someone with you. Check it out. Make sure it's clear."

They needed to move fast; the GOS wasn't that far behind. His comrades were tired. They needed food, medical care, and munitions. Morale hit a new low when one day after another found them in the middle of battle and with hungry bellies.

As soon as the soldier reported the area safe, Ben moved his troops forward. He motioned for them to head across the shallow river and then cocked his rifle. If they were lucky, they wouldn't waste any shots on crocodiles. His trained eyes fixed on what looked like a log—one with huge bulging eyes. More of the treacherous reptiles remained motionless. Ben stifled a chuckle. The GOS had probably programmed the crocs to wait until he forded the river, knowing his habit was to wait until last. His men did a good job. They slipped into the river single file with the new recruits placed between the veterans.

Carrying his rifle above his head, Ben stepped into the water with one eye focused on the crocs. Midway across, two of them slipped toward him, then a third. He was accustomed to moving fast, but not faster than a hungry reptile. Cursing beneath his breath, he fired into the head of the closest one. The movement incited the others. There he was, midstream in the river, and he had stirred up their attention. Another shot from the shore ended the pursuit of a croc situated mere feet from him. Two more shots and, with the aid of his men, Ben reached the other side. The rifle fire was a drawing card to the enemy soldiers, but they would think twice before attempting to traverse those waters. Stirred-up crocs were as good as grenades. At Ben's urging, his men disappeared into the forest.

Once away from the river, Ben pushed aside the heavy brush and tramped deeper into the thick jungle. The calling of birds echoed above him, no doubt complaining of the intrusion. Wild animals, snakes, and an army of insects lived and preyed within the green-canopied fortress, but these were minor irritations compared to the enemy that relentlessly pursued the rebels.

Ben had traveled this well-worn path many times over the past fifteen years. Within the jungle depths hid an arsenal of weaponry for the SPLA. This was not the only facility. Others lay in strategic locations for the other forty-two battalions.

Ben contemplated the years he had spent dedicated to the guerilla army and the people of southern Sudan. In the beginning, even before he joined the southern forces, many of the soldiers were trained outside of Sudan's borders at special command posts. Since then, the army had seized control of many southern cities and kept its forces where it needed them most. Small arms, heavy artillery, ammunition, and trucks came from confiscated GOS arsenals and SPLA's allies. Still, the guerilla forces never had enough munitions, and their soldiers were always outnumbered.

"We have democracy on our side," Ben repeatedly told his men. "The free world supports our cause. They will help." Sometimes he had to remind himself too.

Ben viewed a fork in the stream and calculated another two kilometers before they reached the weapons cache. He signaled, and his men spread out, weapons ready. It wouldn't be the first time the SPLA encountered a traitor within its midst.

Two days ago, he had learned that Farid's MU2 had been shot down. The pilot's life meant nothing to him, but losing the plane left a string of regrets. FTW was the largest distributor of food and medicine to southern Sudan. Farid had done more than his share in flying those missions, but his reputation of escaping enemy fire had aroused enough suspicion that no decent SPLA member would trust him. Given his link to the royal family, his sudden conversion to Christianity sounded like deception.

In the past, FTW had made drops in the north at designated displacement centers where Khartoum had forced thousands of villagers who did not support the Muslim regime. These centers were nothing more than desolate, waterless wastelands. The government would give permission for the starving refugees to receive the supplies, then snatch up the goods for its own soldiers.

Ben remembered Larson's anger when he relayed yet another story about the inhumane treatment of those who opposed the GOS.

"One of my men escaped from a displacement camp," Ben had said. "He told of a group of children who appeared healthier than the others. They received food, clean water, blankets, and medical care. When asked why, the soldier said the GOS used the children's blood to aid Khartoum's wounded soldiers."

"Barbarians," she had said with a curse. "They are worse than animals. Can't anyone get food into those displacement camps?"

"A little here and there, but nothing substantial."

"Do something, Ben. Make the free world understand what is going on in Sudan."

"We're trying. None of us are giving up." Few regrets formed in his mind. All efforts were for the war. No sacrifice was too dear. Ben seized his own thoughts. *Rachel.* Without her, his resolve would make him more of a barbarian than the enemy.

The soldier he had sent ahead signaled for Ben's attention. Not a good sign. They didn't need problems, but adequate rest, food, and supplies before moving on. Four of his men needed medical attention; one had been wounded in the right foot the previous day, and his boot kept filling with blood.

"Colonel Alier," the soldier said, "we found trouble."

"What kind?" Ben asked without a hint of emotion.

"GOS has wiped out the supply camp—killed everyone and cleaned out the storage units. It's a bloodbath, sir."

"Anything left?"

"No, sir. I saw enemy soldiers ready to hit us."

Ben felt the familiar rush of heat singe his heart, the mixture of anger, hatred, and a thirst for Khartoum's blood. The GOS trailed both before and behind them. His men were exhausted.

Paul despised the hospital stay. The treatments were more of a nuisance, especially when he was torn between taking care of responsibilities in California and returning to Warkou. The smell of antiseptic, the tapping of professional heels up and down the hallway, muted voices with an occasional burst of laughter, and the bland taste of hospital food drove him to irritability. He didn't like his attitude, but he knew if the doctor didn't sign a release soon, he would bust out of there like a criminal.

Today, like so many other days, just when he had thoroughly immersed himself in self-pity, he remembered Hank. His long-time friend had a wife and two high-school-aged sons. Hank and Jackie directed Paul's Sunday school class. They were more than friends; they were family. He wanted to be there with Jackie, Tim, and Matt. Sending flowers and a letter explaining how the man had died for the cause of Christ seemed empty, insufficient. He had added special memories, especially the barbecues and family outings, the times of prayer and celebration, and now death.

The funeral service occurred while Paul lay with his leg wrapped in sterile bandages and an IV of antibiotics flowing through his veins. From time to time an efficient nurse offered pain medication, which he always refused. Suffering wouldn't bring Hank back, but to Paul, it eased his guilt. He wanted to put his arms around Jackie and the boys and grieve with them, not be stuck in a hospital, isolated from those he cherished.

No matter how hard Paul tried, he never managed to do enough. Always so many people died. Not that he believed for an instant his salvation came from works, but he wanted to experience the fullness of Philippians 3:10: "I want to know Christ and the power of his resurrection and the fellowship of sharing in his suffering, becoming like him in his death." These were the words of the great apostle Paul, from whom this broken contemporary had taken his name. They had so much in common—so much that Paul wondered if the biblical man had felt the same deep guilt over his prior persecution of Christians. They had both given up family, heritage, religion, political position, and power to follow Jesus Christ, but as the modern Paul stared at the ceiling in his hospital room, he questioned whether he had sacrificed enough. Having a relationship with his Lord was worth any price. He would gladly have taken Hank's place.

Paul swiped at a solitary tear. Hank had been his brother in Christ, the first man who truly accepted him at FTW, who welcomed him into church and Sunday school, who introduced him to Jackie with the immortal words: "This is Paul, my little brother, the one I never had."

Hank lost his life in the MU2—a death aimed at Paul. The GOS soldiers knew on whom they were firing. They had orders from Khartoum to kill the infidel. Muslim terrorists around the world had his name on their hit list. Any of them would have attempted a suicide mission to see Paul dead. His father would gladly slit his throat. His mother would hold the knife.

Paul struggled with the fury welling inside him because of Hank's undeserved death. He clenched his fists and fought the urge to shout at God about the unfairness of it. *It should have been me, Lord! It should have been me!*

The desire to return to Sudan and the village of Warkou stayed on his mind. He pictured Nyok, the boy-warrior who displayed the courage of a seasoned military man. Paul had seen something else in the boy's eyes, a smoldering hatred that often slipped over the cloud of mental torment. Given the opportunity to be relieved of his obligation to Larson, Paul believed Nyok would join the SPLA in an instant. War was for trained men, not angry boys. Nyok's course ought to be focused on an education. How better to serve his homeland than to one day take a prominent position of leadership and service?

Paul sighed and rested the back of his head on his palms. He recalled a discussion some months ago with a group of Sudanese refugees in California. They were young men in their early and mid-twenties who were a part of a group called the Lost Boys of Sudan. As children they had witnessed their families murdered and homes destroyed, then trekked across their country to eventually establish a refugee camp in Kakuma, Kenya. Despite the hardships posed by wild animals, disease, and starvation, these young men had the most profound faith in Christ that Paul had ever seen.

"God has saved us for something in His perfect plan," one young man said. "For me, it is to one day return to my country as a doctor."

"Education is before me," said another. "God will guide me."

"I am studying to be an engineer," said yet another. "I dream of my country rising above poverty. I am among the Lord's remnant."

Paul closed his eyes and prayed that God would protect Nyok from the swirling, evil world threatening to overtake him: *And Lord, use me however You desire. Keep Your angels surrounding Rachel, and bring her back to Ben and Larson.*

Ben ... Paul understood him more than the guerilla leader would ever want to know. He also realized the extent of Ben's ruthlessness. Now that he battled with slave traders, Ben was more than a driven man, a crusader, and a leader. He was a killing machine bent on destroying the forces that battled his heart and mind. Only Larson might dissuade him. She had a power over his actions, a control that Paul wondered whether either of them realized.

He had to get out of the hospital. The waiting with nothing to do but think was driving him crazy. Every day he read the news of GOS and SPLA clashes. Empty promises and prolonged peace talks mounted. The scenario never changed, only the time and the location.

First he must see Jackie and the boys. He wanted to cry with them and laugh about Hank's many antics. They needed to pray together for the future of the family.

"Mr. Farid."

Paul's gaze swung to the doorway. "Hey, Doc. Any good news?"

The coffee-colored man grinned deeply. "I signed your release, unless you want to camp here a while longer."

# 11

Nairobi flocked with people scurrying about, all dressed in Western clothing and always on the go. Energy swept about Paul. The taxi that brought him from the Hotel Inter-Continental to the airport in horn-blaring, bumper-to-bumper traffic made him wonder if dodging the GOS might be easier. Cell phones and fast food, mixed with the scent of outdoor markets and the heat of the tropical sun, livened his spirit, and for the present, he forgot about Hank and the despair of Sudan.

Nairobi was a beautiful city—well-landscaped parks, highly developed business areas, great shopping, and fantastic hotels and restaurants. The poor and the rich made up the city from the slums to the high-rises. To think, not far from here existed the wilds of Africa, untamed magnificence that words alone could not describe. The day before, Paul had taken a jeep outside the city to a game reserve and gazed at the skyscrapers of Nairobi while elephants roamed around him.

His beloved Sudan rose in his mind, a dream of peace and real beauty that soared beyond blue skies, fertile soil, and the calls of birds and animals. True harmony came in the curve of a child's smile, a mother who no longer feared starvation and disease for her children, a father knowing his family would not be persecuted for their faith. Paul shook his head and shoved the despairing thoughts to a remote corner of his mind. Later he would revisit them and continue to pray for God to intervene.

Thinking a cup of strong coffee rather than the Kenyan choice of chai tea would keep him awake for the long flight, first to London, then on to Los Angeles, Paul hobbled into a small restaurant and seated himself in a rear booth. He leaned his crutches against a wall and calculated when he could toss the nuisances and have full mobility. A young waitress approached. Although the national language was English, he knew the people respected hearing an attempt at Swahili.

"*Jambo*," he said to the young woman. She smiled and greeted him in return.

He waved away a menu and ordered *kahawa*. When she presented him with the cup of coffee, he smiled and thanked her: "*Asanate sana*."

Picking up a newspaper, Paul scanned the pages until he found the article he wanted: "Sudan Peace Talks." The moment he began to read, he could tell nothing had changed. In fact, all the articles read the same. Khartoum, the SPLA, and the Sudanese People's Liberation Movement (SPLM) would agree to certain measures, while the bombings continued in the south, especially in the oil-rich regions. No wonder Ben was frustrated and distrustful of anyone resembling the enemy.

Paul sipped his coffee and read through the paper. He had plenty of time before his flight, and spending more than three hours at the airport held more appeal than a similar wait at the hotel room or in the hospital. He had journaled through much of his recovery time and now longed to put his thoughts into practice.

"Excuse me," a young African woman said in Arabic. "Are you Abdullah Farid?"

Suspicion alerted every nerve. He noted the pretty face and the crisp navy blue pantsuit. Her carefully outlined smile looked forced.

"No. You have the wrong man."

She slid in beside him uninvited and tilted her head. "Your brother wants to see you."

*Which one? Does it really matter?* "I believe you're mistaken." She had a large purse, but he knew the tight security at the airport and doubted it could hold anything dangerous. Nonetheless, he glanced about for a police officer.

"Do you prefer Paul to Abdullah?" Her words sounded like a hiss. She continued to smile, a treacherous gesture.

He should be afraid, but after the last few weeks in Sudan, this woman merely served as another frustration. "What do you want?"

"For you to come with me."

Paul lifted the coffee to his lips. He didn't see anyone watching them. Two Arabs sat at a far table, but the others seated in the small restaurant were black skinned and two Caucasian. "And if I refuse?"

"The men at the door have weapons. You will be killed."

Paul picked up the newspaper. He feigned interest while trying to figure out which men had their sights on him. "I'd be killed anyway. I'll take my chances right here."

"You're a fool. We're prepared to kill all these people."

"With what?" He still pretended interest in the paper. He saw a policeman walk past the front of the restaurant. She could be bluffing.

"I have a gun and a bomb in my bag."

*Stall her.* Paul neatly folded the paper. "Why would you want to kill yourself and these people to get me?"

She straightened. "For Allah. For my country."

How well he knew her devotion.

The policeman returned and lingered at the bar.

"Don't try a thing," she said.

The woman had been trained well. To anyone observing them, they looked like cozy friends. Paul wanted to believe the woman lied, but this type of action had been done before. Blowing herself up for the cause of Allah would give her more of a satisfying purpose according to Muslim beliefs.

"Do you have a name?" he asked.

"Doesn't matter. Either we go now, or I set off the bomb."

Paul refused to blink an eye. "Your friends will die too."

"Have you been gone so long that you've forgotten our ways? Now, before I lose patience."

Paul stood from the table and reached for his crutches. He refused to make this easy for them. Again his gaze swept across the restaurant. Two black men from separate tables rose to their feet.

Larson massaged her throbbing back muscles. Hot, tired, and hungry, she watched the last patient move slowly toward his hut. The man had lost an eye during a village bombing and had recently developed a serious stomach problem. In short, he had mere months to live. How many times had she dreamed of a hospital with solid floors and a clean antiseptic smell where the southern Sudanese could obtain proper care? She had had all of that and more years ago in the States, but back then she had taken the professional setting for granted.

She picked up a bottle of water that Paul had left and downed most of it. Perhaps a mobile hospital the size of a semi truck to travel around from village to village was the answer. Of course, Khartoum would confiscate it in no time.

"You look more tired than usual," Nyok said. The two of them, like robots, had begun to clean and disinfect the clinic.

"Depression is playing a hard game with me. I'll get to bed earlier tonight."

"I miss Rachel too." Nyok continued about his business, gathering up instruments to sterilize.

She shook her head. "You know me too well. No matter how hard I try to hide something, you always know."

"It's my responsibility."

Larson bit back a remark about his young age. She saw no merit in insulting his warrior status. "Must everything be a duty?"

"I could ask the same of you."

She studied his face, wishing she could peer into his soul. His age, his wisdom, always astounded her, but with her realization came another heart-wrenching truth. Beneath Nyok's often hard exterior dwelled a deeply troubled man-child. Larson moistened her lips. "Responsibility and duty are the by-products of many happenings bearing down on our lives. They involve emotion and passion."

Nyok stared back at her. For a moment, his hollow eyes revealed the pain tugging at his heart. "You know my story. Nothing has changed with me."

"I know only what you have chosen to tell me, but it festers within you, like an infection that won't respond to medicine."

"Possibly. Perhaps I'm waiting for the right time to lance my wound." His stance had not changed, no emotion creased his smooth skin, and the lack of visible response frightened her. "Tell me why you work yourself into an early grave? What happened in the United States?" he asked.

She shivered in the hundred-degree heat. "I'm a committed doctor. I took an oath—"

"You can be a doctor anywhere. You're not Christian either."

"I told you the story of how the missionary's child died in my care."

He waved away a mosquito. "That story may work for others, but not me."

No one knew the truth but her. "Some things are too personal," she said.

"Not mine to hear, or are you denying what I see?"

*Where are you, Nyok?* Why did the unspoken words between them mean more than the ones they shared? "Are you angry with me?"

He picked up a broom. "No, Dr. Kerr. I speak of the happenings bearing down on our lives—the reasons we take on responsibilities. Isn't that what you said?" He paused. "I think you and I are like mother and son, but because we are not blood and flesh, we cannot open our hearts."

"It would be difficult, I agree." She stopped, before she said more. Most of their discussions merely danced around those things that psychologists insisted brought healing. "I love you, Nyok."

Nyok pressed his lips together. "At times I believe there is no room in me for love. Other times, I feel God calling my name, but I cannot tell you what you want to hear until the pain is gone."

"How can I help?" Desperation clawed at her words. The mother cries inside her begged for his healing.

"Let me carry out my responsibilities."

She knew exactly what he meant. "I cannot."

Paul took his time hobbling to the front of the restaurant. He had experienced many close calls, and each one had seemed like his last. He prayed and looked about for a way to escape. If only he knew whether the woman was bluffing. The lives of innocent people were at stake.

"Paul Farid." A well-dressed Caucasian with a British accent smiled broadly and stood from a small table. "Do you remember me, Roger Welby? We met about six months ago in London at a benefit for the Sudanese."

"Yes, I believe I do." He leaned on his crutch and extended his hand for a shake. "Pardon my manners here." Paul had no recollection of the man.

Welby returned the gesture. "How's the leg? I hear you took a bullet?"

*How does he know?* Tom had taken every precaution to conceal Paul's identity at the hospital. "Almost as good as new," he said. The man was casually dressed in tan slacks and a blue, button-down shirt.

"Do you have time for coffee?" Welby asked, pulling out a chair.

"No, we have a plane to catch," the woman behind him said in perfect English. "Honey, we need to hurry."

"What a shame," Welby said. "I wanted to learn more about your work."

"Another time," the woman said. She glanced toward the men waiting.

"Aren't you going to introduce me?" Welby asked.

Paul realized this might be his only opportunity to elude those who sought to kill him, but foremost in his mind was the crowd in the restaurant. He saw a handful of children. No, he definitely couldn't risk their lives.

"Ah, yes—"

"Rasha." The woman nodded politely and linked her arm to Paul's, the same arm that held her bag. "Darling, I'm nervous about catching our flight."

Paul smiled at her. If only he could get his hands on the bag draped from her shoulder.

"It's a pleasure to meet you, Rasha. Paul has excellent taste." A concerned look passed over Welby's face. "What is sticking out of your purse?"

Instantly Rasha released Paul's arm. Welby snatched her bag. She gasped and struggled, shoving Paul toward the table. Two other men and a woman swung into action. The men headed for the door. The third detained Rasha. Paul lost his balance and sent the crutches crashing to the floor. He reached for a chair but couldn't stop the spiral downward. A shot cracked. Then another. Screams pierced the air, and Rasha fell against Paul.

# 12

"It's all right," Welby said. "We've got them."

Paul felt the weight of Rasha's body pressing against him. Her head lay over his shoulder, and when he reached to touch her forehead beneath a thick mass of black hair, blood oozed between his fingers. She had neither uttered a sound nor moved since she slumped against him.

Someone lifted Rasha's body from him. With the sight of her life's flow pooling around him and the unspoken confirmation of her death, his stomach twisted into a knot. A senseless vendetta in the name of a false god. Now, the young woman lay dead, and when he glanced toward the front of the restaurant, he saw the lifeless form of one of her accomplices. The second man stood handcuffed. The sounds of whimpering women and children shrouded his senses. Their cries seemingly grew until they became a cacophony of all those who had perished under the veil of Islam.

Welby assisted Paul to his feet. His wounded leg felt like liquid fire. "Thank you." Paul bit down hard on his lip. "Who are you?"

"British Intelligence," Welby replied. "We got wind of this attempt when you arrived in Nairobi." He handed Paul the crutches.

"They don't give up, do they?" Paul attempted to sound light, but his inflection betrayed him.

"At least these three won't cause any more trouble." He eyed Paul from head to toe. "We'll get you cleaned up and into some new clothes before your flight leaves at 10:25."

"Again, thank you."

"Did the woman say anything we need to know?"

Paul sighed. "Nothing that you haven't heard or will hear again. They won't stop until I'm dead."

Paul glanced down at his fingers. Blood still was embedded under his right forefinger nail. He unbuckled the seat belt and limped to the rest room, without the aid of his crutches. His leg throbbed, and he considered taking the painkiller tucked inside his carry-on, but he needed time to think through what had happened at the Nairobi airport. Many people, including children, could have died, and for no reason except that Paul's family wanted him dead.

"May I help you?" a male flight attendant asked.

"No, thanks. I'm managing." He saw the scowls of a few seated passengers. He had seen the stares from Arab-haters before.

Paul thanked God for sparing his life, just as he had on past occasions when he had narrowly escaped death. But why had God spared him? What could he possibly do of such vital importance to further the kingdom? Money was not the issue. In the event of his death, his wealth went to FTW. Perhaps he wasn't to know the purpose, and with that acceptance he must go on. If God willed a martyr's death for him, it would come soon enough.

His mind lingered on Jackie and the boys. Hank had loved

his family, and he had devoted his life first to God and then to it. Their concerns had been his concerns. Their victories, his victories; their joys, his joys. Whether Jackie had wanted to see a weepy chick flick, or the boys had decided to look at surfboards, Hank had wanted to be there. Most men let that kind of stuff slip by. He had played violin and touch football, flown food and supplies for FTW, and been able to dig his heels into any Bible study.

Once Paul returned to his seat, he balanced on one leg and tugged on his carry-on lodged between two other pieces of luggage in the overhead compartment. He wanted to update his journal, and unless he took the pain reliever and rested, he would be no good to Jackie. Right now, he wanted to forget everything about his sordid life and where it might end.

His flight touched down in Los Angeles on Tuesday at 2:55 in the afternoon after a four-hour layover in London. Weary and carrying more baggage than he knew a Christian should, Paul took a taxi to his cottage on Malibu Beach. He hadn't been there in weeks, and the thought of home sounded comforting despite the circumstances. Nearly an acre of oceanfront property stood as his private paradise away from the haunting reminders of all the turmoil existing around him. He heard the waves break against the shore like a healing balm. Tension eased from his shoulders, and the knot loosened in his stomach.

Paul paused outside the door and fished for the keys in his pockets. For a moment, he wondered if a bomb might explode the moment he entered. He had grown cynical of the world. It was a trait he did not relish, but one that was true nevertheless.

Here, his worries were minimal. The inside sparkled with the attentive touch of Rosita, who came twice a week whether Paul was there or not. He loved the way she smothered him with affection and an ample amount of enchiladas, rice, and refried beans. What an easy life. His accountant paid all of the bills, and when he needed to simply talk, Hank played the wise counselor. *At least he used to.*

Paul limped to the wall of windows along his living room and peered out over the blue ocean. The waves crashed against the sand and pulled it out to sea. He loved the rhythmic sound, even when the waters grew angry and white-crusted foam boiled fiercely above each wave. He respected its dominance. It kept him humble.

He focused his attention beyond the swaying palm trees and slate-colored rocks to where the horizon blended into everlasting blue. The thought of being swept away in the hypnotic trance tugged at his senses.

Pulling away from his aquatic reverie, Paul sank onto the sofa and pulled out his cell phone. He must call Jackie. He had put it off long enough. Obligation and responsibility lay before him. She answered on the third ring, her voice soft and weak.

"Jackie, it's Paul."

She sighed. "I'm so glad you're home. Are you okay? I mean your leg?"

"It's healing fine. Is now a good time to see you and the boys?"

"I'd rather come there. This house is beginning to close in on me." Her voice trailed off.

"Of course. We can grill steaks later on and talk."

"I'd like that ... very much."

An hour later, Paul met Jackie and the boys at the door. Her pale skin, normally vibrant with color, alarmed him. She had always been slender, but now she was painfully thin with sunken eyes. He invited them inside, wishing away the awkward silence between them. He had watched Tim and Matt grow from Saturday morning cartoons and sweet cereal to sleeping late and devouring cold pizza. They should have had the glow of life on their faces, rather than the downcast features of men twice their age. The cloud of grief and confusion wrenched at his heart. Their long and lanky frames hung just inside the doorway as though they didn't know if they wanted to stay. Paul blamed himself, but did these two young men harbor the same resentment toward him?

Paul reached for Jackie. Her frail body collapsed in his arms. She trembled and sobbed against his shoulder. In the next breath, he shed tears with her.

"I'm so sorry," he said, once he had collected his emotions. "I should have been here earlier. Hank was like a brother to me."

"He loved you." She squeezed his shoulder. "The boys and I felt your prayers."

She released him and stepped aside to retrieve a tissue from her shoulder bag. Paul turned to Tim, the older of the brothers, reached for his hand, and drew him into a hug. Tim shook but did not break down.

"Your father was the best friend I ever had." Paul feared emotion would get the best of him again.

"He felt the same way about you," Tim said and patted him on the back.

The younger brother fell into Paul's arms and openly cried. "I miss him, Paul. He was the best dad ever. I wanted him to be at the diving competition next week. I wanted to make him proud. Now, there's nothing."

"He'll still be there." Paul held Matt against his chest. "And he'll be just as proud. I'm sure he's bragging to Jesus about you and Tim right now."

While Matt continued to cry, Paul glanced at Tim and Jackie.

"He hasn't shed a tear until now," Jackie said barely above a whisper. She linked her arm into Tim's, and the two moved outside onto the deck overlooking the ocean.

Paul's leg ached with Matt's weight, but enduring the pain meant showing compassion for the young man. The teen needed to grieve until every tear pent up inside him had worked its way to the surface. Standing just under Paul's nose, Matt clung to him as though he were a child again.

"I'm sorry," he finally said. "I thought I was strong and shouldn't cry 'cause of Mom."

"A strong man's not afraid of tears." Paul refused to let go of him. "Your dad and I had a few weeping sessions of our own."

"You did?" Matt pulled away.

Paul nodded. "Want to sit down and I'll tell you about it?"

"Sure." He swiped at his damp cheeks and handed Paul the crutches. In the next instant, they sat on opposite ends of the sofa. Matt and Hank shared the same type of personality, deeply sensitive to the needs of others and yet carefully guarded about their own fragile emotions.

"Remember when I first met your dad?"

Matt shook his head. "Seemed like you were always there."

"You were a little guy. I'd attended your church a few times and thought I should get involved with a Bible study. Your dad met me at the door one Sunday morning and stayed glued to my side. I came back the next Sunday, and Hank was there again."

"I don't know this story," Matt said. Paul reached for the tissue box, and the teen wiped his eyes and blew his nose.

"At a Friday night Bible study, a man who had been in the Gulf War made it known how he felt about Arab Muslims. He openly stated the group did not need my presence."

Matt's face softened with the story, so Paul continued.

"I needed to leave, and I made it to the front sidewalk before your dad caught up with me. Hank was equally upset."

"Mad?"

"Hmm, disappointed in the man who said he loved Christ in one breath and despised Muslims in the next. Your dad didn't want to be a part of any Bible study or group that had such open prejudice. Your mom must have missed us, because she came out of the house and announced she'd had enough. She took their car back home, and Hank and I headed for coffee.

"We drank bad coffee and talked for the next two hours. I thought we had the situation under control until I drove him home. There in my car, he broke down and cried for all the people who had been hurt by Christians. He knew I loved Jesus, how my family hated me, and about my plans to aid southern Sudan. Before I knew it, I was crying with him."

Matt's eyes clouded. "That's my dad. What happened then?"

"We ended up praying for the man in the Bible study class, and both of us went to see him a few days later. I shared my testimony and told him about the atrocities going on in Sudan. To this day, he is one of my closest friends. You know him—Tom, from FTW."

Matt's eyes widened.

"Yes, next to your dad, he's my best friend." Paul took a deep breath. "If not for Hank, I wouldn't have returned to that church."

The teen forced a smile through watery eyes. "Thanks for telling me. I remember Dad always had time for me, no matter if I'd done something I shouldn't or if I'd done something good. If Tim or I or Mom needed him, he stopped whatever he was doing. I want to be a dad like that someday."

"You will be," Paul said. "You had the best role model any son could have been given."

Matt glanced out the window. "I guess we should tell Mom and Tim they can come inside now."

"Good idea." Paul patted his shoulder. "If you want, we can all tell the stories we remember best about your dad."

Matt stood from the sofa. "Okay, I'll get Mom and Tim. My stomach's telling me it's time to fill it up. What are we having to eat tonight?"

"Steak, potatoes, salad, sourdough bread, and Rosita left a double-chocolate cake in the fridge."

"Any of her enchiladas?"

"You bet."

Later on while Tim and Matt walked along the beach, Jackie and Paul sat outside on the deck, each with a light comforter in the chilly night air. They had all shared their favorite stories about Hank, laughing and crying together until they were exhausted. Even now, Paul didn't want the evening to end.

Suddenly he remembered one of Tim's comments made at dinner.

"Now I understand how the families of all those people felt from 9/11. It's not God's fault, and yet I want to blame Him. He could have stopped those terrorists, and He could have saved Dad."

Silence had reigned around the dinner table.

"We have all met those same emotions," Jackie had said, resting her fork beside her plate of half-eaten food. "Having someone responsible for tragedies justifies our hatred."

"I don't hate anyone, Mom." Tim swallowed. "Maybe I do. I'm trying to work through Dad's death like he would have wanted. But it's hard. Almost too hard."

"That's why we have God," Jackie said as she reached across the table and placed her hand on his arm. "What we really hate is not people, but evil, and what it does to the innocent."

Now, as Paul reflected on the conversation, he could see and hear Hank in his family's grieving. *It should have been me, Lord. Not Hank.* When one day Paul felt the embrace of his Savior, he would surely ask Him why.

"Let's talk about you," Jackie said, bringing his thoughts to the present. She sat her coffee mug on a small table between her and Paul.

"Me?"

She gave him a "yes, you" nod like the ones he had seen her give Tim and Matt. "Hank and I had a long discussion about you before he left. He had this speech prepared, and since he can't deliver it," she took a deep breath, "then I will do it for him."

Paul searched his mind for what the topic of the speech might be. When nothing surfaced, he bravely responded, remembering how Hank had always played all the possible scenarios before speaking. "Okay, curiosity has the best of me. What did Hank want to tell me?"

"He ... we ... are concerned that you ... have a martyr complex."

When Paul started to protest, she held up her hands in defense. "Hear me out. For Hank's sake, I think you need to listen."

He settled down, and she began again.

"Taking into consideration your past, your faith, and your commitment to the people of southern Sudan, you are one brave hombre," she said, using Rosita's description of him. "But is your dedication based on the desire to follow Christ, or the desire to face a martyr's death?"

Heat rose from Paul's neck to his face. Conviction pressed at his heart.

"Uncross your arms, please. I know you don't want to answer me, but please don't tune me out," she said.

He grudgingly consented and allowed his arms to rest at his side. His heart drummed against his chest. "I want to help those I have hurt and the families of those I have killed in the name of Islam."

"I understand." Jackie's gold-brown eyes pooled. "You love Jesus and want to follow Him unashamedly."

Paul allowed her words to rest first in his mind and then his heart. He knew how he longed to leave this world. Guilt raged through his very soul. Unlike the biblical Paul, most of the time he had no desire to continue living on this earth. All the good he could possibly accomplish would never make up for his sin. He had heard all the reasons why his beliefs were wrong, but they still nestled inside him where they ate away at him like acid.

"I don't expect you to talk about this tonight, not with Hank's death and all of the problems you just left behind in Sudan. But will you promise to pray about it? Will you seek God's will before you go back and risk your life?"

"Why would God not want me to continue my work?" Paul questioned the unfair scrutiny of his ministry.

"I'm not saying He doesn't. I'm just asking you to seek God about what you're doing."

"You're questioning my motives." Annoyance inched through him.

"I'm asking you to explore your reasons for what you do. That's all." The boys ambled their way. "Please, Paul, don't be angry with me. I don't want to lose my husband and his brother."

He stared out at the shadows dancing off the ocean. "Okay."

"It's because we love you."

For those tender words, his mood softened. He didn't want to contemplate her request. He feared the answer.

Larson lifted the newborn baby girl from her mother's arms, a perfectly formed picture of innocence. Nothing else symbolized life more than a mother and child as they became acquainted for the first time. Even in the torrid heat of midday with all the struggles of Sudan, Larson laughed at the infant's squinty eyes and pursed lips.

"She's beautiful, Hannah."

"Thank you, Dr. Kerr. This baby is a blessing. I know God will use her for His purpose."

"Of course."

"When her father comes home from the army, he will be proud."

"I can see Peter now, carrying his little daughter everywhere."

Larson slipped her finger into the baby's palm. "Look at her, grasping my finger. She's strong."

Hannah fairly beamed. Perspiration beaded on her ebony face, and her eyes revealed her lack of sleep. "Her name is Lydia."

A Bible name. She imagined Paul scooping up this precious baby into his arms and planting kisses on her round face. He treasured children more than any man she had ever known. Larson inwardly startled. Why had Paul come to mind? They had spent only a few days together, and she would probably never see him again. Although he did tell Nyok he would be coming back. She caressed Lydia's sweet face, while an image of the Arab Christian stayed fixed in her mind. Dare she hope for his return? Nyok needed a good role model—or was she thinking only of herself?

# 13

Paul decided he would not return to Sudan. He had endured enough. Over the past few years, he had been beaten, shot twice, threatened, almost murdered three times, and now his best friend lay in Forest Lawn Memorial Park Cemetery in Malibu. The SPLA had recovered Hank's remains and made arrangements through FTW to get him home. Finally Paul understood. Sudan could have his money, but not his life. It still had his commitment, but no longer his blood. Hank had termed Paul's obsession with Sudan a martyr complex, and Jackie agreed. For once, he would listen to his friends, and they needed him here.

For three weeks, he had prayed to God and talked to those who offered wise counsel, and the consensus was that he should live out his days in Malibu. Tom had argued all along that by his present involvement in Sudan, Paul was making it far too easy for his family to locate and come after him. Besides, because of his past, many of those he had tried to help distrusted him. He wrote in his journal and read back through the past narrow escapes from death. What a fool he had been.

Jackie needed him to help put her life back in some semblance of order. She found it difficult to understand the legal aspects of her husband's death, and sorting through his affairs left her weeping. Paul and the boys disposed of Hank's clothes while she sat through a counseling session with their pastor. When Jackie discovered what they had done, she withdrew into her room until the following day. Once Hank had boasted that Jackie held the family together like permanent glue, but these days she could barely manage to hold herself together. It was obvious that she was just taking life one day at a time. Supporting Jackie as she learned to cope with widowhood was the least Paul could do.

The doorbell rang, and he hobbled to answer it. Three weeks of healing, and his leg still ached from time to time, fortunately not as badly as before. He had graduated from two crutches to one crutch, which soothed his disposition slightly. Rosita said he needed patience, reminding him that if God took six days to make the world, then Paul could wait the time needed for his leg to heal.

"I'll get the door." Rosita's chubby body waddled from the kitchen. "You rest. Besides you pay me to take care of you."

Paul laughed. "I pay you to mother me and fatten me up." He swung the door open with one hand. Matt met him with a shaky smile, his long arms dangling in front of him.

"Hey, Paul. I know I should have called." He slumped against the doorframe and stuffed his hands into the pockets of his cutoff jeans. "Do you have time to talk?"

"Sure, come on in." Paul studied Matt for a moment, and the youth met his gaze head on. A challenge of some sort radiated from Matt's eyes. Once inside, they chose to talk on the deck.

"What's wrong?"

"Mom."

"Is she all right?"

"She's depending too much on you."

An alarm sounded in Paul's head. "I owe her, Matt."

"Your friendship, but not Dad's place."

Ben scraped the blade of his knife across Quadir's throat. "You told me you had located the girl."

"I thought I had." Every pore on the slave trader's face begged for mercy. Droplets of blood trickled down his neck. "My sources told me the girl from Warkou was found. They lied to me."

Ben's face twisted in rage. His fingers itched to slit the man's throat. "What of the family's money, Quadir?"

"I have it here." He patted his pocket.

"What did you do with your informer?"

"I killed him, Colonel Alier."

Ben pulled out the fistful of dinars from the slave trader's pocket. "I promised this family I would give you 11,000 dinars for their daughter. I'm keeping this and the rest of your slave money. Every day she's not found is a day gone from your money and your life. Do you understand?"

"Yes, Colonel."

He pushed Quadir and smirked at his fall into the dirt. "Find her if you value your life."

Ben watched the slave trader scramble to his feet and race into the distance. The Arab repeatedly turned to see if Ben had picked up his rifle. The frightened looks fueled his anger. Dirty, sniveling coward. Ben wouldn't waste a bullet on him or dull his knife, unless he refused to produce Rachel.

Ben sucked back a sign of emotion. Not an hour passed that he didn't dwell on memories of Rachel. The possibility of her death waged a private war on his mind. If his sister had displayed her usual pride and stubbornness, the soldiers had already killed her. Only her beauty might save her, and then again, it could be the cause of her abuse or demise.

*Where are you, Ben? You once pledged your devotion to Me.*

The voice of the One who knew him best shook his private resolve. He had no room in his life for God. Ben spit onto the sandy-colored ground. *Leave me alone. It's too late. I have a job to do. Peace and love don't enter into it.*

The voice stopped. It wasn't the first time Ben had met the whisper of Truth.

Rain poured from the April sky, ushering in the rainy season. From now until December, those Sudanese who attempted to lead normal lives would be living in their permanent huts, reunited with those who were ill, nursing mothers, and the aged whom they had left behind. The cattle could not be allowed to graze in the swamps for fear they would contract hoof disease. For hundreds of years, the lives of the southern Sudanese had centered on the care of their cattle. These people deserved to have their way of life restored. All they wanted was an opportunity to live as their ancestors and to worship as they desired.

Weariness settled on Ben, a familiar condition, but not one he savored. Every muscle and bone ached, as though his body was a mass of bruises. He craved sleep and a decent meal, but then so did every SPLA soldier. The deprivations succeeded in making them all meaner and more determined to rid their beloved homeland of the hated GOS. Every struggle prepared them for the next one.

Ben had grown to glory in the sight of the enemy's blood. Let it spill until it filled the streams and flooded the banks of the Nile. Perhaps then Khartoum would retreat and leave his people in peace.

Another week passed, and Paul resorted to taking one morning call from Jackie. He no longer made daily visits to check on her. More and more his thoughts touched on Larson and Nyok. He even considered Ben and his infamous temper. More important, Paul wondered if Rachel had been restored to her family. His prayers became more incessant for those he had come to know and care about. As strange as it sounded, Matt's visit had freed Paul. The youth had pointed out Jackie's increasing reliance upon Paul and the dangerous road that lay ahead if he allowed it to continue. Jackie had specific steps to go through in the grieving process: shock, longing, depression, acceptance, and recovery. Currently, she teetered between shock and longing. While outwardly she appeared well into recovery, her sons and Paul saw the despair. She had a wise Counselor, and by Paul's stepping back, she would be forced to turn to Him and not to another man.

Paul sat on his deck and allowed the ocean sounds to relax his body and soul. Glancing down, he saw the day's unopened mail. Thumbing through the various sizes of envelopes, and setting aside those with return addresses from organizations requesting donations, Paul spotted a letter postmarked Kenya. The handwriting looked like Larson's. He couldn't remember giving her his address, but in any event he was glad she had written. With the eagerness of a kid, he tore into the envelope, then slowed to carefully read the letter.

*Dear Paul,*

*I trust you are recuperating well on the California beaches. Being from Ohio, my memories of trips to California consist of beautiful weather and water. Please accept my condolences in the death of your friend. From the information I gathered, I see he left a wife and two sons. Kindly give my sympathies to his family.*

*Nothing here has changed. Each day is much as the day before. I delivered a beautiful baby girl to Hannah. Perhaps you remember her. She promptly named the baby Lydia, and Hannah claims that as soon as the war is over she intends to clothe her daughter in purple. I believe something is stated to that fact in your Bible.*

*Ben has not been here. I received word of fighting and some victories. I also hear he has become more ruthless with the enemy and those whom he feels are informers. I know his fury is due to Rachel's abduction. In the past he did his best to offer Christianity to those he captured. The slave traders haven't been able to locate Rachel, and I am more and more fearful about her fate.*

*Nyok speaks of you often. You obviously made a positive impact on his life. His devotion is the main reason I'm writing this letter. Nyok is filled with bitterness. Even if I felt like relaying his tragic story, I couldn't begin to share the depth of his emotions. Neither do I know its entirety. Unfortunately he attempts to disguise his pain with his status as warrior-protector. In short, he wants to join the SPLA, and Ben encourages it every time he's here.*

*I'm sure you're well familiar with the child soldiers, for both the north and south utilize them in their armies despite the fact that the practice is forbidden by the United Nations. You know how I care about Nyok, and now with Rachel gone, I can't bear the thought of losing him in this horrible war. My dreams are for Nyok to obtain a good education. He's so very intelligent with insight far beyond his years. This could be accomplished in Kakuma, Kenya, at the refugee camp. I know the conditions there are not good, with the shortages of food, drinking water, and medical provisions, but I do believe it's a better place than here. What I'm asking is this: I've already written Kakuma to see if anyone could take over parenting him. I don't want him in a potentially harmful atmosphere. When I mentioned this to Nyok, he was very upset. He refuses to listen to reason about joining up with Ben. Do you have time to write Nyok a letter that might possibly dissuade him from taking up arms for the SPLA?*

*If this is impossible for you, I will understand, but I did want to pose the question.*

*Sincerely,*

*Larson Kerr*

Paul read Larson's letter three times before he folded it and inserted it back into the envelope. Even then he continued to let it rest in the palm of his hand, as though the contents might disappear and he would forget her words. Paul wrestled with the decision to leave Sudan behind him. He hadn't really consulted God. He had simply decided that all the signs indicated he should stay Stateside. How wrong he had been not to consult Him about the future. Paul didn't want to be out of God's will or continue in a downward spiral away from His purpose.

He reached for his Bible and read through underscored passages from Psalms and Isaiah, many of which he had memorized. The phone rang, and he ignored it. He thought about the easy life in California. All he needed to do was write checks, and he could instruct his accountant to handle those matters. He could soak up the sun and listen to the waves crashing against the shores for as long as he lived. If boredom overtook him, he could travel to any vacation spot that struck his fancy. If he desired to step out of the realm of God's will, he could buy all the "wine, women, and song" the world had to offer. In short, Paul possessed the money to do whatever he pleased.

But his wealth came from God and belonged to God. So did his life. Paul's pitiful few years here on earth held no match for eternity. What mattered was God's purpose for him right now.

*Lord, I'm glad You never tire of hearing from me, and I realize that I've been a rebellious son during the past few weeks. Please forgive me for not consulting You about Sudan and Your plan for me there. I'm sorry for not bringing my problems and concerns to You sooner. I have no excuse, except fear of the future. You've heard me earlier about Jackie and the boys, but this is different. I don't know if I should simply honor Larson's request to write Nyok, or if I should get myself another plane and head back to Sudan. I'm not denying that the episode in Nairobi scared me, and since that wasn't the first time, I gather it won't be the last attempt my family makes on my life. Lord, what would You have me do?*

One truth stood uppermost in his mind: God already had all of this worked out.

Reaching for his crutch, Paul pulled himself to his feet. He glanced at the letter and recalled Larson's worries about Rachel and Nyok. His return to Sudan must be for the right reasons. By the time he had hobbled back inside from the deck, he sensed his spirit lifting. As if on cue, the sky looked bluer, the breeze felt fresher, and the flight of the seagulls reminded him of the peace he found only when he piloted the skies.

Paul no longer had a plane, although he had shopped a bit for another one, fully planning to purchase an identical model. With a new aircraft, he could fly without worrying about his leg, but once he was on the ground, he had to maneuver. As much as he hated to admit it, Paul was grounded until the leg healed.

Five days later, Paul purchased another Mitsubishi MU2 and mailed Larson a letter informing her of his plan to return. He had received his answer about returning to Africa, not in an eye-opening sermon or even completely in God's Word, but in bits and pieces from those who valued his work in Sudan and dreams about those he remembered living under oppression there. Each one confirmed his decision to return to the land of his birth.

Four weeks later, Paul flew over Kakuma, Kenya, and checked out the dirt landing strip. Once he had confirmed the wind's direction, he set the plane down. One of the camp's directors was waiting to escort him around the camp and answer his questions.

Joseph Kaei met Paul as soon as he stepped from the plane. The tall, broad-shouldered man with signs of gray weaving through his hair offered a wide smile and a firm handshake. "Welcome to Kakuma, Mr. Farid. I've heard much about you."

Paul grasped his hand. "I'm honored to make your acquaintance. And please call me Paul."

"And I'm Joseph. Our accommodations are meager, but we welcome you in love and hospitality."

"That's all I could ever ask." He met the man's dark eyes and detected the sincerity he desired. "I'm anxious to see the camp." Paul glanced up and studied the crowd ahead of him held back by Kakuma security. He waved, and many returned the gesture with shouts of welcome in a mixture of languages, mostly English.

Joseph greeted the crowd in the same manner. "Your e-mail said you had a particular interest in our education facilities?"

"Yes, I do. I have a young friend inside Sudan whose guardian would like to see him out of the war zone. Naturally, education is critical to the boy's future."

"I would not turn away anyone seeking our help, but remember we are in crowded conditions, and supplies run dangerously short." He spoke to a boy who retrieved Paul's baggage. "What do you know of Kakuma?"

"Little, except what I've learned through recent research. I know the camp originated in the early nineties when thousands of Sudanese boys entered Kenya seeking asylum from the GOS. These boys told of their families and homes destroyed in the civil war and recited a tremendous tale of their walking first to Ethiopia and then here."

Joseph smiled. "You know more than most people in the free world. Currently, the camp houses approximately 80,000 refugees from Burundi, Ethiopia, Somalia, the Congo, Uganda, and Sudan."

"What are the most crucial needs?"

"Food and sanitary water. Typical of refugee camps, we have a list of other things: clothing, housing, medical personnel and supplies, educational tools, and additional volunteers."

Paul surveyed the area. The massive undertaking looked overwhelming. "I assessed many needs from the air." He didn't want to say the area looked like an African slum, but based on what the officials had to work with, they did remarkably well.

"We've taken great strides, but daily we receive refugees. We are blessed to have so many churches and worldwide humanitarian organizations working together to help us."

"From the way I look at it, these people are the survivors, the hope of their countries," Paul said.

"True." They stood in front of a grass hut near the camp's operational structures. "This is where you will be staying. Once you're settled, you can let me know when you'd like to get started."

Paul stepped inside the hut, and the young boy trailing them placed his bag inside. "How does right now sound?"

Joseph introduced Paul to many workers involved in the day-to-day operation of the refugee camp. They appeared tired, but enthusiastic.

"We have the camp divided into zones, so the different groups can stay together. It helps morale and gives the people a sense of belonging," Joseph said. "Most of the refugees are women and children, and their needs are great."

Paul listened as Joseph talked on about the varying degrees of needs and how Kakuma worked diligently to eliminate the problems. To minimize the fighting, an activities director kept the men and boys busy with sports. To avoid disease, classes were held for the women about health and sanitation. Prenatal classes and infant care helped lower the mortality rate.

Staring out over the desolate area, Paul realized that only the commitment of godly people could keep the camp going. "Can anything be grown in this red clay?"

"No. That's why we are solely dependent upon contributions from around the world," Joseph said. "The United States provides approximately 70 percent of the food and supplies here, and that helps provide the refugees one meal a day—a tasteless mixture of maize. As you can guess, the population is malnourished."

Paul clenched his jaw. He didn't need to ask about depression and hopelessness. He saw it in the faces of too many men, women, and children. The condition of the refugees, their slumped shoulders and haggard faces lined with frustration, said it all.

"How do you bring any happiness to these people?" Paul asked.

Joseph clapped a hand on his shoulder. "Later on, we'll watch a soccer game. This is the highlight of the refugees' day. Although it's temporary, this, along with faith and education, gives them something to look forward to."

They strode toward a primary school called Malakal, where Paul heard children's laughter. This was the hope all countries needed. The building was constructed of a type of plaster made from water, dirt, and whatever filler materials the workers could find. "Do you mind telling me about your education system?"

The two men stood facing the school. "Education has top priority here, and it's one of the major factors in keeping peace among the people. Because the schools are open to all, English is the spoken language."

"What percentage of the population is involved in the education process?"

"Approximately 35 percent. We have three levels: early childhood, primary, and secondary. Those students who have good marks are eligible for a distance learning program through the University of South Africa."

"Where do you get your teachers?"

"Very few are university trained. Most are recruited from among the refugees. We work with all of them, so they can utilize their strengths. We also offer a vocational program for all interested persons, as you can see from the concrete building on the right. Those classes are taught by the refugees who have these trade skills."

"What about programs for special-needs kids? The boy I have in mind is bright, but I wonder about those who have disabilities."

Joseph released a sigh. "The International Rescue Committee and Lutheran World Federation have developed a program on the primary level to teach sign language to the deaf. They are also working on future programs for the blind and other learning-challenged children."

Paul processed all of Joseph's words. Nyok could do well here, and Kakuma was doing its best with its massive undertaking, but this wasn't the best situation for the boy. He needed to be in the United States or England.

Paul stayed at Kakuma for three days. He mingled with the people, the volunteers, the children, and those involved with the church. The spiritual leaders in Kakuma had a tougher job than those who attended the poor in U.S. cities. Before he climbed into his plane and left for Warkou, Paul phoned his accountant and added Kakuma to his list of monthly contributions.

"Thank you," Paul said as he shook Joseph's hand. "I appreciate your taking time with me these past few days. You're doing a mighty work here."

"We are blessed," Joseph said with a smile. "God is good, and He continues to meet our needs. My prayer is that He will touch the hearts of those who are able to give, so these refugees can have some sort of dignity and hope for tomorrow."

The situation Paul left at the refugee camp settled heavily on his heart. The age-old question swelled within him: *Why must the innocent always be the ones to suffer?*

# 14

Rifle fire kicked up dirt across Ben's path. "Get back!"

He aimed his weapon toward the top of a ridge and pumped out cover fire. His men scrambled into the underbrush. Except for one. He continued to move forward.

"Fata, get down."

Ben had suspected for some time that the man had lost his hearing on one side.

A rifle cracked. Fata's body twisted, and he fell hard on his face. Ben cursed. The man was a loyal friend, a trusted soldier from the Nuer tribe. For eight years he had fought under Ben and trained new recruits. Only logic stopped Ben from racing toward the injured man. All Fata had wanted was a chance for his children to grow up free. Now life drained from the still body into a ditch. A ditch of useless dreams.

Ben crawled back on his belly. Several more shots zipped over his head. He reached inside his shirt and pulled out a grenade. Signaling for cover, he hurled the death charge into the ridge. The explosion raised screams of anguish. Signaling again, he directed his men as they fired into the smoke. When they stopped, silence reigned.

Ben rushed to Fata and turned him over. His face was ripped open, his rugged features a mass of torn flesh. Ben pointed. "You three, bury him. The rest of you, search the area." Fata would not be left for the hyenas.

Once more, Ben had the task of bearing devastating news to an anxious family. When that unpleasant chore was finished, his lost friend would become a forgotten face, stacked in the cold, dark closet of his heart where emotions were banished. He would say a brief prayer and move on. So far, the desolate corner inside him had been escape proof. Except for James, his childhood friend and brother.

Into his rooted thoughts about Fata came unbidden memories of James, and always Rachel. Ben fought hard to focus. They had another battalion to meet four kilometers ahead. The two groups would march toward a camp of GOS who had confiscated SPLA munitions. From there he would head toward Fata's family; on to Quadir, the slave trader; then to Warkou.

Unlike the others, war kept him sane. He identified with it. It was linear and accomplished with action. The cost he could deal with, although often severe. For Ben, the difficulty began in Warkou. He needed to see Larson. Maybe she had information about Rachel.

Larson listened to the steady rhythm of the afternoon rain tapping against the thatched roof of the clinic. Sudan woke with the sun promising a new day and the evening's assurance of a magnificent sunset, but the afternoon brought earth-growing showers. In the past, she had found the rainy season comforting; it marked a temporary reprieve from the GOS. The crude roads flooded, making it difficult for the soldiers to get through. But since Rachel had been abducted, the rains served to deepen Larson's despair. The waiting to have the girl redeemed from her abductors plunged Larson into an ill-fated abyss.

If Rachel had been taken to one of the oil-rich regions, the likelihood of getting her back increased. The foreign oil companies had built high roads to carry their equipment through the rainy season. With transportation enhanced, Larson could levy a little hope that the slave traders could get in and out. Of course, better roads also meant the GOS could take advantage of the rain-soaked villages along the concrete path.

Larson wiped perspiration from her face with her arm. She squeezed a sponge soaked in warm, soapy water and scoured the medicine cabinet. She expelled a heavy sigh. No matter how she looked at the situation, the GOS was successful in destroying any hope of happiness for the villagers.

"Dr. Kerr," Nyok said from the clinic's entranceway. "Come see."

"What? Can't you see I'm cleaning?"

He linked his arm into hers and guided her to the doorway. "Look, over there."

A double rainbow spread across the sky with a backdrop of green mountains in the distance. For a moment, she tasted the overwhelming grandeur of nature. "Oh, it's magnificent."

Nyok leaned against the door. His slow smile sealed the moment. Too often her sweet warrior allowed the dismal circumstances of the day to affect everything he did. Seriousness was good in appropriate times, but she fretted that Nyok had long forgotten small pleasures. This moment relieved her concerns.

"My mother used to say rainbows were a sign of God's promises," he said.

"You rarely mention her."

"She was quite beautiful. My sisters looked like her." He cupped his hand under the raindrops and lifted it to his lips. "They believed in rainbows."

He had never spoken about them before. "Do you?"

"At times. I think one would have to trust in God before believing in His promises."

"I want to hear more about your mother. I used to make wishes on rainbows."

"What do you wish for now?" Nyok asked.

"Does it matter?" She had grown used to Nyok basing his understanding on emotion and the unspoken.

"Maybe not to me. Let's play a game. Give me a wish for every color."

She tossed the sponge into a bucket behind her. "I don't want to do colors, but I'll play as long as you will." When he nodded, she began. "I want Rachel back unharmed. I want the war to end. I want you educated at a fine university."

When she paused, he poked her in the ribs. "That's three; you need one more."

"I can't tell you the fourth. It's personal."

"I already know what it is." He laughed.

"Hush. It's your turn."

"I want Rachel returned. I want to join the SPLA. I want an independent south, and ..." He paused in midsentence.

"Was she gentle?"

"Very."

"Tell me about her." Larson spoke barely above a whisper and waited.

"Sarah, the one who has grown so old that you cannot tell if she's ever been beautiful, she is my mother." He watched a child play in a puddle of water. "Every time she picks up a crying child or gives her food away, she is my mother. When she sings praises to God over one who is dying, she is my mother. When the villagers seek her counsel, she is my mother. When you look at her and see the gold beneath the silver in her hair, she is my mother."

Larson swallowed a lump in her throat.

"One day when I marry, I want my wife to be like Sarah ... and you."

Larson sucked in a breath. "Me? Thank you, Nyok. That's quite a compliment."

"I might never find her." The child outside slipped and fell, her naked body coated in mud. "I'll get her," he said.

The comical sight broke the seriousness. Nyok held up the little one and allowed the rain to wash her, scrubbing her bare behind with his hand. Larson laughed with him. Relief eased into her bones. He would not have wanted to hear that Paul's return was her fourth wish. With the pilot's presence, she sensed new hope of finding Rachel—and maybe new purpose for Nyok.

Three days later, shortly after sunup, she heard the sound of cheers and lively voices. Larson set aside breakfast and raced to the center of the village. Ben had arrived. Her stomach fluttered, and the thought of seeing Rachel—touching her and hearing her musical laughter—made Larson tremble as she raced toward the soldiers.

Ben searched the familiar sea of black faces for the white woman with sapphire-colored eyes. The healer, the Sudanese called her, the one who had God in her fingertips. Ben chose to keep his sentiments to himself.

The moment he caught Larson's gaze, elation left her face. He could tell by her look that she expected to see Rachel. The grim look on his face had revealed the truth. She stopped amid the enthusiastic crowd and offered a wave and a faint smile while he and his men wove their way through the milling villagers. Sometimes she displayed the respect he deserved. Other times she rebelled over the slightest issue and argued her viewpoint. Discussions he enjoyed. Squabbling over different viewpoints reminded him too much of the conflict. If Larson had chosen to practice medicine in the north, she would have been tortured and killed a long time ago. He hoped the Sudanese never learned the mannerisms of American women. This one plagued him.

"Hello." Ben studied the tiny lines fanned from her eyes. Two months ago she didn't have them.

"You look tired, Ben."

"We've been on the move constantly, our supplies stolen and our men ambushed."

"I'd hoped the talk of peace negotiations would bring a halt to the fighting," she said.

"It's increased. Discussing give-and-take measures in Kenya hasn't changed a thing."

"Even in the oil-rich areas?"

"Those are the worst." A boy tugged at his pants leg, and Ben patted his head.

"With all the criticism of some of the European-based oil companies, wouldn't you think those firms would want to put up a good front?"

"Money speaks louder than humanitarian efforts." Ben spoke to a woman who had lost her husband during the last raid on the village. Once she stepped by, he turned back to Larson. "The oil companies want the profits, and Khartoum wants their slice to fund the war."

"I remember what you said the last time."

"The war's become an exchange of blood for oil."

She raised her shoulders as if to speak, then released a sigh. "I can cook for you. My patient load is down."

He knew her reasoning was to learn about Rachel, but he didn't mind. As long as they both recognized her ploy, they would surely not argue.

"I need the rest," he said, and indeed he did.

"Who did you lose?"

"Fata."

"I'm sorry."

"He had six kids."

She set her jaw. "I'll make coffee."

They walked to the clinic. Not a word passed between them, and for that he was grateful. Once inside he lay on a cot normally occupied by a patient.

"Why don't you rest while the coffee brews and I cook? You can't lead your men when you're exhausted."

"I'm no more tired than they." Immediately he regretted his harsh response. "Sorry, Larson. It's not the demands of war."

"I know." She kneeled beside him. "You're doing everything you can to bring Rachel back."

He placed his hands behind his head and avoided her scrutiny. "I nearly killed a slave trader—the one who has the best chance of finding her." A moment later, he added "It's as though she's disappeared."

"I keep dreaming about her."

"Is she safe in your dreams? Has some dirty Arab sliced her face or taken the light from her eyes?"

"No, Ben. She's always smiling ... and fine."

"Coffee sounds good."

Hours later, after the afternoon rains had lulled his men to sleep, Ben continued to stare outside. Larson had patched up his men and shared food from the FTW provisions. With full stomachs and the villagers hailing them as heroes, they would be ready to pull out in the morning. He needed to sleep, and wanted to, but no matter how heavy his eyelids, rest would not come.

"Do you want to talk?" Larson placed a stool by the cot.

"I'd ramble." Her nearness affected him in a way he dared not venture.

"I'd listen."

This was the Larson Ben enjoyed. "I read a report that one of the European oil companies donated funds to construct a huge hospital. Of course the facility would be named after them."

"How appropriate. Are they painting the hospital red?" she asked.

"My thoughts exactly."

"The report came out after an investigation cited that the company was behind the ethnic cleansing in the oil-rich regions." Ben cursed.

"What about the United States? Haven't they been conducting a report?"

"Yes. Their envoy visited twice. Met with Khartoum and the SPLA."

"Did you talk to him?" Larson asked.

Ben nodded. "And a few of my men. The findings went to their president, but I don't have much faith in any action on their part."

"The United States tends to be swayed by their own interests," Larson said.

"They haven't pulled much leverage yet." A weight pressed against his chest.

They sat in silence, just as most of the day had been. He wanted to look at her but feared his own wavering emotions. Why did Larson make him feel vulnerable and unsure of his own name in one breath and invincible and proud of his family heritage in the next?

"Do you want another cup of coffee?" she asked.

"I'd like that." He stole the opportunity to watch her. She possessed the grace of an elegant lady. He imagined her in a silk gown with her light brown hair flowing from her shoulders and diamonds around her neck. Her delicate features didn't belong in the midst of Sudan's war and poverty, neither did the easy sway of her hips. But he didn't want her anywhere else.

He rose from the cot, like a huge cat. Stealing up behind her, he wrapped his arms around her small waist and buried his face in her hair.

"Ben."

"Please." The scent of her enveloped his senses. He couldn't stop himself, and didn't want to.

"We can't—"

"Who says we can't." He turned her to face him. Her lips were but inches from his.

"Let me go, please. This won't work."

"Why?"

She trembled in his embrace. Was it fear or repulsion … or desire?

"Why?" he repeated.

"Because I don't love you."

"Does that matter?" He tried to mask the anxiety rising in him.

"To me it does. We're friends, Ben. Don't ruin it with this."

He ran his hands up and down her arms while the longing refused to dispel.

"Please, you're scaring me."

"I'm used to getting what I want."

"And I can't stop you." Her clouded gaze pleaded with him. "Do you really want me this way?"

A warning sounded in Ben's brain. His heart had betrayed him. He stepped back. "I … I don't know what came over me."

She sighed. "It's Rachel." She touched his shoulder. "We're both upset about this."

He knew his sister had nothing to do with it. "It won't happen again. I promise."

Larson nodded and reached to the small counter that held his coffee. Her fingers shook as she offered it to him. Larson knew the truth.

Nyok stayed close to the fire with Colonel Alier's soldiers. He enjoyed the talk intermingled with the crack of a spitting flame, although he preferred the clinic with the colonel and Dr. Kerr. She had told Nyok that the man needed rest and not a bombardment of questions about the war movement. He didn't believe her. She wanted him as far away from the colonel as possible. Any talk of enlisting in the rebel army would have caused a quarrel among the three of them. Dr. Kerr's emotions were fragile right now, and out of respect for her, Nyok chose to honor her request.

"When are you joining us?" a soldier asked.

"Soon," Nyok said. He felt the attention of the four other soldiers.

"I saw you kill the lion when we were here before," the same soldier said. "The SPLA needs courageous men."

"I'm not afraid."

"What's stopping you?"

"A commitment."

"What could be more important than your country?"

He formed his reply carefully. "Colonel Alier has given me a task, and I'm fulfilling it before I ask to serve under him."

The man gave a thin-lipped smile. "We will welcome you when the time comes."

Relieved, Nyok rose from the fireside and walked toward the clinic. From the doorway, he heard the colonel approach Dr. Kerr. Nyok held his breath. He dared not interrupt either of them. Irritation picked at him for the way she refused the colonel. Couldn't Dr. Kerr see how the colonel felt about her? How could she turn away from such a respected man, a leader among leaders? Suddenly Dr. Kerr's frightened voice alarmed him. If the colonel pursued her against her will, Nyok would have to intercede. He slipped into the shadows beside the clinic. The conversation veered in a different direction. A few moments later, the colonel left the clinic.

Once a proper amount of time had elapsed, Nyok made his way to the doorway. He had to make certain she was not harmed. He wanted the colonel and Dr. Kerr to find mutual love, not what almost happened. Inside she straightened the bandages. She swept a finger beneath both her eyes.

"I wanted to see if you had any chores for me," Nyok said.

She didn't turn to greet him. "I think we're fine."

"Any news about Rachel?"

"No. The slave traders are looking."

He maneuvered to her side and viewed the tears. "The colonel will find her. He always gets what he wants."

# 15

A week later, the low rumble of an aircraft seized Larson's attention. She held her breath and listened for the distinct whirl of GOS helicopters. She expected the sharp pop of gunfire and the cries of the frightened and wounded. The memory of a thousand other bombings paralyzed her body and assaulted her mind.

"Nyok, who is it?" she asked.

"Listen, Dr. Kerr. It's not the GOS." He hurried outside the clinic.

Larson opened her mouth to call him back, but he knew how to avoid the dangers. The two of them had been up since before dawn tending to an elderly woman and a nine-year-old girl who complained of fever, shaking, chills, and headaches. Their listless bodies now lay in a catatonic state. Shortly after daybreak, a toddler demonstrated the same symptoms. Larson sent the children's mothers home. They kept falling asleep while cradling their young.

Malaria. The women probably had it too.

Without enough proper medicine, many would die. Some strains were resistant to the inexpensive antimalarials, and many of the people contracted the disease despite taking an antibiotic. Mosquitoes. Larson hated them along with all of the other insects bringing disease to the Sudanese.

"It looks like Mr. Farid's plane," Nyok said. "I know his crashed, but it looks the same."

Her heart beat faster. Paul had written that he would return to help with Nyok. Yet she had expected him to change his mind. It made no sense to ask him to walk barefoot into a viper's pit. Guilt mixed with excitement mounted as she watched the plane descend and touch down on the damp earth. With Paul back on the scene, she had everything to gain for Nyok—a chance for education and a ticket out of persecution. If Larson forced herself to admit it, she needed to see Paul again too. What was it about him that had captured her senses and kept her remembering their encounters? She knew better than to consider involvement. It must surely be a link to civilization and their lengthy conversations.

If Ben discovered her feelings, no matter how insignificant, he would kill Paul with his bare hands. Another reason to hide her unexplainable reaction to him.

"Go, meet him," Larson said. "I have things under control."

"I won't be long. He may have brought medicine." With that, Nyok disappeared.

Proper medications would stop the spread of malaria, and she had mentioned it to Paul when he was in Warkou weeks ago.

Earlier she had administered the last of the chloroquine, and now she could only treat the fever and chills. The disease had attacked many of the villages, depleting what she had once felt was a generous supply of antibiotics. The toddler whimpered. He had soiled himself and vomited. The stench permeated the air. She rose to her feet and poured fresh water into a basin. This was only the beginning. These poor people didn't have a chance. If it wasn't the GOS, then starvation or disease attacked them.

Had it been only two days ago when she had laughed with a group of women who planned a garden? They had seeds, and with those nuggets came hope for fresh vegetables and healthier children. Now this. The laughter should come more often. Some days she forgot its healing powers.

Rachel had often rippled with laughter. If Larson dared to dwell on the memory, Rachel's sweetness echoed around her.

Several minutes later, Larson felt Paul's presence and whirled around to see him standing in the doorway, his arms laden with boxes. He stood shoulder to shoulder with Nyok. Odd she remembered him much taller.

"Hey. I'm ready to go to work."

The gentle voice echoed in her ears, and she turned away. "This is a messy business."

"Nyok told me. I have antimalarials—two types since resistance is a problem."

Tears pooled in her eyes. In the deepest part of her, she realized this was why Paul had found a home in her heart. "You remembered."

"I thought since I was coming, I might as well stock you up." He set the boxes in the corner.

"You're a saint."

He chuckled. "Now that we've settled my status, I'll get the plane unloaded."

"I'm glad you're here."

Relief eased the tension in her back and shoulders. She wanted to throw her arms around his neck and thank him for coming, but she dared not. A doctor had responsibilities and a duty to her patients. She could reveal gratitude, that was all. Anything else would be foolish and inappropriate.

The toddler began to cry. She scooped him up into her arms and drew him to her chest. Bare, hot skin radiated through her T-shirt. His name was Timothy. The joy of birth, the despair of death, she would never adjust to it. Nineteen months in this world, and he had been reduced to bones, fever, and chills. Now his limp body didn't have the strength to cling to her.

"Can you spare Nyok to help me?"

The question pulled her from the sadness. "Sure." She glanced beyond the dark-haired man and nodded to the boy.

"We'll hurry," Paul said.

She didn't say it might be too late with the precious medicine, that this little one couldn't take any more antibiotics until later. Besides, she doubted that he would survive the disease that was tearing through his tiny body. The villagers expected her to cure everything—and she couldn't.

While Nyok and Paul sorted through the various supplies, she scanned the boxes' contents until she found the one she needed. Larson calculated she would have enough antibiotics left to help other villages suffering with malaria. She had traveled to some of them and had used up a large supply. Always something threatened them: either some form of sleeping sickness or cholera, hepatitis, meningitis, yellow fever, and a long list of other diseases.

The toddler in her arms calmed and closed his eyes. Larson boosted him onto her shoulder and held his little body against her. So hot. His breathing sounded ragged. She hated for babies to die in her arms. No matter how many children played at her doorstep, flashed their smiles, and smothered her in tender hugs, the ones who didn't make it stayed fixed in her mind.

"I made reservations for dinner," Paul said over her shoulder. He planted a kiss on the sleeping toddler's forehead. "Can you get a babysitter?"

She startled. The unexpected invitation was just the kind of distraction she needed right now. "Depends on where we're going to dinner."

"Seafood on Malibu Beach."

"Little late notice, don't you think?" Larson turned to look at him. Her stomach fluttered. For a moment she felt like a girl again. Flirting, for heaven's sake in the middle of the stench of death.

Paul shrugged. "I just flew in."

"I don't know if I can get anyone to watch the kids at this late date."

"I'll triple the hourly."

His warm breath tickled her neck while he studied the ill toddler's face. She shivered. Ben had been this close a few weeks ago when he approached her. He had frightened her. Her mind had rippled with pity for the emotions he tried to hide. Later she had wished she could conjure up feelings for him, at the least stop the arguing that erupted most of the times when they were together. "I don't have a thing to wear."

"We'll stop and get you something on the way." He massaged her shoulders. His familiarity didn't bother her. In fact, his fingers kneading the knots in her shoulders brought comfort.

Her thoughts trailed back to yesteryear when life's cares centered on friends and parties. Closing her eyes, Larson allowed college days to shower her with sweet memories—fall leaves in scarlet and gold that ushered in football games and parties with hangovers the next morning, all-night study sessions with gallons of coffee and piles of milk chocolate bars. She remembered the sound of snow crunching under her feet and the first warm days of spring that brought the lazy days of summer. She loved the taste of watermelon, buttery corn on the cob, and juicy hamburgers on the grill—the thrill of convertible sports cars and the wind weaving through her hair. Umm … Dairy Queens and ice-cream trucks.

"Where are you?" Paul asked.

His quiet words broke the indulging spell. Oh well, she didn't need to be lingering in the past anyway. The present was what gave her purpose and walled off the bitterness from days gone by.

This suffering toddler, the child, and the woman needed her attention.

"I was thinking about college days," Larson said as she rose to her feet, "instead of administering antibiotics to my other patients. I feel stupid, selfish."

"No need to. Don't you ever take a few weeks off to rest?"

Given other circumstances, she would have laughed. "I took three days off two years ago. I'm always afraid of what will happen in my absence."

"Life goes on with us or without us." He touched the toddler's head. "He's burning up. Let me take him."

Larson relinquished her hold and allowed Paul to gather up Timothy. Reality snaked up her spine. "I've had malaria outbreaks in other villages."

"I can help. That's why I'm here."

The emotion in Paul's words touched her, but she refused to comment or look his way. "Okay, since you offered, I'll put you to work." She wanted the conversation back where it stood before, light and teasing. Perhaps weariness had tugged at her long enough.

Hours later when the afternoon rains had gently lulled the infant to sleep, Larson eased down to sit on the floor beside Nyok. She could easily nap, but fought it. Patient charts and reports sat unfinshed.

Nyok read through an astronomy book that Paul had brought him. He sighed, lost in a world not his own. Good, her dear boy needed to challenge his mind.

Paul wrote in a thick book. Now and then he lifted his head and looked about.

"A journal?" she asked.

He nodded. "I don't keep it up every day, but whenever I think of it."

"I used to keep a journal, but then I noticed my entries were all depressing."

"Me too. Now I make it a point to include the good things too."

She tilted her head and blinked to hold the sleepiness at bay. "Paul, I believe you're an optimist, one of those 'the glass is half full' types."

He stuck the pen behind his ear and closed the journal. "I'm a Christian. I believe in hope rather than despair, victory more than failure." He paused. "I once heard a journalist who said that a pessimist is an optimist with experience. I don't intend to ever soak up that attitude. I serve a mighty God who promises life."

Like Rachel. What was it with these Christians?

Nyok lifted his head, and an unspoken word passed between her and the young man. She sucked back a remark. A little more time in Sudan, and Paul would realize how foolhardy his beliefs were. He might be an Arab Christian, but he had no idea of the suffering in this country.

"Do you feel up to discussing Rachel?" Paul asked as he shoved his journal and pen into his backpack.

"I need to. We haven't heard a thing." She yawned and stretched. "I know the slave traders are looking, and Ben has paid a good price."

"I thought of offering a larger amount," Paul said. "But I feared Khartoum would get wind of her importance."

"Wise decision," Larson said. "Sometimes I wonder about this whole slave redemption process."

Paul nodded and glanced out into the rain. "You mean the logistics of filling the trader's pockets while they carry out their treacherous work?"

"And the increasing number of slaves traded more than once."

"How else do you propose to get them back?" Paul stood and took a glimpse at the sleeping toddler in his mother's arms. Fever raged in his little face.

"I don't have any answers. Right now I'd pay anything for Rachel. Before that, I believed slave redemption increased the likelihood of other kidnappings."

"It's a circle with no end," said Nyok as he closed his book. "I wish someone could stop it, but as long as Khartoum is in power, slavery will go on."

"Unfortunately yes," Paul said. "I say, pay whatever it takes to buy back the slaves."

Larson used to believe the opposite, but that was before ...

"Do you have friends in the U.S. government who could do something about it?" Nyok asked.

"It's complicated ... and involves political agenda. In the United States, it's called 'The squeaky wheel gets the grease.'"

Confusion etched Nyok's face, and his lip curled. "Do you mean Khartoum pays the United States not to say anything about what's going on here?"

"Not at all. I'm saying that U.S. politicians have a list of what is important to them and the people they represent. Whoever shouts the loudest gets the attention and the action."

"I don't know if I like your government's way of doing things," Nyok said.

"Well, that's how the system works. It's a democracy—the people decide the outcome of the issues."

"How can the American people hear about us so they can help?" Nyok leaned forward, his every nerve tuned in to Paul's words.

"By the Sudanese getting their message out to the people through churches, humanitarian organizations, and refugees who have sought asylum in the States. The media are picking up stories, and Washington is taking notice. I don't know if you are aware of this or not, but our government has condemned the GOS's inhumane treatment of the Sudanese. Legislation is under way. Those who care about Sudan are doing what they can."

"Like you?"

Paul nodded. "Yes, like me. I'm only one man, Nyok, but many voices together can make a loud noise."

Larson listened to the two continue discussing politics and the slave issue. She clung to the questions and answers. This was what Nyok needed—to hear a viewpoint other than Ben's. The colonel would poison Nyok's mind with the ways of a warlord. Fighting might be necessary, but it was not the way to bring about peace. The Sudanese problems—slavery, religion, and politics—had been going on for years. Nothing had been settled. Temporary peace with unfulfilled promises at times calmed the country, but not for long. Paul offered intelligence and a clear, rational method of looking at Sudan's problems. Someday she intended to find out what had divided the country in the first place.

But Paul's ways didn't have answers either, just like Ben's. To her, neither man had a sure solution. Who did? Could it be that Sudan was destined to destroy all its people?

# 16

*A* "A village called Xokabuc, about four hours from here needs my attention," Larson said after a week had passed. "They sent one of their people for me. Many are sick, more malaria."

"I'd like to go," Paul said. "Until Ben contacts you about Rachel, there's nothing much I can do to help the situation." He didn't want to say how every day that went by lessened the chances of finding her.

"I appreciate the offer. We could leave early in the morning and be back the next evening. I might even let you drive."

He chuckled. Larson had a rusted, beat-up truck that he swore came from a World War II army surplus pile. "I'll try giving it a tune-up."

"Don't you dare. I have that baby just the way I want her. She responds to my touch—only."

"Remind me of her attributes when we're stuck somewhere." Paul glanced about the clinic. Would Larson leave Nyok in charge of the patients? No new cases were reported, but that could change while they were gone. "What about the clinic?"

"Nyok's capable of taking care of these people."

A rustle snatched his attention, and a boy about ten years old entered the clinic.

"I'm Joshua," he said to Larson and reached to shake her hand. "I'd like to learn medicine and be your assistant."

Her eyebrows lowered, and she stared at the thin boy with a smile. "Did someone send you?"

Joshua's eyes darted about like a trapped animal. "My mother knows I came."

"She sent you then? Why didn't she come too?"

"I don't know."

Larson glanced beyond the sun-drenched clearing outside the clinic. "Was it Nyok?"

"I told him I wanted to be a doctor someday." Joshua shrugged. "And he suggested I come here."

"I have Rachel, Nyok, and Mr. Farid. Why would I want to replace them?" She spoke in the same gentle manner that she addressed her patients.

"Rachel is gone. Nyok is getting older ..."

She bent to his level. "And."

Joshua stared at his bare toes.

"Did he send you to me to take his place so he could join the SPLA?"

Still the boy said nothing.

"Why don't you think about whether you really are interested in helping me?"

He nodded. "I am. I really am."

"Wonderful. I'm glad. But I need you to be a few years older. In the meantime, work hard at your studies." She watched Joshua leave, and when he turned she waved. A tear trickled over her cheek.

Paul saw the fear in Larson's clouded eyes. What she had expressed to him now nibbled at her resolve to keep Nyok safe. He clenched his fists to keep from touching her, but he lost the battle. Moving in front of her, he reached out.

"Don't touch me," she said as she moved away. "I'm fine."

"You don't look like it."

Fire raged from every pore in her face. "What would you know? You aren't fighting every evil known to man. Ben ... I hate him. He wants my Nyok, and I won't allow it."

For a moment, Paul thought she would break down into a pool of emotion.

Larson rubbed her palms together. "I'm sorry. This isn't your fault. It's just that I despise the helplessness." Her gaze flitted from one thing to another in the clinic but not to him.

"I see the despair, Larson. I'm not blind to it or your love for these people."

She lifted her face to meet his. The sprinkling of brown freckles across her nose and cheeks looked out of place with the sadness. A little girl in a grown-up body. "I'm not normally this emotional."

"I know. It's Rachel and Nyok—and you're tired."

"I live with tired, but my children ..." she gulped, "... my children are my joy."

He considered talking about his joy and his faith, but a nudging stopped him.

"I've seen too many mothers bury their children." She crossed her arms and scuffed at the dirt floor. "I vowed a long time ago that it wouldn't happen to me. I simply forgot to guard my heart when it came to Rachel and Nyok."

"Did you really want to file them under responsibility?"

"No." Her words came out weak.

"You don't have a shield over your heart. To care is to admit we're human. No one wants to think of life without someone to love."

Her fists clenched. "Not when they're taken away. That's too big a price."

Scripture rose in Paul's mind. Someday he wanted to share the hope expressed by his namesake in Romans 15:4: "For everything that was written in the past was written to teach us, so that through endurance and the encouragement of the Scriptures we might have hope."

Paul longed to look deep into Larson's soul. Bitterness festered there—something more than the pragmatic problems, something beyond her own understanding, perhaps issues she had never dealt with or wanted to. Why he sensed this revelation was beyond him, but he knew it as well as he knew his name.

He wanted to help, even prevent her pain. The problem he had run into with Jackie surfaced. That had been a situation of guilt over Hank's death. Paul's protective nature toward Larson didn't compare to what he had felt toward Jackie. Larson's despair stemmed from his family's power, and he knew that only Jesus could calm her tormented spirit.

Paul looked in on the recovering nine-year-old child who had contracted malaria. She slept, a healing sleep that showed in her peaceful features. The elderly woman and the toddler had not been this fortunate.

With all the persecutions these people faced, what he wouldn't give to help find Rachel. She was the angel the villagers looked to for hope and encouragement. The young woman prayed for them and sang God's praises with them. Paul glanced up from the child. Right then he understood what he needed to do.

The following morning as a fiery sun crept over the horizon, Larson and Paul loaded medicinal supplies and a few bags of grain onto the truck bed and covered it with a tarp. Nyok scowled in the doorway. He had been in a foul mood since Larson had asked him about Joshua, although he hadn't denied his part in the attempted deception.

"I should be accompanying you," Nyok said. "I'm your protector."

"That you are." Larson refused to allow Paul to help her heave one last bag of grain under the tarp. "But until tomorrow evening, I need you to protect the patients."

"Don't treat me like a child, Dr. Kerr."

She bit her tongue to keep from commenting about immaturity. "I wouldn't leave a child in charge of my clinic. You have my instructions, and you know how to handle emergencies."

Nyok startled, which was exactly what she wanted. She hadn't offered Rachel this much trust, but Larson knew she had to relinquish control over Nyok—or she would lose him.

"Thank you, Dr. Kerr. I will take care of everything."

She allowed herself to smile. "I know you will." Climbing into the truck, she turned to wave.

"Are you letting Mr. Farid drive?" Nyok asked with a teasing grin.

She studied the smirk on Paul's face, then swung a glance at Nyok. "Not for one minute." She snatched the keys from Paul and laughed—the first good laugh she had enjoyed for a long time.

Half an hour later, she still felt an extraordinary carefree attitude. She didn't know where it originated, only that she welcomed the diversion.

"Okay, Miss Mirth, I'm assuming we can get through the roads?" Paul asked.

"I've done it before."

"In this?" He raised a brow, his serious face causing her to laugh again. "Remind me to drop you a new vehicle—and soon."

She wiggled her shoulders and settled into the torn seat. "Can I pick out whatever I want?"

He closed his eyes and shook his head. "I've created a monster here. Sure, why not?"

"Options, options. This will be fun." She glanced his way. "At your expense, of course." She drummed the steering wheel—what there was of it—with her palm. "I would like a Hummer, but not a red one. The GOS would spot it a mile away and confiscate my fun."

"Absolutely."

She enjoyed his feigned annoyance. With the giddy feelings of a schoolgirl, she purposely hit a bump, sending them a half-foot into the air.

"Whoa," he said. "Who taught you to drive?"

"My granddaddy. He went through World War II, drove a truck like this one."

"I'm not surprised. So tell me more about your Hummer options."

"Camouflage and hidden compartments."

This time he laughed. "If you're trying to hide things, the GOS will find them."

"I'm thinking about Ben." And she was serious. "He'd steal me blind if I didn't watch him, including my new Hummer." Sleeping with him would take care of that problem, but she couldn't, wouldn't.

Shaking aside the ever-present dilemmas, Larson turned her attention back to Paul. "Until we get to the village, I don't want to think about malaria or any other disease, the GOS, starvation, unsanitary water, politics, oil, slavery, or Islam versus Christianity."

He placed his arm over the back of the seat. "Good, that gives us a whole lot of other topics."

"Name one."

"The weather and your childhood."

"That's two."

"Take your pick."

Larson braved a deep breath and thought back to the days in

rural Ohio when she rode a country school bus and carried peanut butter and dill pickle sandwiches in a Barbie lunch box. "I was terribly skinny, terribly shy, and too smart for my own good. We lived on a farm. Daddy raised everything from soybeans to Yorkshire pigs—"

"What kind of pigs are those?"

"Those were first brought to Ohio around 1830. I know because I did a report on them in the fifth grade. They're the typical pinkish white pig." She gave him a sideways glance. "Back to my story. I went to school and then became a doctor."

"You sure left a lot of years unaccounted for," Paul said. "I read about the missionary child who died and how that experience moved you to come to Sudan."

"And here I am, probably until the day I die. Some days that gets closer than I'd like." Larson's heart pounded. No one knew the truth but her parents.

"No special man?"

"Nope. I'm married to my profession. How about you? What's your story?"

"I'd rather talk about the GOS."

"That bad, huh?" Larson remembered she had never questioned Ben about Paul. Curiosity needled at her.

"My story is boring. Ben hasn't told you?" Paul opened his backpack and took out his journal. When she shook her head, he continued. "I'll tell you my side of it after you hear his version."

"Why?"

Paul grinned. "His may be more colorful."

Larson didn't believe him for an instant. A sordid past? Ben had made the comment about Khartoum taking Paul as trade for Rachel. How could she push him for more information? She decided not to prod. She didn't want to tell all either.

Paul could have easily occupied her time for the next three

hours with his life story. But the idea of revealing his roots left a sinking feeling in the pit of his stomach. Instead, he kept silent.

The truck bumped over the narrow road to Xokabuc. Actually it resembled nothing more than a path. The village's name meant "we still struggle." From the size of the ruts, not many vehicles traveled this way. Paul reached for the rifle in the backseat. He trusted neither two-legged nor four-legged animals.

"Thanks," she said. "Nyok or Rachel has been with me in the past, and they rode shotgun." She hesitated. "Ben took this jaunt with me once too."

He started to say she and Ben had a strange relationship but thought better of it. Paul had determined the first day he delivered supplies that Colonel Ben Alier felt more than a passing interest in Larson. His eyes gave away his heart. His words betrayed his façade. A man of Ben's caliber didn't put up with a woman's independent, stubborn nature, not even a woman doctor, which had to frustrate him. Why Larson acted unaware puzzled Paul. A woman of her intelligence recognized things in people. Realization struck him hard. She knew the truth and might even share the same feelings.

A twinge of something akin to jealousy pinched at Paul's heart. He wondered if a feisty, beautiful woman like Larson would ever consider the scrawny Arab Christian beside her. He had no power, stature, looks, or intellect. *I'm losing my mind—been in the jungle too long.*

"Talk to me," she said, interrupting his ponderings.

"I'd rather listen to you," he said. "Tell me about the area where you grew up in Ohio."

She giggled, as though she enjoyed the sound of it. Paul did; it reminded him of music.

"We had a creek winding around the farm. If I close my eyes, I can still hear it gurgling over moss-covered rocks. Slippery ones, I might add. Sometimes my granddaddy and I took a picnic lunch and fished in it. We never caught much, but we sure had a good time. Granddaddy always told me stories about the war. Not gory ones, but sentimental tales about his buddies and how the war turned them from boys into men. Granddaddy didn't talk about the bad parts until just before he died. Guess he needed to get it out." She hesitated. "Now, I know how he felt. Some days you wish someone cared."

"Sounds like a great man."

She nodded. "He pastored a church for over forty years."

"And you went every Sunday?"

"I did until shortly before graduation from medical school."

Paul lost her there. She appeared to lose her thoughts in a place in time where he couldn't set foot. Larson did know the Lord. Whatever drove her from His arms had to be deep—and ugly.

"Did you go wading in the creek?" he asked.

She blinked, then tilted her head. "Sure did. There were these little crabs that used to tug at my toes, and in the winter I ice-skated on it."

"A dog?"

"Of course. What's a farm without a dog? Mine was a collie and shepherd mix. I called him Huckleberry. Sometimes at night, I sneaked him in through the kitchen and let him sleep beside my bed. My mother didn't appreciate it, but it never stopped me. I loved Huckleberry. In fact, I loved all those animals. We always had plenty of pigs, calves, chickens, ducks, and rabbits. Without brothers and sisters, those animals were my pets. I nearly became a vet."

"If you'd done that, we wouldn't have become such great friends."

"And under such pleasant circumstances too."

"Do you ever think about going back?" Paul understood he was treading on treacherous ground. How close could he get to Larson before she pulled back?

She nibbled at her lip. "I don't think I'm supposed to. Everything would be changed, spoiled. I'd rather keep it in my memories and visit there when I choose."

"And your parents?"

"We don't keep in touch. I get cards and letters at Christmas and my birthday." She shrugged. "We don't have anything in common."

# 17

Late that morning, Larson and Paul approached the remote village of Xokabuc. Larson attempted to put her thoughts in order. The freedom of expressing those old days had raised the curtain on her life and, for a brief moment, she had become a girl again. For the past hour, she had made a point not to say a word. Humiliation clung to every breath, and in the intense heat, chill bumps jogged up and down her arms. Paul hadn't coerced her. It was her stupid mistake. She had not revealed this much to Rachel, and they had been in constant company. Her careless accountings of home and childhood left her feeling somewhere along the spectrum between embarrassed and violated.

What if she had ventured too far? The truth be known ... she would have told him, the treacherous, accusing truth. The thought frightened her. He had no right to learn about those things dear to her. Once more she realized that something about Paul calmed her. He managed to release the pain and stress of the clinic and its score of problems. How long had it been since she had heard Granddaddy play the banjo and Daddy croon an old Hank Williams tune? How long since a kitten had brushed against her leg and she had lost herself in the awe of silky fur? She remembered baby ducks in the front lawn, impersonating dandelions in spring; the aroma of Mom's warm baked bread and freshly churned butter, dozens of molasses ginger cookies frosted with sweet cream and sugar ... all before she ruined it, before she destroyed everything that symbolized love and life.

Larson couldn't take back those moments she had shared with Paul, but today she had learned something. While the memories wrapped a comforter around her, they also held up a warning sign to her. Only in her private moments would she dare journey there again.

The sound of the truck's engine prompted a welcoming committee from the villagers. Women and children stood in the path waving. Larson's visits were always like this, even when the villagers buried more of their number than survived.

"This is it," she said to Paul. "Are you prepared to work?" *Is this the time I'll contract a fatal disease and find my rest among a people not my own?*

"Yes, you just point me the way."

His enthusiasm irritated her. "You think this past week was rough? Wait until you drag in tomorrow night."

"Larson." The sound of his voice gripped her attention. "We're friends. Thanks for telling me about your childhood."

She glanced ahead and shouted a greeting at a familiar face. "You frighten me, Paul."

Ben lifted a canteen of cool, clear spring water to his lips. The village of Wulu had been alive with activity for two days. Southern economists, political figures, and SPLA members had met to discuss southern Sudan's future. Usually these meetings gave him the strength to go on.

He leaned back against a chair and closed his eyes. Last night he had slept long and hard, but today his body craved more rest.

Age, no way of preventing it. He was forty-four years old, and the tasking hours of keeping pace with the younger men over rough terrain had sunk its claws into him. He shouldn't feel exhaustion or the ache in his bones. His head throbbed.

Some labeled this condition as depression, and why not? The one person who gave him joy and loved him despite of his faults had been snatched away. His fault. His selfishness. His torment. Ben deserved whatever happened to him, but not Rachel.

She had been gone almost three months, and he could recall every grueling moment—the guilt, the regrets that compounded by the hour, the sleepless nights. And when he did catch a few moments of rest, nightmares exploded with scenes that left him sweating. He had even prayed.

Slavery. The practice was centuries old. It filled pockets. It served as a means of exchange: the rich grew richer; the poor were exploited. The British outlawed slavery during their rule, and when they granted Sudan its independence, slavery raised its venomous head again.

He whisked away his thoughts. After all, he could do nothing more for his sister, or could he? If he knew where to look, he would head north.

"The meetings went well," said Solomon Thic as he entered the hut and interrupted Ben's thoughts. The man, a member of the southern banking and currency committee, was a trusted friend.

Ben shook the respected man's hand. "We now have a plan once the war is over."

Solomon eased into a chair. He looked older, grayer than Ben remembered from their last meeting six months ago. "It saddens me that our country cannot rely on a common currency."

"Unless you count goats."

"Ben, I want so many things for our country, but using four-legged animals to do business is not one of them."

"We need our oil."

Solomon folded his hands in his lap. "Sometimes I feel like a fool dreaming about what we could have. Can you imagine hosting tourists, leading safaris, developing industry?"

"Dreams keep men alive." Ben paused. "And send good men to their death."

Solomon shifted in his chair. "For twenty years we've struggled. We've always struggled. I don't know about you, but I'm tired. At first it was for my children, now my grandchildren. Makes me wonder if I'll live to see peace and a good quality of life."

"Where is your hope?"

"Perhaps I've turned into a cynic, my friend." Solomon smiled.

"Not you." Ben shook his head and chuckled. "We won't allow it." He stood and walked to the door. Leaders of the southern movement gathered outside in clumps, no doubt discussing the future.

"As agreed upon this morning, southern Sudan must have an economic infrastructure before the war is over. We must fight and build at the same time. I don't see any other way."

"I'd rather try than do nothing." Ben released a labored sigh. "I'm concerned with the plans to maintain a southern bank and extend that vision to other branches. What's going to stop the government from bombing the buildings?"

"Good question. For that matter, Khartoum is likely to circulate counterfeit bills to ensure our failure."

"Like I said before, I'd rather try."

Solomon studied Ben. "I heard about your sister. I'm sorry, my friend."

*If I could only get her back.* "I hope they don't know who she is. I don't want to think about what could happen."

"How old is she?"

"Sixteen ... beautiful ... high spirited." Ben swallowed. "This is difficult. I made sure she knew the value of standing up for her beliefs. Now I'm afraid it may have got her killed."

"Slave traders turning up nothing?"

Ben gazed away from Solomon's piercing glare. "Not a thing."

"I'll alert our people in Khartoum."

"Thanks. That's the one place I don't want her to be."

"No one will know about this but you and me—and the Weathered Gazelle."

"That's why so many of these people are sick." Larson stared at the well and kicked at the dirt. She knew from the number of patients that something had happened. Xokabuc had always been a favorite, a respite from so many of the others. "Looks like the GOS thought they'd do themselves a favor and fill up the well."

"Right. They didn't have time to wipe out the village, so they ruined its water supply."

"And brought on the disease. Add malaria, and we have an empty village in no time at all." Larson rubbed the back of her neck. "I could stay here a week and still not be through."

"Who dug the well?" Paul asked.

"Living Water International." She walked around it. "I remember when they brought in their drilling equipment." She crossed her arms. "After they had ensured these people safe drinking water, they gave classes on cleanliness and nutrition and took care of medical needs." She didn't mention they were Christian. She assumed that Paul knew that.

"I've heard of them. Nonprofit?"

"Based in Texas, I think." She shrugged. The old familiar anger swelled. "No matter, look at their effort now. Did you know that every six seconds someone in the world dies because of contaminated water?"

"Makes sense. How deep is this pipe?"

"About 120 feet. Why?"

Paul bent and peered into the hole. "I'm going to pull it out—that is, if you can spare me."

She pointed to the sun directly overhead. "I know you're no stranger here, but it'll reach 120 degrees this afternoon."

"Before or after the rains?" He grinned and pointed to his T-shirt that read "All Muscle."

"Are you always this energetic?" She wanted to ask why he had accompanied her in the first place, but something told her she wouldn't like his response. He probably had designs on converting her to Christianity. "All right. I'll tend to my doctoring while you clean out the well."

"We're a team, Dr. Kerr, like Batman and Robin."

"Please."

"The Lone Ranger and Tonto?"

"Laurel and Hardy."

Later, after the rains had subsided enough for Paul to work, he started tugging on the water pipe. Foot by foot, it emerged from the ground like a giant serpent. Children gathered around to watch, and a few of the men assisted. At least he could talk to the adults in English.

Sweat streamed down his face. Memories of his life in Khartoum slipped in unbidden. Larson's questions must have brought those days to the present. Back then, he wanted for nothing and asked for more. His home was a palace. The marble, gold, and luxurious fabrics now embarrassed him. He ate the finest foods and threw away more in a week than most Sudanese consumed in a month. His clothes sported the labels of the finest European clothiers. When the time came for him to drive, Paul's father picked out a Ferrari. Then each year he received a new one. He was the oldest son of his father's first wife, the most privileged of the privileged.

The flip side of his lifestyle happened outside of his family's wealth: the unspeakable things, the plaguing things—those atrocities committed under the umbrella of the Muslim faith—because that's just how things were then. He had studied the Qur'an and followed the *sharia*. He had adhered to the strict rules and practices of Islam. He had moved against those who did not share the same beliefs and loved those who embraced his faith. While he had enjoyed the good life, others in his country were persecuted for their beliefs.

And Larson wanted to know about this? He assumed Larson knew his history. At the least, he thought Ben would have shared his lurid past—in rich detail. Why Larson had displayed regret in relaying her idyllic childhood confused him.

The media had taken Paul's story and twisted it into a humiliation for the Muslim world and an act of heroism for the rest. Christian magazines had slapped his picture on the front of their publications as one of the century's biggest converts, while the secular media had questioned his newfound faith. In any event, one's view of Abdullah Farid depended on where one sat on the proverbial fence.

Paul lingered a moment on Larson's enthusiasm this morning in talking about rural life in Ohio. Her eyes had sparkled, and a little girl's lightheartedness had worked its way to the surface. She had laughed. She had teased. The lines in her face had softened, and he had seen a woman who embraced life. That was the Larson Kerr he had observed in those moments when children played at her door. And those characteristics had pushed Paul to grow as close to her as she would allow.

Back in California, he had merely wanted to help her, but now he knew that his purpose was to bring her back to Jesus. This past week had proved otherwise. His heart had got involved. Of course, she had never looked at him with anything more than friendship in her eyes. What did he have to offer such a woman anyway, except money? She would scorn wealth rather than be captured by its lure. Larson Kerr's person, perspective, and purpose all went deeper than materialism.

This wasn't the proper time for Paul to dwell on anything but Larson's relationship with the Lord—and doing what he could for Sudan.

Colonel Ben Alier would have Paul drawn and quartered if he knew his thoughts. In a way, Paul found the truth amusing. Here they were, two Sudanese natives caught up in their country's civil war, with nothing more in common than a shared love for the land and a common interest in the welfare of a good woman.

Paul worked until dusk. Some of the men stood around him with clubs in case lions prowled the area. One man began to sing an old hymn in English, and the others joined in. The sound of worship spurred Paul to continue working, despite the ache in his arms and back. He listened until "What a Friend We Have in Jesus" filled the evening air, and then he had to sing too. When the group had finished, he taught the men a few of his favorite praise songs.

"I am Jacob. How did you come to know Jesus?" a toothless old man asked.

Paul didn't hesitate to tell this part of his life. He understood the curiosity in light of his Arabic heritage. These men had every right to despise him.

"I met an old man who was suffering for his faith in God. In fact, his hand had been chopped off for lifting it in worship. He told me about Jesus. He told me how God came into the world in the form of a baby to save the world from sin. He told me how Jesus allowed evil men to nail Him to a cross and kill Him when He'd done nothing wrong but preach love to a hurting people. When the old man said Jesus rose from the dead after three days, I didn't believe. I thought it was a child's story. Then the old man looked at me, and I saw something in his eyes that I wanted. My spirit cried out for this Jesus. That's how I became a Christian."

"Are your family believers too?" Jacob asked.

Paul shook his head. That was the one part of his life that was left unfinished. "No. I have twelve brothers and four half sisters. I am the only member of my family who is not Muslim."

"They are trying to kill you," Jacob said, as though he knew Paul's nightmares. "We will pray for your safety and that your family comes to know Jesus as Lord. You are a good man to help us."

"Thank you." Paul peered into the old man's dark eyes. "May God bless you and your village."

"Praise God," another man said. "We pray that one day the whole world will know Jesus."

"God sent you to fix our well, just as He sent the Living Water people to dig it," Jacob said. "We will never forget you."

Paul fought the emotion rising in him. He stood from the mud and wiped his hands on the grass nearby. He embraced Jacob. The others lined up behind him, and Paul hugged each one of them. Just when Paul needed encouragement, God sent a messenger.

In the distance, a lion roared.

"The Lion of Judah is among us," Paul said. "We have nothing to fear with Him in our hearts."

# 18

The well took an extra day to get back into working order, but Paul didn't mind. He had made new friends and intended to visit again. Larson treated the sick and left medicine for the others in capable hands. Exhaustion tugged at both of them, and the drive back seemed to take twice the time. Larson even let him drive the war-torn truck part of the way. In the late afternoon, they saw the familiar grass huts of Warkou.

The moment Larson and Paul entered the village, excited villagers waved and shouted greetings. Glancing about, Paul expected to see Ben, but there was no sign of him or his men, only an inexpressible sensation that left Paul breathless and unsure why.

"Bishop Malou must be here," Larson said. "I feel his presence."

Paul whipped his attention to her, taken aback by her statement. It confirmed his earlier beliefs that before Larson came to Sudan, she knew Jesus, and once the Lord had embraced His children, He pursued them relentlessly.

She stopped the truck outside the clinic. Instantly Nyok

appeared. Worry lines creased his young face. "Where have you been?"

"I pulled up a 120-foot water pipe," Paul said. "The GOS had filled it with dirt, and the people were without sanitary water. I'm sorry."

Nyok took a deep breath. Paul caught his belligerent stare, the stiffening of his shoulders.

"I'm sorry. Many were sick, not only from malaria but from the dirty water."

The boy's shoulders lifted. "I ... was worried."

"I don't blame you." Larson swung open the truck door with a loud creak and gave him a hug. "I'm better at keeping my word than that. Truth is, I could have stayed a lot longer." She grabbed a tattered bag from the back of the truck. "Is Bishop Malou here?"

"He arrived yesterday," Nyok said as he took the bag. "He preached last night and held a service for the dead. He's staying with Sarah."

"At least he's not staying at the clinic." Larson pressed her lips together. "Did you go?"

Nyok startled. "I had patients to watch."

She stepped into the clinic. "Good."

Paul watched Larson's demeanor change from the flirtatious woman who had challenged his wit two days ago to the hardened professional he had known before their trip to Xokabuc. Even in treating the villagers over the past three days, she had shown compassion and understanding. What had happened to build this wall around her heart? She had lived a pastoral life as a child and had obviously treasured it. The change must have come later, perhaps from a professor who succeeded in convincing her that science held all the answers, or maybe it was a lover who took priority over God. A family tragedy? A disappointment? He didn't think the missionary's losing the child had turned her away from God. Rather it must have been a series of events. He wondered if she remembered the story of the ninety-nine sheep and the one lost lamb. She might have crossed a continent to flee the Good Shepherd, but she still recognized God's presence—and He still sought His wandering lamb.

Once Paul had unloaded the truck, Nyok helped him camouflage it with brush. Then Paul began looking for Bishop Malou. His reputation as a courageous, dedicated man of God was known at FTW. Meeting him would be a pleasure.

Paul found him standing beneath a sausage tree, talking to a group of men and women. The bishop possessed a soft voice, causing those who listened to lean in closer and not miss a word. Paul had learned this method of keeping attention from volunteering in a Sunday school class of three-year-olds.

Bishop Malou had the proud carriage of a Dinka—tall, slender, ramrod posture—and the God-given peace of a Christian. Envy bit at Paul's heart. He saw in this stranger what he desired to be himself—a man of influence. Some said that Paul had displayed those qualities in his dramatic conversion and aid to Sudan, and as a result he had an impact on the entire world. An evangelistic magazine had even termed him the modern-day apostle Paul. The words had encouraged him, but he felt so unworthy.

As he was approaching the group under the tree, Paul heard Bishop Malou say, "He who began a good work in you will carry it on to completion until the day of Christ Jesus."

Recognizing the words of Philippians 1:6, Paul felt a wave of love sweep over him. Man's recognition meant nothing. God's good work meant everything.

Bishop Malou continued his message using the apostle Paul's letter to the Philippians to bolster the villagers' faith. He stressed joy and perseverance. Paul had memorized this book, and hearing the bishop speak from it affirmed God's presence with him—and his calling to Sudan. Afterward Paul introduced himself.

"I've heard about your work with the FTW," Bishop Malou said as he gripped Paul's hand. The bishop looked to be in his late thirties. Judging by his facial scars, he had gone through the warrior's rites.

"And I've heard about your ministry. How many members do you now have in your churches?"

Bishop Malou grinned, displaying a smile that revealed several missing lower teeth, the obvious result of a tribal practice for many Dinka. "Over 17,000. God has blessed my work."

"If you have the time while you're here, I'd like nothing better than to talk."

"I'm free until tonight's service." The bishop's compassion reminded Paul of another man, another time. "The people of southern Sudan owe you many thanks for your bravery and generosity."

For the next two hours, Bishop Malou and Paul discussed the spiritual growth of Sudan. Although Christianity flourished in the north, the number of believers and the work accomplished there was difficult to measure.

"I read a report that approximately two and a half million southern refugees live in displacement camps in the north," Paul said. "It came from an International Christian Concern article."

Bishop Malou nodded. His eyes held the pain of an oppressed people. "I'm told the non-Muslims are sent there in an effort to clear out animists and Christians from the south."

"Jesus is everywhere," Paul said, "and He's not leaving."

"Amen. It is inhumane that these people are being denied basic needs—food, shelter, medical care—just because of their faith." The bishop picked up a rock and threw it into the river near them, as though the strength in his arms could eliminate the frustration. "Many are thrown into jail and forgotten unless they renounce Jesus."

Paul looked to where the rock had caused ripples across the water. "I knew a man who refused the government's mandates to embrace Islam." He struggled with the emotion that always rose in him when he remembered Abraham. "I will never forget him."

"Martyrs for the faith," Bishop Malou said with the reverence of a prayer. "Friends of mine had their home and church destroyed. He was arrested and charged with opposing the government. The GOS killed him and one of their daughters, but his wife and other children escaped."

"Ever wonder why we have escaped death? Why others have fallen, but we still stand?" Paul stared into his new friend's face, seeking the answers to his most perplexing questions.

"The Bible says that God does not show favoritism, and He has a plan for everyone's life."

Paul needed to accept this simple explanation. He had tried to do so ever since saying yes to Jesus.

Larson smiled again at Nyok. "You did an excellent job while I was gone. I'll not hesitate to leave you in charge again." They were alone, and she planted a kiss on his cheek.

Nyok stared down at his bare feet. "I just followed your instructions."

"You did even more. You went beyond, Nyok. What a gifted doctor you would be."

"That's what you said about Rachel."

Larson searched for the right words to express his talent, his intellect. "Right, I did. Rachel has healing in her hands and in her words, but you have foresight and organizational skills." She picked up the chart of one of the patients. "You saw that this man's fever rises in the middle of the night, so you got up and bathed him before his condition required it. He's already lived longer than I ever expected, but you didn't see his hopeless condition. Instead you saw an old man who needed the best care."

Nyok continued staring at the earthen floor. "I felt good when I helped the patients."

She laughed, and his gaze flew to hers. "That's the goal of every good doctor, to help those in need."

He glanced about the clinic, spotless in every area. "Attending medical school would be good. I'd like to be a doctor someday." He turned to meet her gaze. "When I've helped the SPLA win the war, let's talk about it more."

Nyok's words could not have hurt more if they had been thrust through her heart with a knife. She sucked in her breath, determined not to cry. Weary from the past three days, she didn't have the strength to confront Nyok's declaration. They would argue, and he would withdraw into his protective cocoon of quiet defiance. Tonight she would talk to Paul. He must know a way to convince Nyok of this foolishness.

Every time Ben entered the village, she feared Nyok would leave with him.

Paul shifted his backpack onto his shoulder and did a mental check of what he needed to take with him. He had prayed about this trip with Bishop Malou and felt confident about accompanying him for the next few weeks to various villages. They would minister to those who knew the Lord and evangelize the ones who did not.

He would have to take the chance that Ben might return to Warkou before his return. An idea had burrowed into his mind, and he couldn't let it go. To proceed with it meant asking Ben for help. Knowing the man wanted him dead left Paul wondering if he had lost his senses.

"We will be a great team," Bishop Malou said while clasping his arm around Paul's shoulder. "Like Paul and Barnabas." Paul felt like a boy next to the towering man.

"I'm honored and humbled," Paul said.

"Some of the people will expect you to prove yourself. They will be skeptical."

"I understand completely. Will any of them be Muslim?"

Bishop Malou nodded. "One village is a mixture of animist and Muslim. It has been the site of bloody disputes, but I feel God is leading us there. You and I will show how two different races can live together as brothers in the Lord."

*My new, dear brother, races can exist peaceably, but not Christians and Muslims.*

# 19

Larson hated the thought of Paul leaving with Bishop Malou, but she couldn't bring herself to protest. He wasn't her private servant. She wanted him there for Nyok, to persuade him to pursue an education and give up his crazy notion of joining the SPLA. At least that's what she told herself. Deep down she knew that depending on Paul to make things happen the way she wanted wasn't fair to him. Despite all the excuses she mentally conceived to keep him in Warkou, the fact was that Larson wanted him there with her, and her selfish thoughts irritated her. She knew she simply needed to wave good-bye when they climbed into Bishop Malou's truck and then go on about her business.

Paul had spent an entire morning with Nyok explaining the basic points of aerodynamics and identifying parts of the plane.

"Thank you for taking the time with him," she said when Nyok left them alone in the clinic.

"I enjoyed it," Paul said. "I talked to him about the future of Sudan, how our country will need educated professionals to lead the nation, and he agreed."

"Wonderful." A vision for the boy began to take form in her

mind. "Did he indicate putting aside his ridiculous plans to join the SPLA?"

Paul released a sigh. "Not exactly. The plans for his education and leadership goals are for after the war—after he has helped his country establish its freedom from Khartoum's tyranny." He punched his fist into his palm. "I'm sorry. Those were his words exactly, no doubt put there by someone else."

"Colonel Ben Alier." Anger simmered just above Larson's boiling point. "I wish I knew how to persuade Ben to leave Nyok alone." As soon as the words were spoken, her mind slipped back to the last time she had seen the colonel. She knew exactly how to convince him. Larson swallowed hard. Her legs nearly gave way beneath her.

Paul grabbed her and led her to an empty patient cot. "Are you all right?"

"Just dizzy. Tired, I guess."

He lifted her chin and studied her face. "Fever, chills?"

She couldn't help but smile. He actually cared about her health. "I'm fine, really. I'm too stubborn to contract malaria."

He frowned. "Why do I not believe you?"

"Trust me. Once a diseased mosquito heads my way, it turns tail and runs. It's the color of my eyes that scares them off." She forced a chuckle, but it sounded weak. Between the realization of what she would have to do to deter Ben from encouraging Nyok and the closeness of Paul, Larson wondered if being ill had better appeal.

Paul glanced at a pregnant woman outside the clinic. "Is it necessary for you to see her now?"

Larson shook her head and rubbed the back of her neck. "Not unless she's having problems."

"Then lie down, and I'll ask her to come back in the morning."

"Thanks." She did as he requested and remembered that Rachel had always shown this concern. *Rachel, where are you, my sweet daughter? If only I knew that you were all right.*

Paul whirled around from speaking to the pregnant woman. "Why are you crying?" He bent to her side. "You are sick, aren't you?"

She shook her head. "It's Rachel. I miss her terribly, Paul. Sometimes I think I'd rather find out she's dead than to consider her living among those barbarians." Tears rolled from her eyes. She couldn't stop them, as though the floodgates of emotion had broken.

Paul gathered her up in his arms. He held her head against his chest and urged her to cry. "You haven't grieved, Larson. You can't expect yourself to be some extraordinary human being who isn't supposed to feel."

"I thought we'd know something by now." She sobbed.

His fingers wove through her hair, his touch sparking a mixture of comfort and fear. "I came here to help find Rachel. I know I've done nothing in that direction yet, but I'm waiting on Ben."

She lifted her head and stared into his dark eyes, those pools that radiated compassion and understanding when she needed them most. "Why? He despises you. He tried to kill you and will probably try again."

"I need his help." Paul released a ragged breath. Could it be she affected him in the same way? It couldn't be. His concern was for Rachel and the way he felt responsible for her abduction. "I have a plan."

"What kind of plan?"

"I want to go north, to Khartoum. If they've discovered Rachel's identity, I have a few ideas where they'd hold her."

Bewilderment assaulted her senses. "How would you know?" She tried to clear her mind. "If they knew they held Ben Alier's sister, wouldn't they send word to him?"

"Possibly. They could be trying to extract information from her first."

Larson held her breath. His words cast terror, and her anger rose as though truth came from uttered words.

"I'm sorry," he said. "But it stands to reason, especially the way they think and do things."

"What could you do?" Just because Paul was Arabic didn't mean he had the market on how Muslims treated their prisoners. Ben's words on trading him for Rachel echoed across Larson's mind. Of course Paul intended to make an exchange. The GOS would like nothing more than to get their hands on the man who had dropped tons of food and supplies all over southern Sudan.

Paul's features tightened. He drew her close.

"Paul, what you're thinking is dangerous. Khartoum doesn't want you as much as they do Ben. There has to be another way." She pulled away from him.

His hand brushed against her face; his thumb wiped away the tears. "Larson, you have no idea the history behind me. The things I know. The things I've done."

"I don't care. I see a good man, one who cares, a man who exceeds any code of bravery."

He lowered his head and brushed a kiss against her lips. Every ounce of her told her to stop. Involvement invited disaster. She feared it worse than the forces from the north, but her heart won over.

"Dr. Kerr!"

Larson swung her attention in the direction of the voice. There in the doorway stood Nyok.

"How long have you been preaching?" Paul asked Bishop Malou. They had visited two villages in the past week and had spent a few days in each, encouraging the believers and evangelizing the others. As in Warkou, the Christians accepted their persecution from the GOS as part of their faith. And the church continued to flourish.

"Ten years I've been serving the Lord." Bishop Malou stopped the truck to stare out over the plain. In the distance, Paul saw the tops of huts like huge straw hats. "I was studying philosophy in Nairobi and about to graduate when I received God's call."

"Did you go on to seminary?"

"Not at first. I wrestled with that aspect for a long time. I wanted to jump into the mission field and get started, but God wanted me learning first, to deepen my relationship with Him." He gave Paul a sideways glance. "I know some ministers step right from the call into preaching, but God had something else in mind for me."

Envy settled onto Paul. How many nights had he lain awake asking God about the future? "I'm still looking for my life's calling."

"I think you already have it," Bishop Malou said as he stepped on the accelerator and moved the truck toward the village.

"Maybe for now, but I can't see myself dropping food and supplies over Sudan for the rest of my life."

"What if God wants you to continue what you're doing?"

The thought frustrated Paul. He wanted something grander, finer. "I can't imagine that. Maybe He wants me to preach Jesus like you do. I could get used to this life."

Bishop Malou pointed to his chest. "You have to listen with your heart. We forget God wants us to hear Him. It does no good to serve until we understand His plans. Listen to your heart, my friend."

*I wish God would nudge me a little, so I'd know what to do about … life.*

"What else is bothering you?" Bishop Malou asked. "We've been together for a week now, and I sense there's more going on in your spirit than what you've told me."

All of the ways God speaks to His children rolled across Paul's mind like credits in a movie. Perhaps he could touch on the latest, the issue tearing at his heart like a wild animal seeking to devour him. "Have you tried to share the Gospel with Dr. Kerr?"

Bishop Malou stared ahead. His brows narrowed, and he nodded slowly. "I learned enough from her to realize she knows much about the Bible, but her heart is hardened. I've met many educated people who feel they have no use for God."

Paul digested his words. "I believe she once made a decision for the Lord. Her family is Christian. In fact, her grandfather was a minister."

"Medical school could have swayed her. For many, the theology of science is the answer to all things."

"I think something happened to turn her against God, and I don't believe it was the missionary child who died in her care." Paul wiped the perspiration dripping down his face. The kiss he had shared with Larson picked at his conscience. He knew better.

"The Bible says for us not to yoke ourselves with unbelievers."

Paul startled.

"You don't have to say a word," Bishop Malou said.

"I thought I was interested in Larson in that way, but the more I think and pray about it, I see that my job is to lead her to the Lord." He attempted a laugh. "Besides, if I were interested in her romantically, Ben Alier would kill me. He's looking for an excuse anyway." Paul wondered how much he should say about Larson. "I did kiss her a few nights ago, and I have regretted it ever since. I apologized, but now I worry if I've ruined my chances to share Jesus with her."

"I believe you have two solutions to your problem," Bishop Malou said. "Whether she is away from the Lord or has never asked Him to be a part of her life, you have a responsibility to guide her in the Lord's direction. The second choice is to leave the area; run as fast as you can from potential sin. Now, the colonel is a whole different matter."

A mixture of frustration and compassion swirled in Paul's brain and tingled throughout his body. "I've prayed about those very things. To complicate matters, I've made a commitment to help find Ben's sister and help Larson get Nyok out of Sudan. The boy wants to join the SPLA, and Ben is encouraging it."

Bishop Malou chuckled. "You don't live an easy life, do you?"

Paul returned the smile. "Never have. I'd consider it an honor if you would pray for me."

"I have been doing so, and I will continue. Where do you think God is leading you about all this?"

They continued a bit farther in silence. Paul's thoughts refused to cease. "To do both. Lead Larson to the Lord and honor His Word."

Shouts of villagers captured their attention. A young boy rushed to greet them with words of welcome for Bishop Malou. For now, Paul's anxiousness must wait. He loved ministering to these people, talking about the Lord, and watching Bishop Malou baptize new believers.

Tonight when the hush of sleep crept around the village, he would ponder and pray about it all again. He would remember Abraham and the quest to find his family. He would ask God for purpose and direction. He would pray for Ben to find the God of his family and his sister. He would recall Larson's sweet kiss and the sadness of her troubled mind. Last of all, he would deliberate on what to do about Nyok. Since Nyok had found Larson and Paul together, the boy's anger had surfaced again.

"Dr. Kerr! What are you doing?" Nyok's words had spit venom.

When Paul's gaze flew to the young man, Nyok had reached for the rifle leaning in a dark corner. "Leave her alone. She's not your woman. She's—"

"Watch what you say," Larson said. "You're right. I'm not Paul's woman, but neither do I belong to anyone else." She sat upright, and Paul stood.

Nyok shook. Even in the dim light inside the clinic, the boy's eyes narrowed. "I will kill him for touching you."

"He kissed me." Her voice rose. "He held me while I cried. Furthermore, it's my business, not yours."

Paul took a deep breath and sensed an amazing calm. Too many times he had seen what happened in the heat of anger. "Let me have the rifle, Nyok."

The boy lifted it and aimed at Paul's chest. "First you promise me that you'll never come near her again."

If Nyok was this possessive, how would Ben react? He remembered when Ben tried to strangle him after Rachel's abduction. Fear was not a stranger to Paul. He recognized the chills, the tightening of the chest, and the way his breath came in short spurts. He shuddered but maintained his stance. "I can't speak for her. Dr. Kerr is capable of making her own decisions."

"Put down the gun." Larson's soft voice contrasted with the turmoil registering on Nyok's face. She stepped toward him. "Here, let me have it."

"No." Nyok kept his attention on Paul. "This is the duty given to me by Colonel Alier."

"He never asked you to commit murder." Larson inched forward. She reached for the barrel and turned it away from Paul. "I appreciate your devotion. I love you for it, but this man is innocent of anything you might be thinking."

"Colonel Alier will be angry," Nyok said.

"You will not tell him." Larson's words were firm. "He has enough to worry about."

Resentment hit Paul hard. "What are you going to tell him? Alier doesn't rule this village."

"Easy, Paul." She used the same gentle tone to soothe Paul's anger. Shame flooded him.

"I'm sorry," he said to Nyok. "You are the warrior-protector, and you have pledged to uphold Dr. Kerr's honor. I assure you nothing wrong has happened here."

Nyok scowled, but he lowered the gun. Larson pried his fingers from the weapon and lifted it from him. "Stay away from her," he said to Paul. "Go back to the States where you came from."

"Enough," Larson said. "Neither you nor anyone else tells me or Paul what to do."

# 20

Ben tramped through the thick green foliage in the late afternoon sun. Judging by the familiar acacia trees and the high waters to the south, he would be in Warkou by evening. He had marched his men since dawn on through the midday rains, a trek he hadn't planned on taking for another month, longer if he could put it off. After what happened the last time, Ben intended to avoid Larson for as long as possible. He had never been turned down by a woman, but pride wasn't the only issue. Seeing too much of her caused him to lessen his focus. Ben wouldn't be heading to Warkou now except for a message from Farid.

The Arab had sent word through one of Warkou's warriors that he needed to talk to him. Ben had repeatedly mulled over the matter, until he was tired of wondering why. Farid could have decided to lend his financial support to the SPLA. Maybe he had decided to tell what he knew about Rachel. The confession ought to set Larson straight about her saintly pilot. The idea of those two working together bothered Ben, bothered him a lot.

Since the meeting in Wulu, Ben had tried to focus on the economics of Sudan and what the leaders envisioned. They painted a bright outlook for the country—once the GOS met their demands. With this hope, the leaders planned the infrastructure necessary for a new southern Sudan. Ben was pulled in different directions. As tired as he was of fighting, war flowed through his veins. What would he do without it? How would he serve southern Sudan?

Larson's back ached from leaning into the swollen river and washing clothes. She and Rachel used to enjoy this together, not the work, but the reprieve from the clinic's demands. The other women crowded around her, as if their presence would bring back some of the magic. Only Rachel held that distinction. Nothing could replace her musical laughter. Larson stood and stretched. She craved the sound of Rachel's voice and the way she made the day sparkle. Glancing around her, Larson saw the anguish in the other women's faces.

"We miss her too," said Sarah, her round, wrinkled face glistened in the morning heat. "Rachel was God's messenger."

*Must it always lead back to God? I crossed an ocean to escape Him.* The longer she stayed in Sudan, the more the believers gathered around her. At times she thought God was chasing her. What irony, especially when she didn't believe a God existed, certainly not One who promised love in the midst of pain. No thanks, she believed in the tangible, not illusions.

Paul believed in God as strongly as Bishop Malou and the other Christians. The two men's enthusiasm reminded her of little boys caught up in a game of good guys and bad guys. They preached that the good guys always win, when in fact she knew otherwise. Everything about Paul except his faith drew her in. Larson touched her wet fingers to her lips. He had kissed her like she was porcelain—fragile, special. She appreciated every second of his embrace, although the mere thought was forbidden. His mannerisms reminded her of someone else, and she shuddered.

*No more. I can't use Paul to recapture the past.*

The kiss. She had to make sure Nyok didn't tell Ben. But how? She refused to bribe the boy, neither did she want to resort to the same tactics Ben used. If only she had the right words to convince Nyok that what he saw was innocent. She wondered if Ben had instructed the boy to spy on her. The thought sent an angry current through her veins that left her tingling. Ben didn't need another reason to kill Paul, and Nyok could push him over the thin edge between rivalry and the SPLA commitment.

Pulling the last T-shirt from the river, Larson wrung it out and contemplated whether Ben had mistaken any of the conversations between her and Ben for interest. Goodness, they fought most of the time … and then he wanted her. The thought still upset her. The idea that he could have followed through with his intentions despite any protest from her twisted in her stomach. She couldn't picture herself with him, not in a million years. He took lives. She fought to save them. A gnawing reminder surfaced. Larson would sleep with Ben, if it meant keeping Nyok out of the SPLA or Paul from being butchered. What an exchange, but she would do it.

Tonight she would talk to Nyok like old times, and when Paul returned from his missionary journey, she would discuss what couldn't happen between them ever again. And once Rachel was found, he would be back flying food and supplies over Sudan. This would all be forgotten. Satisfied that she had solved her dilemma, Larson gathered up the wet clothes and headed for the clothesline near Sarah's hut to hang them out, so they could dry before the afternoon rains.

Larson lifted her gaze to search out Nyok. He always stood in the background and guarded the women, children, and elderly, just like the other warriors. She waved at him, but he glanced away. He looked like a silhouette against the blue sky, a proud boy too soon called to be a man. His response tore through her heart. He had been aloof since that uncomfortable night, and she had searched her mind for a way to restore their relationship. Today she would ask him about the astronomy book, to see if he would like any additional reading material on the subject. One of her contacts in the States might be willing to send a telescope. A flash of guilt danced across her conscience. She was guilty of bribery too. With a heavy sigh she walked toward Sarah's hut. If bribery worked, then why not?

While throwing her clothes over the clothesline and tucking her bras and panties under her arm—these had a way of disappearing—an eerie chill raced up her spine. Whirling around, she saw the subject of her distress standing with Nyok.

"Hi, Ben. I didn't expect to see you this soon." She shielded her eyes from the sun and looked to see if Rachel could be with them.

"Where's Farid?" he asked.

"We'll be in Warkou by nightfall," Bishop Malou said. The rain had started, and the truck's windshield wipers scraped across the glass.

"Remind me to get you a few extra blades before your windshield is destroyed," Paul said.

"I have it on my list when I return to Kenya." Bishop Malou laughed. "Not a smart move during the rainy season. Actually, I need to map out the next month. The roads will be impassable by then."

As much as Paul wanted to travel with his newfound friend, the journey steered him away from his commitments in Warkou. He hadn't visited with Nyok since the night before he left with Bishop Malou. The relationship took a turn for the worst then and might still be severed. Ben's face settled in his mind. Paul had a plan, but he needed the colonel's support. Support meant trust, and Ben despised him. Only God knew if the colonel would agree.

"I hope this is not our last meeting," Paul said. "Just being with you has encouraged me in my Christian walk."

"Good." Bishop Malou grinned. "I think you and I together could win all of Sudan for the Lord. The people don't expect to see a black man and an Arab working side by side."

"Maybe in the future." A bittersweet sensation filled Paul. He started to ask Bishop Malou about an old man fitting Abraham's description, but he changed his mind. Sometimes finding Abraham seemed more like a dream than reality. "I'll be praying for you."

The fiery sun had just met the horizon when the two men arrived in Warkou. Nothing in the world compared to an African sunset in deep shades of amber and blue. Paul loved his beach home in Malibu, but his heart was here amid the rugged beauty of a land centuries old.

He thought of Larson, her sprinkling of freckles and the depths of her blue eyes. Strong and spirited just like Sudan. He thought of the many ways he could present the Gospel to her, but wariness led his emotions. Concern for her soul must take priority.

Weary, Paul headed to the clinic to speak with Larson before finding his cot next to Nyok in the adjacent hut. He shook his head in remembering the night before he left with Bishop Malou. The thought of Nyok slitting his throat had kept him awake most of the night. Whistling a Michael W. Smith tune, Paul stepped inside the clinic.

There sat Ben with Larson, drinking coffee.

# 21

Ben hated the sight of Farid. He represented everything the SPLA fought and died to destroy. The Arab's small frame and weasel-like features wrapped in a phony Christian façade reminded Ben of the hundreds of years his people had been persecuted and enslaved. He would line up every last one of them and blow them all to hell if his conscience didn't keep reminding him it was murder. The thought of Larson calling Farid friend made the situation even more repulsive. If not for the slightest chance the Arab might lead him to Rachel, he would kill him just to make Sudan a better place to live.

"You sent for me?" Ben forced his sight on the animal before him.

"I did. Thank you for coming." Farid turned to Larson. "How are you?"

She smiled, and the gesture fueled Ben's anger. "Good. Would you like some coffee?"

"I'll get it," Farid said.

Ben fumed. *That's my coffee.* "What do you want? Is this about Rachel?"

Farid nodded and poured a mug full of the strong brew. "Would you like more, Colonel?" he asked.

Ben stuck out his mug. "I've come a long way, Farid. This had better be worth my time."

The Arab took a seat on an empty cot. "I understand your responsibilities, Colonel. I have an idea, and I need your help." He glanced at Larson and back to Ben. "Can we take a walk?"

Ben stood. "Let's go. I'm tired of wondering what this is all about."

Outside, the two men walked beyond the thatched-roof clinic toward the Lol River. There they would have privacy. Impatience coiled around Ben's senses like a snake squeezing its prey.

"I want to search in Khartoum," Farid said. "If the GOS learned Rachel's identity, then they will likely have her there."

Stories about the ghost houses—torture chambers—and their tactics left Ben's mouth dry. "I have contacts there."

"But I doubt if they're the same as mine."

Ben attempted to think through the deceit in what the Arab proposed. "Why? Aren't you wanted there?"

"I am, but I'm not stupid enough to announce my presence. Look, Colonel, Rachel was with me when the GOS abducted her. I have a stake in this whether you want to acknowledge it or not. I'd feel the same if Nyok had been taken."

"What are you going to do once you're there?"

"Call on a few people I trust. Find out what we need to know. Do whatever I can to find out if the GOS has your sister. And," he took a breath, "if they do, see if we can get her out."

"How would you manage that?"

"I'm relying on God for an answer. I'm willing to make an exchange—me for her if necessary."

"How noble." Ben glanced into the darkness. He didn't trust the Arab, but Ben's heart pounded with the thought of Rachel under interrogation. He had sent out a few feelers, but nothing had resulted. The longer time lapsed without locating her, the more the likelihood she had been killed. "What do you need me for?"

"SPLA protection up the White Nile for as far as you can provide it. I don't want to be captured or killed before I get there."

Ben hesitated. This could be a trap, but did he have a choice? "How many men do you need?"

"I have no idea. That's your specialty."

*Right. It's you and me the GOS want anyway. Farid's heroics. Does he not think I'd trade my life for my sister?* "So, at a certain point, you'd take off alone?"

"Yes. I wouldn't risk anyone else's life in the north."

"No, I don't think you would." Ben smirked. "I'll give you your escort. Just you and I will head north."

Farid studied him. "What good is the south if you're killed?"

"If I am, who do you think they'll blame? Think about it, Farid. The north is already out to get you, and if I'm dead the south will be too." The night sounds of insects rose as dusk took over the sunset. Farid became a shadow.

"Have it your way," the Arab said. "How soon can you leave?"

"Day after tomorrow. We can take a truck until the roads are impassable. I'll arrange for a boat. Can you handle it?"

"I can handle anything you throw my way."

Ben laughed. "I doubt it."


Nyok watched Colonel Alier and Paul disappear into the shadows. He couldn't make out what they were discussing, but they weren't arguing. That fact alone surprised him and angered him just a bit. Nyok knew that Dr. Kerr hadn't expected the colonel this soon. He could tell by her pale face.

When Nyok thought about the situation between Dr. Kerr and Paul, he realized that she hadn't talked to him about it. She was frightened, and she should be. Nyok held the power of life and death over the Arab. He rather liked the position.

A brush against his conscience seized him. Nyok cared about Dr. Kerr. He didn't want her upset. She gave of herself in taking care of his people, and she had been good to him. Nyok blamed the pilot. Paul was trying to take the colonel's place in her heart, and Dr. Kerr belonged to Colonel Alier. She needed to understand her position.

He stole back into the village. As Dr. Kerr's protector, he must remind her of the seriousness of this mistake. If she failed to listen, then he would be forced to tell Colonel Alier what he had seen. Nyok tightened his jaw. He hoped all that had happened was a kiss.

A twinge of regret settled on Nyok. He liked Paul, and he didn't want him dead. Another plan formed in Nyok's head. He would explain to Paul the situation between the colonel and Dr. Kerr. That way the pilot could leave Sudan unharmed.

Nyok studied the soldiers who sat around the fire, laughing and talking. Usually he joined them, and he ached to do so now, but not tonight. He had to take time to form the proper words. Paul must leave Sudan and allow the colonel to find Rachel. Nyok knew how to be persuasive.

Inside the clinic, he helped Dr. Kerr straighten the area. She still looked uneasy.

"Can we talk a little?" she asked.

"Aren't you waiting for Colonel Alier and Paul?"

"Yes, but we have a little time."

"What is this about?" As if Nyok didn't already know.

"You saw something, Nyok, and you misunderstood what happened."

He strained to hear her soft voice. "Do you think I'm stupid?"

She moved closer to him. "Not at all. You're very intelligent."

"Don't praise me because you want me to keep quiet."

She touched his shoulder, and he stepped back. "Please listen to me." When he said nothing, she continued. "I have no feelings for Paul. I was upset, and he comforted me. That's all there was to it."

Nyok raised his hand in protest. Children might believe those lies, but not him.

Her forefinger tapped against his mouth. "Let me finish before you speak. I know Ben would be angry if he found out. For that reason only, I will speak with Paul to make sure he understands that we are only friends."

"And you are asking me to ignore what I saw?" Nyok hid his satisfaction. This might work out fine. Another plan formed in his mind.

"Yes. Once Rachel is returned to us, Paul will leave. Everything will be back to normal."

Nyok thought about her words. He had seen women and noted their ways with men. As much as he cared for Dr. Kerr, he didn't believe she would keep her word. "I have a deal for you," he said.

She gave him her attention.

"I'll say nothing in exchange for you not stopping me from joining the SPLA."

Her eyes flared. "I will not. Who are you to make demands on me?"

"Who are you to make demands on me? I have a duty to my country."

She pointed a finger into his chest. "You are too young to join this war. You are brilliant, much too smart to die in this godforsaken country. How many times must I say how much more valuable you would be serving your country as an educated man? Listen to Paul. He can guide you to a good school."

Nyok stiffened. "Paul, the jackal? I see how he's guided you."

"You have no right to say that. Paul is here to help your people and you. Please reconsider your decision to join the army. I'm afraid you're making a terrible mistake."

"You don't understand. You weren't there." Once he flung those words at her, Nyok stomped off. He knew exactly what he intended to do, whether she liked it or not.

Early the next morning, Larson learned about the Khartoum trip while the three watched the dawn usher in a new day. She couldn't believe their idiocy, the self-imposed danger.

"What good will you do Rachel dead?" she asked them. Both men had refused breakfast, and she knew something weighed on their minds to cause them to turn down food.

"I suggest you ask Bishop Malou to fast and pray for us," Paul said.

"A whole lot of good that will do." Ben forced a laugh. "Have a little faith in the SPLA. We're the fighting force of Sudan."

"The SPLA?" Larson turned to keep from spewing her thoughts on that subject. "Why not let the slave traders handle finding Rachel? After all, you're filling their pockets."

Paul stood from his chair. "Larson, I appreciate your concern, but what choice do we have? If Rachel is in Khartoum, she's in trouble."

Larson stood and eyed him squarely. "You and Ben will kill each other before you get there. How can you get along traveling together when you're at each other's throats now?" She sucked in a breath. Would she not go if given the opportunity? "I understand. I really do." She stopped before she said any more and sank into a chair beside them.

"We have a job to do," Ben said. "I have no intention of killing Farid until Rachel is found."

"That's wonderful news." She gave him a smug look. "You two deserve each other."

Larson had no idea how she would endure the days until the men returned. And the problem with Nyok hadn't been solved either. The boy refused to speak to her. He had stayed with the soldiers the previous night and hadn't yet returned. She refused to mention the matter to Ben, simply because it involved more explanation.

A short while later Ben ordered his men to stay in Warkou until he returned or sent them marching orders. The time promised much needed rest for his weary soldiers. In addition, Bishop Malou decided to stay and conduct a daily prayer vigil. He knew Rachel and how the villagers loved her.

*So what if Ben and Paul are killed?* Larson asked herself. It wouldn't be the first time she'd lost someone dear to her. What was one more?

Paul and Ben headed east to the White Nile in a truck driven by one of Ben's soldiers. As always, the mosquitoes swarmed around them. Paul swatted at the buzz near his ear. He hated those disease-carrying demons. The three were crowded, hot, and just short of miserable. Paul said nothing. No point in arguing with the colonel.

The truck knocked them against the doors and each other as it bounced along and wound through the thick green forests until it could not go another foot. Twisted limbs sought to curl around the tires and hinder them from turning. All three men tugged at the branches and brush lying in the narrow path, too overgrown to call a road.

"We have to keep off the regular routes," Ben said as he tossed aside the heavy brush they had cut to get the truck through. "Spies are everywhere."

"Do you have passage at the river?" Paul asked, wiping the sweat stinging his eyes.

"Yes. We'll get into the city; then it's up to you."

They drove until dusk and at night slept on the truck bed beneath mosquito netting. Each one took a turn at keeping guard, but Ben didn't sleep during Paul's watch, not that it surprised him.

"What do you think I'm going to do, Colonel?" Paul asked.

"Doesn't matter," Ben said. "I don't trust you."

Paul wondered if in the darkness he could be honest. "Guess I wouldn't either." He hesitated. "What would it take to earn that trust?"

Ben chuckled. "Not a thing—unless the GOS would take you as trade for my sister."

"I've already agreed to that."

"We'll talk about it when I have Rachel." Ben turned over to face up at the stars. "Don't be calling me Colonel until we're finished with this."

"What, then?"

"Mohammad sounds good."

Paul agreed. "Larson doesn't know my link to the royal family."

The scream of a cat echoed across the night. "If you make it out of here alive, you're going to tell her. Her opinion of you will hit zero with that news. Your coming back makes no sense. Why did you do it anyway?"

"I've told you before, other than Rachel, it was Nyok. Larson wanted me to convince him he needs an education, not the army."

"That won't happen." Ben spat the words. "I need him, and he's too old to play around the clinic with her."

"He needs an education."

"What do you know? I need every man in this country to carry a rifle. He's not a child, and he's not afraid of anything."

Paul considered mentioning the United Nations' viewpoint of the matter but assumed that his words would fall on deaf ears. During the rest of his watch, Paul tried to get Larson out of his head. He hadn't been honest with her about his past. That was wrong, and she would be furious. How could he ever expect her to listen to him talk about the Lord when he had kept his past from her?

Behind the truck seat were the civilian clothes they planned to wear into the city. With a sigh, Paul hoped they found out what they needed to know fast. He didn't want to spend any more time with Ben Alier than necessary.

Midmorning the following day, floodwaters caused them to abandon the truck and the driver to take a small boat toward the river. There, a fishing boat followed the White Nile until reaching the point where the water converged with the Blue Nile. The mighty winding river ran south to north, the ancient waterway that men had fought to control since the beginning of history. On the left bank sat Khartoum, the largest city in Sudan. Bahri lay on the right side, and Omdurman lay on the left of the White Nile. The three cities composed the tri-capital of Sudan. Paul's old home. The site of those who wanted him dead.

*Lord, I don't know if I should ask to find Rachel in Khartoum. My logic tells me we don't want to find her there, but You know what is best. Guard her and keep her safe.*

# 22

Khartoum, the second largest city in northern Africa, had once been Paul's home. Now, the high-rise buildings of the business area looked menacing, reminding him of shrines to a society caught up in a false god. The wealthy citizens flourished because they obeyed the fundamental laws of Islam and were loyal to the government. Paul had despised the poor, ignoring their needs for his own gratification. He too had encouraged the persecution of Christians and followers of tribal religions.

*How could I have been happy here?* And when Paul considered his past, he realized that he had flitted from one materialistic whim to another.

Dressed in worn white shirts and light-colored pants, Ben and Paul walked on the outskirts of Khartoum until Ben phoned a friend who picked them up in a rusty, fifteen-year-old Ford. Ben climbed into the front, and Paul sat behind him. Ben called the driver Vo—a thin, wiry fellow who had little to say as they drove into the city.

Paul had let his beard grow out since he first conceived the idea to look for Rachel in Khartoum. He hated the thing. Anyone who might think he recognized him would remember his dislike for a beard. At least he hoped so. Both men wore kafiyyehs and carried their cell phones and 9mm Helwan pistols inside their bulky pants.

Everything around them complemented the blue, cloudless sky: tall, green palms; shades of brown buildings; black-skinned people; and Arabs clothed from ancient dress to today's latest fashions.

Domed mosques caught Paul's attention and provoked a sinking feeling in his chest. Five times a day, loudspeakers sounded the call to prayer. The ritual, the cleansing, the god who could easily send a man to hell or paradise, dominated every breath. It sickened Paul to think of the millions of Muslims caught up in the lies. They would never bow to Mecca again if they could experience Jesus Christ. Someday he would find Abraham's family and tell about the man who showed him the Light.

"Where to?" Vo asked.

Ben scowled and stared out the window. The rain had begun. "Do you know a man by the name of Babrak Kayra?"

Ben turned his gaze to Paul. "How do you know him?"

"He was a friend to me years ago before I fled Khartoum. We have common contacts."

Vo focused his attention on Ben as though waiting for permission to speak or act. "I know how to locate him."

Ben motioned him on, then drummed his fingers on his knee. "Do not get this man killed."

"I have no intention of doing so. He helps the Christians here in the city and those in the displacement camps." Paul paused. "I also know he assists the SPLA."

"I have already contacted Babrak, and he knows nothing," Ben said.

"My business with him is just the beginning."

Vo moved through the narrow, wet, unpaved streets of what was once considered the upper-class quarters. Now the area resembled the middle-class sections of other Arab countries. Billboards of the president rose like warning signs. The whole city seemed to be in a holding pattern, as though waiting for something to happen.

"I read on-line that Khartoum's tourist attractions are unrivaled by any other Sudanese city," Paul said. "Made me laugh."

"Yeah, look at those mosques," Ben said. "Why don't we stop and you can take my picture outside one? We'll send it to Larson with a note that wishes she were here."

*First decent words he's said to me yet.*

Vo weaved in and out of the narrow streets until he reached a familiar concrete house. His windshield wipers screeched across the glass worse than those on Bishop Malou's truck. Vo stepped on the brakes and glanced at the backseat.

"I'll be back in a minute," Paul said.

"I'm going with you." Ben tapped Vo on the shoulder. "Take a drive in case my comrade decides to turn us in."

Paul ignored him and exited the car. The rain splattered against his body like tiny needles, reminding Paul of what the GOS would begin to do if he were caught. Forbidding those thoughts to deter him, Paul turned his attention to the home of his old friend. How long had it been since he had seen Babrak Kayra? Countless e-mails from him and others with southern sympathies filtered through his mind. This reunion with the craggy old man would be good, if not for the circumstances.

He heard Ben slam the car door behind him, and Paul chuckled. Foreign turf obviously ruffled the colonel's feathers. Without stopping, he walked to the iron gate and waited for someone to ask about their business.

A familiar face emerged, a man nearly as old as Babrak. He didn't appear to recognize Paul.

"I'd like to talk to Babrak," Paul said.

"Who are you?"

"A friend. Tell him the lion roars at dusk."

The man peered into Paul's face and glanced at Ben. Releasing a pent-up breath, he turned and ambled beyond the gate. A few moments later, Babrak rushed toward them. Tears streamed down his face, matching the rain. He couldn't pull the gate open fast enough.

"My dear friend, my brother." He drew Paul inside and wrapped his arms around his shoulders. "I've been blessed," he said in a hushed voice. "Shall the Lord call me home today, I will rejoice that I have seen and touched you again."

Paul forced down the lump in his throat, but a tear still slipped over his cheek. Babrak stepped back and reached out to grasp Ben's hand. He had aged, but he was far from frail. "You are welcome here, Colonel. Let's go inside where it is dry. We can eat, drink, and talk."

"Thank you, sir." Ben took Babrak's hand and covered it with his other.

"We can't stay long," Paul said. "Although I'd like nothing better than to spend the day with you, a critical matter needs our attention."

They entered the home where his old friend lived alone. The modest furnishings appeared the same as they had years before. Babrak produced towels, then led them to a sitting area. Once they were comfortable, the man who had met them at the gate brought cool water and slices of bread.

"Shall we pray?" Babrak asked. In the next breath, his raspy voice began. "Lord God, we ask Your blessings on us this day. Thank You for bringing Paul to me. Watch over him and bless him in his every endeavor. Thank You for men like Colonel Alier who bravely lead soldiers to free us from tyranny. Draw him closer to You. Be with us now as we seek Your will. Amen."

Paul smiled into the old man's face. Although layered wrinkles and a humped back marked his physical body, his spiritual body was alive and basking in the love of the Lord. "Tell me what's going on with you, Babrak."

"My oldest son fled to England with his family. His brother and sister live here in Khartoum, and we are working with other Christians. And my youngest ..."

"I know what happened to your son. I'm very sorry," Paul said.

Babrak pressed his lips together. He turned to Ben. "Do you remember Thomas?" When Ben nodded, he continued. "He became very sick. The doctors refused to treat him because he was Christian." Babrak took a deep breath. "He died—almost three months ago. The Bible says to expect persecution, but I never imagined it would be so hard."

"He was a good man." Ben's respectful tone told Paul that there might be hope for the man after all. Then he remembered that Ben often brought bad news to families of deceased soldiers.

"Thank you. He had no family, which is both grievous and a blessing. A wife and children might have suffered too." Babrak lifted the glass to his lips.

"And the others working here in the city?" Paul asked.

He rested the glass on the table. "We do what we can. Thanks to you, dear brother, we are able to do so much more. The tracts are distributed, but no one knows where they are coming from. The church is growing."

"The Lord is blessing your work." Uneasiness crept through Paul. He didn't deserve any praise. "I do what I can."

"This man," Babrak said as he turned to Ben, "he is a saint. When the Lord sets the great banquet table, Paul Farid will have a seat of honor."

*I'm sure Colonel Alier is enjoying this conversation.*

Ben coughed. "We all contribute something in a small way." He glanced at Paul, his impatience evident in the lines across his forehead.

Paul leaned in closer to Babrak. "We have a serious problem with a missing young woman …"

"I see." The old man settled back in a worn overstuffed chair and folded his hands over his lap. The lines deepened in his face. "What does she look like?"

Ben cleared his throat. "She's Dinka, sixteen years old, very beautiful, and she has an inch-long scar on her left shoulder." He took a breath. "Her name is Rachel."

"I'll find out if she's being held in any of the prisons here or in nearby displacement camps. I heard there was a search for such a young woman." He stared directly at Ben. "And I'll find out if there are any fitting her description held in other parts of the city."

Paul appreciated Babrak's discretion.

"Thank you," Ben said. "How long do you think this will take?" His huge weathered frame slumped. The signs of fatigue and sun weighed down on him.

Babrak shrugged. "Three days perhaps. I would be honored if you two stayed with me."

"We can't," Paul said. "It's too dangerous. Can you give me the names of three places where we would be safe?"

The old man blinked back the wetness pooling his eyes. Without a word, he wrote down the names and addresses. "These you know by name, but probably not by sight. All would welcome you in their homes."

Paul stood, and Ben followed. They shook hands. "Thank you for everything," Paul said. "We'll contact you in three days."

Outside they waited in the rain by the iron gate until Vo appeared. Once in the car, Paul asked to be taken to an address.

"Drive around the city for a while. Take your time—just in case. Keep us out of downtown and away from the presidential palace." Paul studied the names and addresses from Babrak, then handed the paper to Vo. He scanned the information and handed it to Ben. "Memorize it," Paul said.

"Where are we going?" Ben asked. "That address isn't one he gave us."

"To a safe place for the next three days."

"You don't trust Babrak?" He spit the words.

"I trust him completely. I don't want him killed."

Ben clenched his jaw and thrust the paper with the addresses at Paul.

"Burn it."

In an instant the car smelled of sulfur.

"You think of everything, don't you?" Ben blew out the match and stomped the remains to dust on the floorboard.

"No, I don't claim to." Paul wondered if the black ashes represented Ben's feelings for him. He found it humorous, but he dared not laugh and instead peered out the window. A half-dozen black-skinned youths kicked at a ball in the street. Paul remembered playing soccer with Tim and Matt. "I'm not the enemy, Ben."

"That's your opinion."

More than an hour later, Vo pulled into an area befitting the car. The homes were slapped together like concrete bricks fortifying a garbage dump. They smelled the same too.

"There." Paul pointed to a house on the left. "No need to wait." He turned his attention to Ben. "Can you call Vo if we need him?"

The colonel nodded. He shook Vo's hand. "Thanks. Ten o'clock Thursday."

"I'll be here."

Once Vo disappeared, Paul took off in the opposite direction of the house. The stench from rotting garbage and sewage tore at his stomach. To think he had lived in a palace while the citizens of Khartoum existed in this rat-infested hole. The conditions brewed both anger and compassion. The rain continued. Too bad it couldn't wash away the filth.

Ben said nothing until they were nearly a kilometer away. "Just where are we going?" Rancor bubbled beneath his words.

One of Hank's sayings reminded Paul of Ben's predicament: *Like a fish out of water.* "A safe place, like I said before."

"I want to know where."

"A house about ten minutes from where we stand."

"Is that the final stop?"

Paul swung his gaze at the demanding colonel. "Maybe."

"Do you trust anyone in this city?"

Paul laughed. "A few, a choice few. I have learned a lot from you, sir."

A labored sigh broke an awkward silence. "I despise you, Farid, but you have shown cunning today. For your sake, it had better be for the good of southern Sudan."

Paul stopped in the middle of the mud-coated street. "My number one priority is the Lord. He has called me to do specific things for the good of southern Sudan. That commitment is not up for discussion."

# 23

Ben followed Farid inside an iron gate that had once been painted black. The aged Arab who met them did not appear surprised. He had the mannerisms of a Muslim and greeted Farid like an old friend. Ben calculated how quickly he could retrieve his pistol.

"This is my friend, Mohammad," Farid said in Arabic.

"It's an honor to meet you." The Arab gestured low. "Come in, please. We've been expecting you."

The man led them up a stone entranceway to a small concrete house. The secrecy and the switching from place to place without an understanding of who or where left Ben outside his normal realm of control, and he didn't like it. He was the one who issued commands. Besides not having the power he normally possessed, he detested Farid's calling the shots. As soon as they were alone, Ben intended to find out everything about the next three days— in detail. In particular, why were they in the home of a Muslim, and why did they have to continue speaking Arabic?

Up to this point, Farid had demonstrated cunning and shrewdness with his plan. It was another source of contention, but

Ben wasn't stupid. He refused to trust him for an instant.

Inside the house, the Arab ushered them to a table where bread, vegetables, fruit, and a meat that looked and smelled like chicken set ready for them to eat. He left the room once an old woman dressed in black shuffled in and greeted Paul. She asked for God to grant him success—and it wasn't the God a Christian served. She disappeared while the two men ate.

"What's going on here?" Ben took a quick glimpse at the food, and his stomach growled. He ignored the inconvenience and swung his attention toward his partner—of sorts. "Who are these people, and why are we here?"

Farid rested his fork beside his plate. "We're with friends where no one would suspect us."

"Arab Muslims?" Ben cursed. "I need an explanation fast."

"I want to eat first; then I'll tell you about it." He sat on the floor, as was their custom.

Ben touched the 9mm pistol. His fingers ached to unload it on Farid and anyone else who got in his way. "I want to know now." He pulled out the weapon.

Farid filled his plate, piling high the meat dish and vegetables. "Shoot me, and you won't know a thing. Besides that, my friends will slit your throat." He proceeded to eat. "Try some. It's good."

"Do you have a death wish?" Ben tightened and released his right fist.

Farid chuckled. "I've been asked that before." He waved his fork in the air. "Maybe I do, but until I decide for sure, you may as well eat because I'm not telling you anything until I'm finished."

Never had anyone angered Ben on a regular basis like this man. Never had Ben wanted to find a reason to kill anyone as much as he wanted to find a reason to kill Paul Farid. Time. Ben needed time and patience. He laid his gun on the table until the weasel had finished eating.

Twenty minutes later, Farid pushed back his plate, wiped his mouth with a napkin, and turned to Ben. "I'm ready."

"Are you sure you don't want dessert first?"

Farid grinned. "No, thanks." He scooted back from the low table. "Gadwa is the old woman's name. Nearly eleven years ago, just before I fled Sudan, I learned of two political prisoners—a father and son—who were being framed and used as scapegoats. At the time I was a new Christian, zealous for God and for defending oppressed people. I pulled a few strings and got the two men out of the country. Gadwa is married to the father. She chose to stay in Khartoum and help others persecuted by the GOS. They believe she is loyal to the current government."

Ben expelled a heavy sigh. "The old woman owes you."

"Exactly. Some refer to her as the Weathered Gazelle."

*Impossible.* "Not here; I don't believe it," Ben said.

"Ask her yourself." Farid called for Gadwa. She dragged her feet across the floor. She was tiny, frail, old …

Farid stood and thanked her for the fine meal. She stared at Ben. "He hasn't eaten yet, but he will shortly. He feels a little ill. Would you be so kind to tell my friend how we met?"

Gadwa nodded and smiled a toothless grin. Word for word, she told the story of how Farid helped her husband and son escape death and find asylum in Egypt.

"What else do you do to help those who oppose the GOS?"

She hesitated. Her stare hardened. "I help the SPLA. I am known as the Weathered Gazelle."

"Prove it." Ben's pulse raced.

"I don't have to prove anything to you, Colonel Alier." Gadwa stared at Ben openly. "But think of me the next time your men pick up a shipment of Kalashnikov rifles or you need a message gotten through to your contact within the president's advisers. You don't believe me or my friend? I don't care. I have nothing to lose. Your approval means nothing." She moved toward the door, then turned back. "Solomon Thic has already tried to locate your sister through me. I have no information, but Farid has additional contacts. Listen to him."

Ben stiffened. No one could have known about his conversation with Solomon except the Weathered Gazelle. "I understand."

"Now, stop insulting me and eat the food I have prepared for you."

Ben opened his mouth to protest but changed his mind. He lowered himself to the table and filled his plate with food. He hated Farid. He hated him because of his heritage. He hated him because of Rachel. He hated him because of the way Larson looked at him. And he hated him because he had been right.

Larson packed the truck with medical supplies and necessities for her and Nyok. She had closed the clinic for the next few days. Her patients were well enough to have others care for them. She needed Nyok to help her at a Red Cross center at a Khartoum-approved site a few hours north of Warkou. A woman, whom she had not seen in almost a year, planned to be there.

"I can stay at the clinic," Nyok said for the third time. "You said I did a good job the last time."

"The patients are okay for now."

"You don't want me here alone when Colonel Alier returns." His accusing glare stoked a fire in her, but she refused to give in to an argument with a twelve-year-old.

"You're right, I don't. But more important, I need you to help me. There will be medical personnel there, but I'm the only doctor, and you know my ways."

Nyok stomped back into the clinic for the last box of bandages and valuable medicine. "You can't stop my destiny."

Larson slammed the door on the truck and wondered if this would be the time it fell off. She whirled around to face him. "I've had enough of your disrespect, Nyok, and I'm not an idiot. Your destiny can't be stopped, but I will do everything within my power to guide it."

"You know nothing about what I think or the things I must do." Her breathing came in short spurts. "Try me." When he said nothing, she returned to packing the truck. These outbursts of his were becoming more and more frequent. Were all twelve-year-olds this difficult? A thought struck her: *hormones.* Could all of this animosity stem from Nyok's leaving his childhood behind and facing adolescence? His childhood had been a nightmare anyway, but this full-blown rebellion was a little more than she could handle. She would talk to Sarah. She would know how to handle a growing boy after raising five of her own. Relieved with that prospect, Larson waited for Nyok to bring the last box.

"Whether Rachel was here or not, I'd still need you to help me the next few days."

"I don't see why. She did everything I'm doing." He positioned the box in a secure spot and leaned against the truck beside Larson.

For a moment she considered asking him not to lean too hard. The truck side was nearly rusted through. "Rachel is good with patients. You're good with assisting me in medical procedures. There's a big difference."

He didn't reply but stared ahead, obviously contemplating what she had said. "So you're saying Rachel acts as your nurse, and I am more of an assistant?"

"Exactly." She reached for the truck door and sounded as enthusiastic as she could muster. "Are you ready?"

"I don't have a choice, do I?"

Larson bit her tongue to keep from hurling words his way. This would be a long day.

Unlike the road trip with Paul, the time with Nyok dragged

by. He refused to talk, and she refused to prod him any further. Instead she bounced along and thought about seeing Marty at the Red Cross location. She was a friend to talk to and laugh with, not a patient or someone who didn't understand all the idiosyncrasies of a Western woman. The last time Marty brought chocolate—mouth-watering, irreplaceable, intoxicating chocolate. And she had magazines, and they weren't medical journals, but popular periodicals full of information about fashion and makeup—and fiction stories about interesting women. How Larson had enjoyed the escape the publications provided, and Marty had written that she had brought more.

Right now, this very minute, Larson believed she wanted a furlough home. She thought maybe her parents had pushed the memories to that part of their minds where forgiveness chose forgetfulness. Maybe the three of them could drive to the old farm and reminisce about days gone by. She hoped the new owners had taken care of the place. Perhaps she and her parents could visit Grandma's and Granddaddy's graves and take flowers. A picnic sounded nice, or a trip to the Amish country. Larson allowed her mind to linger on the pleasantries. She had done quite a bit of that lately. The longing started with Paul.

She must establish heart boundaries with him. Just because the only man in the area who exhibited some remote interest was Ben, she didn't have to act like a fool over the next one thrown in her path. If she admitted the truth, she was looking for a diversion until Rachel returned. Thinking about a man, no matter how mismatched the relationship, pushed her sweet daughter from her mind. How selfish of her.

She didn't really have an interest in Paul. He filled the aching void of her beloved children, and she simply wanted Rachel back unharmed. And Nyok, she didn't want to think about raging hormones and ridiculous plans. She wanted him safely out of the country and continuing his education. Larson glanced at the troubled boy. He stared out to his right, no doubt deep in thought about how many GOS soldiers he would kill when he was able to carry a rifle. The truth echoed around her. She stood powerless to stop him, no matter what she conceded to do with Ben.

The powerful colonel was another matter. Congeniality between the two of them must exist. She much preferred battling with him over the rights of the Sudanese in her village than wrestling with him in the heat of passion. *Why must everything be so difficult and so complicated?* She tilted her head back and stretched her aching neck muscles.

These problems were all her own fault. She had decided a long time ago to live a solitary life. At the time, the decision meant survival of the astronomical pressures closing in around her. Yet, sometimes she longed to be a little girl again, to wrap her arms around Daddy's or Granddaddy's neck and hold on for dear life. She needed someone to tell about all the woes building inside of her until she thought she would explode—an aneurysm of the soul.

Up ahead she saw the outlines of the Red Cross plane and the roughly constructed center. For the next two days, she intended to enjoy herself and push all the junk out of her head. The closer the images came into focus, the more Larson studied the workers for signs of a dark-haired Western woman—young, vibrant, and always laughing. Pulling the truck to a halt, she scanned the crowd again. The sound of a female's voice rose above the others.

"Larson. Over here."

"Hey! How are you?"

"Hot, tired, and thirsty, but what else is new?" Larson asked.

Amid the boxes and people, Marty motioned for Larson to join her. In the next breath the two hugged and cried at the same time.

"You look dazzling." Marty's short-cropped hair lay plastered against her head, and perspiration dripped from her temples.

"How do you manage out here in the wilds?"

"It's a secret, but I'll tell you," Larson said. "It begins with sweat and ends in ducking bullets."

"How horrible. Whatever, it's working. Can we get together later? I know you have a ton of patients, but—"

"Nothing will stop us from catching up," Larson said.

Marty motioned toward two other Red Cross workers handing out bags of rice. "I brought chocolate, like I promised, and six months of *People*."

Larson nearly squealed but thought better of it considering the Sudanese and other relief workers were watching. Besides, people waited to see her—the sick and dying. Too many children with skeleton limbs and swollen stomachs needed her attention. Later she would relax with her friend.

"We're going to be busy," she said to Nyok.

They each grabbed a box of medical supplies and trudged toward the front of the line where the Red Cross had set up a small tent for her. Almost an hour later, she heard helicopters approaching. Thinking the GOS was simply checking out the humanitarian efforts, Larson ignored the sound of whirling engines.

"Helicopter gunships," Nyok said, lifting a child from the makeshift examining table to the ground.

"Don't say that," Larson said. "You'll frighten these people."

Nyok stepped out of the tent and glanced up. "Dr. Kerr. Those *are* gunships."

His words were no sooner spoken than the GOS soldiers leaned from their aircrafts and started pouring fire into the crowd. Screams mixed with the whiz of bullets echoed around Larson. Nyok grabbed her and a child, then dove under a mass of boxes.

# 24

By Wednesday evening Paul realized that he had stretched his limit with Ben. The confinement within Gadwa's home had left both of them irritable. She had fed them and made sure they were comfortable, then withdrawn to her own affairs or asked to speak to Paul privately. He didn't blame her. Ben seemed to look for reasons to quarrel, and Paul was tired of dodging barbs.

He prayed and read the brown Gideon New Testament tucked in his backpack. He had tossed around the idea of whether to bring it, but decided that if he was searched he would rather die for the Lord than save his skin. In the afternoon he phoned Babrak to see if the old man had learned anything about Rachel. So far nothing.

"Would you consider dissuading Nyok from joining the army?" Paul asked Ben once darkness had spread its cloak around the city. "He's extremely bright and needs to be in school."

Ben paced across the floor of the small living-room area, reminding Paul of a caged animal. "I've heard that before, many times."

"And?"

"What do you care?" Ben stopped and planted his hands firmly on his hips. His gaze threw poisonous darts in Paul's direction. "The SPLA needs him."

"I agree Sudan needs him, but in a few years when he's ready to serve them in his best capacity."

"You spend too much time with Larson."

Paul knew he should not say another word, but he couldn't stop himself. "Is the problem Nyok, or the fact that Larson has spoken to me about her ambitions for him?"

Ben glared. "What are you saying?"

"The obvious. You're in love with the woman."

"That's the stupidest thing you've said yet."

"But it's the truth." Paul watched Ben's features stiffen. *The man already despises you. Don't push him.*

"You're wrong, Arab. I have no feelings for the woman."

"Then I must be blind."

"I can arrange it."

Paul's phone rang. "All right. Suit yourself." Before Ben could respond, Paul answered his cell phone.

"Are you safe?" Babrak asked.

Paul moved so he could peer around the blinds to see onto the street. In the night, the shadows all blended into one. "I believe so. What's going on?"

"We have a problem, my friend," Babrak said. "The three addresses I gave you have been searched by the GOS."

"I chose not to stay at any of them."

"No matter. That you are not in custody is an answer to prayer. Who else knows you are in the city?"

Paul trusted Gadwa with his life. The ones remaining were Ben and Vo the driver. "I have an idea. We'll be careful."

"Do you still plan to be here at ten in the morning?"

Paul hesitated. Babrak's or Gadwa's house could be tapped, or Vo could have betrayed them. "We'll be there."

"God be with you and the colonel."

Paul set the phone on a small table and stared at Ben. "The three safe houses that Babrak gave to us have been raided. Someone has betrayed us."

"Who?"

"I suspect Vo. How well do you know him?" Paul rubbed the back of his neck.

Ben ceased his pacing and sank into a worn sofa. "If it's him, then why wasn't Babrak questioned? Unless he figured the old man is—"

"Our contact."

"My thoughts."

Ben pulled his phone from his shirt pocket. "If it's him, we need to find out." He punched in a series of numbers. "Hey, Vo. How are things? Good. We'll be ready in the morning for the ten o'clock appointment." He paused. "Yes, pick us up where you dropped us off."

He dropped the phone back inside his pocket. "Now we'll see who has betrayed us. I'm not beyond suspecting you."

"I understand," Paul said. Ben's relentless distrust was beginning to wear on him. "What time do you want to leave in the morning?"

Ben said nothing for several seconds. "Can Gadwa get us there by eight? Perhaps Babrak can get us out of the city before Vo realizes we're gone."

"I'm sure it can be arranged."

"If this is true, Vo will be dead before this time tomorrow."

"Can you use him? Feed him wrong information?" Paul asked.

Ben forced a laugh. "You're beginning to sound like one of us."

"I am one of you."


At eight o'clock the following morning, Ben and Farid slipped through the gate at Babrak's home and hurried inside to see the old man. Ben had mixed feelings about the meeting. As much as he wanted to find Rachel, he didn't want her near the city. The issue wasn't getting her out of Khartoum, but what she had endured while she was there.

After sharing a few pleasantries and making sure Babrak could transport them out of the city, Ben could wait no longer. "What did you learn about my sister?"

"Nothing. No one has heard or seen her in or around Khartoum. I understand you were hoping to find her, and I'm sorry." Babrak touched Ben's arm.

"I did want to find her, but not here … where she could be harmed."

"A blessing perhaps?" Babrak asked with a tilt of his head.

"I think so." Ben took a deep breath. "I hope so. Slave traders are looking."

The gatekeeper halted their conversation. "I see two GOS cars coming down the street. They're up to something."

"I think so too," Babrak said. "Please escort these gentlemen out the back. A driver has been waiting since you arrived. Hurry now, before you're discovered."

"Thank you," Farid said. "We will talk soon."

Ben shook Babrak's hand and followed the gatekeeper through the back of the house.

Slipping between concrete houses and buildings, they made their way to the car. A moment later the vehicle moved down the street and toward the outskirts of Khartoum.

"Vo betrayed you," the driver said. "Babrak had me follow him. Colonel, what would you have us do?"

Ben glanced about to make sure the GOS wasn't following them. As much as he disliked Farid, the Arab did make sense about using Vo. If Ben had taken the time to consider the situation, he would have come up with the same idea. "Continue to treat him as though we are ignorant of his treachery. Watch him.

He can be used to our advantage."

"Very wise, Colonel," the driver said.

Farid coughed. Ben wished he could wipe the smirk off the weasel's face.

Once they reached the Blue Nile, the two men boarded a fishing boat and headed south. An hour into their journey, Ben attempted to relax. The sleepy Nile, often called the water of life by the Sudanese, was as revered as the Garden of Eden to the Christians. Some speculated that the original paradise lay between the White Nile and Blue Nile. Ben could see why. Its beauty rivaled that of any river on earth, and its waters irrigated their land while providing fish for their bellies. Along the banks, palm trees rose like giant statues guarding the river, while colorful birds appeared to lead the way.

Someday Ben intended to live an easy life along the Nile. He allowed his eyes to drift shut. Just before nodding off, he punched in a number to catch an update.

"Reported helicopter shootings near a Red Cross center," his contact said.

"What happened?"

"GOS opened fire on civilians, mostly women and children. Two of the Red Cross workers were killed."

*Larson and Nyok were there.* "It was an approved site!"

"Yes, sir. We've sent men into the area."

Little good it would do now. "Keep me posted." Ben replaced his phone and stole a look at Farid. "Helicopter gunners fired on a Red Cross center."

"How many casualties?" Farid buried his face in his hands, then abruptly raised his head. "Larson and Nyok," he whispered.

"I know. No totals yet, only that a couple of the workers were killed. The rest were women and children."

"Animals," Farid said.

Ben shot his attention at the Arab. "Aren't those your people?"

"What do you mean 'my people'? Just because we're the same race doesn't mean I condone what they do." Farid's face reddened. "How quickly can we get names or find out if Larson and Nyok are all right?"

"I'll keep checking." The familiar rise of anger threatened to overtake Ben. *Not Larson and Nyok.* They had to be safe. She had been in a lot of tough situations before and knew how to use her head, but she would risk her life for those in trouble. At least Nyok was with her. He would keep her out of harm's way. The boy would die for that woman. "We'll push on through. Not stop and rest until we get to the site."

The lines across Farid's forehead deepened. "At least we agree on that." His jaw tightened. "I'm getting her a phone, a global one. She should have had one a long time ago."

Ben hated to admit that the Arab was right again. Why hadn't he thought of providing Larson some means of communication?

"When your sister is found and I'm back to flying for FTW, Larson will need to have a source of help," Farid continued. "And a good computer too. She could e-mail FTW for supplies and keep in contact with … with whomever she wanted."

"What kind do you mean?"

"One that is intended for rugged use—a notebook designed to handle the extreme temperatures, one equipped with the latest of satellite communications. It could have a built-in global positioning receiver, long battery life—all the latest technology. In fact," he said as he peered intently at Ben, "you need one too."

"How could she charge up the battery?" Ben asked, leaning in closer.

"She has a generator for the refrigerated medicine. I believe FTW or one of the other humanitarian agencies supplies her with gas. I know I've seen the tank."

The Arab confused Ben. He understood Larson's need, but his? Money might not be a problem for Farid, but why should he help the SPLA? "That would be a valuable asset."

"And for you, Colonel, I'd think the technology of the global positioning satellite and its ability to pinpoint where you are and the surrounding terrain would be invaluable. What about digital imagery?"

Incredulous best described Ben. "Why would you do this for me?"

"Why not?" Farid asked. "We're on the same side. We both want southern Sudan to one day know peace and be able to assume some type of autonomy. We both want freedom of religion and a democracy. We both want the children to grow up educated in the best schools." He took a deep breath. "It isn't going to happen unless one of two things takes place: either the peace negotiations are successful, or the SPLA gets a step ahead of the GOS."

Ben said nothing. He twisted and turned at the thought of Paul Farid being the man the media claimed he was. *Had he really fled the royal family due to his new beliefs?* Ben didn't want to admit he had been wrong one more time, but everything Farid said and did pointed to a man committed to the good of Sudan.

"It's hard to trust you," Ben said. The rhythmic sound of water slapping against the sides of the small fishing boat soothed his troubled mind.

Farid nodded. "I would feel the same way if I were in your shoes. You know my past, and I know you were raised in a Christian Dinka home. Despite what I did then, I now serve Jesus Christ. That's it, plain and simple."

The man was too good to be true, and Ben refused to take him into his confidence. His offer to purchase needed equipment for him and Larson had to be a trick. Somehow, someway, he would uncover the deceit of Paul Farid.

Larson swiped at the mosquitoes swarming between her and the critically wounded woman before her. She couldn't stop the bleeding. Without surgery the woman would die. She would make six dead and ten wounded. To make matters worse, the woman was pregnant.

"Marty, check on that little girl over there." Larson pointed. "She has a few scratches and bruises, but she keeps crying."

"That's because you're working on her mother," Marty said.

"Oh no."

"Mama's not going to make it?" Marty whispered, then turned her attention to the little girl, who was not much more than three years old.

"It doesn't look like it." Frustrated, Larson cursed. "I didn't bring supplies to perform surgery. I intended to see you, perform some routine medical procedures, and then go home. I can't do a thing for these people but dig out bullets with local anesthetic and bandage them up."

Marty touched her shoulder. "No one expects any more than what you give."

Larson swallowed the emotion rising in her throat. *These people expect a miracle.* She glanced about at the makeshift tents set up to shelter the wounded—pieces of canvas held down by boxes. Yesterday the afternoon rains had drenched them all, mixing blood, dirt, and sweat in a swirl of confusion.

Larson caught her breath. The woman before her was dead. "One more for the count," she said, easing away from the cramped position on her knees and stretching her back. How many bodies had she seen since coming to Sudan? Sometimes in the dark of night, they opened their eyes and pointed their boney fingers at her. "You could have done more," they said.

Larson pulled a worn sheet over the dead woman's face.

Marty rubbed her temples. A tear slid from her eye. She said nothing but rose from her position across from the body and walked over to the little girl. The child seemed to sense what had happened and cried harder. Larson watched as Marty gathered her up and held her close. The child laid her head against Marty's chest, sobbing.

It was the sound of Sudan: children weeping.

SPLA soldiers had been at the site since a few hours after the attack. They surrounded the Red Cross area ready to assist if the need arose. Larson wished Ben were leading them. His presence made her feel safe—as long as he kept his distance. Not far away, a group of women and children began to sing. Larson and Marty turned to hear them.

"'Jesus Loves Me,'" Marty said. "How sweet the words. We can't forget the Lord is here with us. He sees all the suffering. How fitting that a child's song should usher in the love and peace of our Lord."

The thought tore through Larson's mind. "How can you even think a loving God would permit this kind of barbarity?"

"Are you blaming God for the government's sin?"

"I can't blame something that isn't there."

Another tear slipped down Marty's cheek. "How can you not believe when you see the love in these people's faces? It's a miracle we weren't all killed."

Larson couldn't stop the bitterness clawing at her chest. "Have you been blind too? What has your God done for you?" She pointed to the sky. "Nearly got you blown up?"

Marty held the child as though paralyzed while tears flowed unchecked over her cheeks and onto the child's head. "Jesus Christ is my reason for breathing in this sin-infested world."

Larson detected the distinct odor of death and sickened bodies. She would never grow accustomed to it. Never. "The stench of what the GOS is doing to southern Sudan wrenches at my stomach. Don't tell me you can't smell it. Sometimes I think I can taste it before it happens."

"But God doesn't bring evil." Marty's words were gentle, quiet, not like the explosion in Larson's heart and mind.

"I agree. It's the roar of a million demons plaguing a helpless land."

Marty shook her head and clasped her hands together as if in prayer. "If you believe in demons, then surely you believe in God."

"I can't." Larson stood from the ground. "I refuse to mask life with this God-loves-everyone veil. It's a sad joke played on unsuspecting fools."

Marty gasped. "Are you saying I'm a fool to trust the Creator of the universe? How did you become so bitter?"

Larson detested the words spewing from her mouth. She took a deep breath and willed her shattered emotions to calm down. "No, Marty, you're not a fool. You're a wonderful, giving person. I'm sorry. I … I simply don't believe in a God of love. I look around me and see nothing but waste and carnage."

"What *do* you believe in?"

Larson had never been asked that question before. In the past, her cynicism about the subject had always stopped others from pursuing the subject any further. Where did she put her faith and trust? In medicine? In democracy? In the law of the jungle—only the strongest survive? Larson cast her gaze beyond Marty to the thick forest.

"I don't know," Larson said. "I grew up in church. My grandfather was a Methodist preacher. I went through all the motions of a Christian, until life proved unbearable. I decided that I would rather be in charge of my future than see the disastrous results of those who served God."

Marty's chin quivered. She shook her head and blinked. "What do you think will happen to you when you die?"

"I'll rot somewhere and probably smell worse than these poor Sudanese bodies."

"I don't think for one minute that you have completely forsaken God." Marty pressed her lips together before continuing.

"When I recall the many times He has saved you, then I understand He is after you. God wants to return you to His fold, and He's waiting."

"Marty, don't. The past two days have been a nightmare. We're exhausted and emotionally spent. Let's not talk of this anymore."

"I love you, my sister, and I won't ever stop praying that one day you will seek God with your whole heart."

*Create in me a clean heart, O God; and renew a right spirit within me. Cast me not away from thy presence; and take not thy holy spirit from me.*

Larson covered her ears. The words of David shouted above her senses. She didn't want to remember. She wanted it all to stop.

"Larson. Larson." Marty touched her cheek. "Are you all right?"

Larson uncovered her ears and peered into her friend's face. "Ah yes, I'm fine. I'm very tired right now."

"You did work through the night."

"And so did you."

Marty shifted the little girl in her arms. "The wounded are tended to. Why don't you lie down for a few hours? I rarely pull an all-nighter. I think you do it on a regular basis."

Larson glanced around. She had forgotten that Nyok had been sitting there listening to the conversation. She sucked in her breath. He didn't know about her growing up in church or about her grandfather being a Christian minister. His deep brown pools met hers. All the hostility of the past days had vanished.

"Please, Dr. Kerr. Miss Marty is right. You need rest, or you will be sick." He nodded at the body. "I'll take care of the woman and help with the burial. The soldiers dug the other graves. They will dig this one."

The bodies of the Red Cross volunteers who died would be

sent home. Larson wondered if their families had been notified. How sad. All they had wanted to do was give of their time, and now they had no time left to give.

"I'll help you get situated for a nap," Marty said, "and manage things until you wake up."

Too spent to argue, Larson nodded. "Thanks, both of you. The rains will begin soon."

"It will be like a lullaby," Marty said. "Go. Over by the plane is shelter. Nyok and I have things under control."

Contrary to her obstinate nature, Larson agreed and allowed Marty to lead her around shattered boxes, broken crates, and other vestiges of the recent mayhem to the shelter beneath the plane's wings. She would merely catch an hour's nap, just long enough to refresh her body.

"I will continue to pray for you," Marty whispered.

Larson smiled, the fight drained from her. *Someone needs to. Jesus loves me, this I know ...*

# 25

The truck rumbled along, splattering mud as high as the windows. In some places, Paul wondered if they would make it through the water at all. A rickety bridge creaked and moaned as the truck jolted across. For Paul, the vehicle couldn't go fast enough. As before, the bumps threw them against the sides. The sounds of birds and screeching monkeys ordering them away from their forest homes contrasted with the fumes from the antiquated vehicle.

Ben snatched up his cell phone and placed a call. "Any word about the attack on the Red Cross center?" He listened, his face showing no sign of emotion. "I'll be in touch."

"Any news?" Paul asked.

"Seven dead, two more critical. No count on the wounded. Soldiers are posted there, but the GOS haven't returned."

"I don't imagine they'll be back. They've done their dirty work, and they enjoy the element of surprise," Paul said.

"And the tactics of taking civilian lives."

Paul shook his head. What would it take to end this war? "This latest attack ought to get worldwide attention."

"At least until the next news break. Maybe we'll get coverage on CNN—as a one-liner about Red Cross workers killed while helping the needy."

"How special." Paul stopped before he produced a whole string of ungodly statements. In the next instant, he realized that he was getting as derisive as Ben. For once they were in agreement. What a paradox. At least for the moment, he and the colonel weren't arguing.

Shoving aside his convictions, Paul prayed for Larson, Nyok, and the others involved at the center. Larson had mentioned how she looked forward to seeing a friend there, a woman who had volunteered for the Red Cross. He hoped the friend hadn't been one of the two workers killed or among the wounded. Paul prayed for something in that tragedy to speak to Larson about Jesus and His love.

He could almost feel Larson's loneliness and the wall she had erected around her heart. Once again he regretted kissing her. He had taken advantage of her emotions in losing Rachel, because he too was alone and needed the touch of another human being. His actions hadn't mirrored Jesus; neither had they cured the ache inside him from unanswered prayer. Earlier he had told Ben that when Rachel was returned, he would go back to flying missions for the FTW. Paul didn't feel any enthusiasm about his pilot's job or anything else. His future looked more and more like a maze with no exit.

Right now getting to the attack scene and helping the best he could occupied his senses. Maybe *simply doing* was part of the answer—just living each day as though it was his last. He had read that in Og Mandino's *The Greatest Salesman in the World*. Odd he remembered those words now, or maybe God had placed them in his mind for a reason.

Paul sighed inwardly. Trying to outthink God proved futile at best. He would keep praying for direction and take one moment at a time.

"Have you decided to deter Nyok from joining?" Paul asked.

Ben's eyebrow rose sharply. Not many men could do this effectively, but the colonel had a way with gestures. He easily put fear into the hearts of the most robust of men. "Don't ask the question if you don't expect your jaw broken."

Paul chuckled. "Never hurts to ask."

"For some maybe, but not for you, Arab."

*Some things haven't changed. Oh, Lord, again I ask You to spare this boy—now and in the future. Bring him to a realization of his worth in You. I have a difficult time believing You'd want him fighting as a child soldier. Lord, I don't know what else to say.*

"God must be with us," the soldier driving the truck said. They had just forded a low point in the road. "Normally, this is impassable."

Ben said nothing. Paul agreed with the soldier. A moment later, Paul and the driver began a conversation about God's blessings. It continued until Ben announced that he had heard enough. Paul laughed but complied.

Hours later in the darkness of night, they reached the Red Cross center. Several SPLA members stopped the truck at gunpoint, then briefed Ben on what they had done since the helicopter attack.

Paul realized that the soldiers had done nothing, but what else could they have done? Not able to stand the waiting any longer, he asked the driver to let him out. Although anxiety about Larson and Nyok ate at him, Paul wasn't so sure he wanted to know the outcome.

"You can wait on me." Ben's voice rose over the night air. He swung his attention back to the soldier who was briefing him on the current situation. "What about Dr. Kerr and the boy from Warkou?"

"They are fine, Colonel."

Ben spit at Paul's feet. "Farid, are you satisfied?"

Paul stared at him. His temper inched out of control. "Thank you, Colonel Alier. Your generosity is exceeded only by your compassion."

In the shadows, a soldier stepped forward and swung a blow alongside Paul's face. The slap of flesh against flesh stunned him. A fiery hot pain shot up his cheek. Dazed, his head spun, and he fell backward, mud sloshing between his fingers.

"Get up." The soldier straddled Paul's body, his fists hooked. "You speak to Colonel Alier with respect."

Paul couldn't move. The pain in his jaw raced up the side of his head. The soldier grabbed him by the shirt and started to yank him up.

"That's enough." Ben's orders echoed across the night air. "Leave the Arab alone. This one is not the enemy."

Paul bit back the angry words begging to surface. Ben could have stopped the soldier earlier. *I have to maintain control.*

Ben reached down and pulled him to his feet. "Stay out of my men's way. The next time I might not be around to save your neck."

Paul maintained his placid demeanor. The things he longed to say continued to march across his mind like the army of mosquitoes buzzing around his face.

The soldier who had hit Paul towered over him. He could feel the man's hot breath.

"Easy," Ben said. "I said leave him alone."

The soldier said nothing. A tense moment followed before the man stepped backward.

Paul could taste the blood rolling over his lip and chin, yet he refused to swipe at it.

"I've got things to do," Ben said. In the next instant he pushed past Paul and strode toward the lights ahead.

Taking a deep breath, Paul eyed the three soldiers standing by the truck.

"Get out of here," one of them said. "We won't be as kind as the colonel."

Seeing where Ben had headed, Paul ambled to the colonel's right. *I need water.* Thirst mounted inside him, and he realized that he should probably wash the blood from his face. His mud-caked clothes stuck to him, but the throbbing streaking up his face left him dizzy. He reached up to touch it and felt slimy blood beneath his fingertips. His jaw didn't feel broken. At least he hoped it wasn't.

Someday he would learn to stay out of the SPLA's way.

Paul stumbled over a rut and nearly fell. Glancing up, he made out a few lanterns and makeshift cots surrounded by crates. A dark-haired white woman sat in a folding canvas chair and stared out into the night.

"Are you all right?"

He recognized the voice to the rear of him. "Larson, it's Paul."

"Have you been hurt?"

Paul held his breath while the pain thundered through his head. "A little."

"I'll bet it's little. Step into the light."

Paul moved toward the lanterns, hoping he looked better than he felt.

Larson gasped. "What happened? Did the GOS do this?"

"I got roughed up."

"I'm so sorry. Did Ben get hurt too?" She took his arm and led him to a small work station neatly organized with a bucket of water, a basin, and an assortment of bandages and other supplies.

"He's fine." Paul leaned on the table and took a few deep breaths. He hadn't noticed it before, but the area smelled of death.

"This is my friend Marty," Larson said. She picked up a roll of paper towels and tore off two of them. "Marty, this is the pilot I told you about."

Marty waved her hand but didn't budge. From the tired lines etched around her face and eyes, it was obvious that the woman teetered between exhaustion and passing out. "Pleased to meet you. I'm not trying to be rude here. I can't muster enough strength to move."

"I understand." He lowered his shaky body into a canvas chair beside her. "You two have been through quite an ordeal. What can I do to help?"

Marty smiled. "Take care of yourself first. You don't look so good."

Larson peered into his face and dabbed at the blood. "This just happened. Why do I have this strange feeling that Ben looks pretty good right now?"

"I fell." Paul winced when she touched his jaw.

"Liar."

He had missed her sense of humor. "There's a rut out there by the truck."

"Probably with knuckle prints." She placed her hands on her hips. "You don't need stitches, thank goodness. What about your stomach? Ribs?"

"Fine, I'm fine. Some sleep will cure me."

Paul's gaze caught Larson's attention. She looked more rested than Marty. "Rachel was not in Khartoum. No one had seen her either."

Larson stiffened. "I believe we established that would be good."

"Yes, and we'll keep looking."

"I know." She saturated a cotton ball with antiseptic and patted it over his cuts. "You remind me of a dog I used to have."

"Ouch, that stuff stings. Is this another one of your stories from the heart of Ohio's farmland?" He groaned. "And I suppose it's supposed to keep my mind off what you're doing?"

She continued to dab the wounds. "Hush and listen. We had

this old hunting dog named Prince, one of those long-eared, slobbery kind. He didn't bark, just howled. Well, my grandmother hated this old dog, but Prince loved her. He dug up her flowers, sang to the moon outside her bedroom window, jumped on her with kisses. I mean, the dog was just a big-ol'-overgrown, friendly puppy. One day Prince dug up her prize rosebushes. Grandma piled him into the truck and drove twenty miles to the middle of nowhere and ordered that dog out. Told Prince never to come back. A week later, Grandma stepped out of the house, and there was Prince, wagging his tail and wanting to give her kisses."

Paul attempted a chuckle, but it hurt too much. "And how do I remind you of Prince?" For a moment, he wondered if she had learned the truth about him.

"Oh, it's simple. No matter what happens, you come back for more. Your commitment to Sudan is bigger than your fear of those who don't like you." She captured his gaze and lowered her voice. "Be careful, and I want to know everything, start to finish."

He started to suggest that she ask Ben, but he heard the colonel heading their way.

"There you are," Ben said, crossing his arms over his ample chest. "Glad you're all right. The director just filled me in on what's been going on."

Larson finished tending to Paul's cuts. "It wasn't a picnic. Nyok has been a big help."

"When do you think you'll head back to Warkou?"

Still ignoring Ben, she capped the antiseptic bottle. "Tomorrow or the next day. Depends on my patients." She pointed to Paul. "He sure took a bad fall by the truck. I didn't realize there were so many ruts and brush there."

Ben nodded. "He's clumsy. Not sure how he tripped." He glanced around, then peered at those lying wounded on cots. "Where's Nyok?"

"He's with a group of soldiers on the other side of the plane,"

Larson said. A man cried out, and she stepped to his side.

"No, he's not. I was just there."

Ben studied the Arab sitting alone near the plane's wings where cloth bags of grain were piled. A lantern cast an ethereal look about his face, and Ben knew from Farid's calm features that he was praying.

Ben also saw the swollen face and eye. A twist of guilt hit his gut, and he rubbed the back of his neck as though he could erase what his soldier had done. He moved toward Farid, not really wanting to speak with him, but sensing a need to make some type of amends.

Farid lifted his gaze. He neither smiled nor frowned. The look always bothered Ben; he took too much pride in evaluating a man's facial expressions.

"What are you reading tonight?" Ben asked.

Paul smiled. "About King Ahab."

"And his lovely wife Jezebel?"

"That's the couple." Farid closed the book. "I have just the New Testament in my backpack, but Marty lent me her Bible. Don't know how I got into their story. Ahab and Jezebel have the distinction of being the most evil of all Israel's royal leaders."

Ben nodded, not sure what to say. He leaned against a wall of grain sacks.

"King Ahab reminds me of how I used to be." Farid's voice rang soft over the night sounds of insects and distant animals. "I closed my eyes and ears to everything going on except what pleased me. Talk about a worldview. The world existed for me, and I took every advantage of it." He paused. "Makes me sick thinking about it."

"We all feel that way from time to time," Ben said. He sensed Farid's gaze penetrating his very soul.

"Thanks."

"Are you okay?"

"Sure."

Ben took a deep breath. "I should have stopped him before he threw a punch."

"Don't worry about it."

Ben realized that Farid meant exactly what he said, and he felt more convicted of his past treatment of him. But he couldn't bring himself to fully apologize, not when he didn't fully trust the man. He couldn't. Farid represented the enemy, no matter what he claimed or did. Turmoil continued to pick at Ben.

"I understand your father is proud of your work with the SPLA," Farid said.

*Strange question.* "Yeah, seems to be. He's a strong Christian—lives in Nairobi. When I took my post with the SPLA, he sent a letter congratulating me along with a verse."

"What's the Scripture?"

"Second Timothy two, verse four: 'No one serving as a soldier gets involved in civilian affairs—he wants to please his commanding officer.'" Ben chuckled and wondered why he had brought up the matter. "I understand my father meant for me to be a soldier for Christ instead of for man, but those things are for later. Right now, I have a war to finish."

"You can do both," Farid said, barely above a whisper.

"No, I can't. War's a cruel master, and I'm a slave to it."

Farid expelled a heavy breath and stared out into the night. "I'm sorry to hear that."

Irritation made Ben restless. He had stated his business, and he had no desire to make friends with the Arab. "I need to get going."

"Sure. Have you seen Nyok?"

"Not yet. He's here somewhere. Larson is overreacting, as usual."

"She's still up, tending the wounded."

Ben glanced in the direction of the makeshift beds and painful moans. "I'll see what I can do to calm her down."

# 26

The morning sun beat down hot on Nyok's back, and sweat soaked his shirt. He didn't care. For the first time in years, he was doing exactly what he wanted. Each step brought him closer to collecting on the revenge he sought for his family's murder. He kept pace with the soldiers ahead of him. They had even given him a rifle—a Russian Kalashnikov.

Nyok longed to use the weapon on the GOS. He planned to kill ten men for each one of his family members. When he had finished, every dead GOS would have increased Sudan's chances for freedom. Clenching his fists, he allowed his loved ones' memories to wash over him. It fueled his anger and kept him from thinking about Dr. Kerr and how upset she would be to learn that he had left the Red Cross center with the soldiers.

She had pushed him to his limit by always telling him he was smart and that southern Sudan needed educated leaders to make the country stand and grow. Of course Paul agreed.

*I am smart. I saw through Dr. Kerr's need to mother me. I'm a warrior, and I need to fulfill my destiny.*

Rachel had been taken captive, and Dr. Kerr wanted to hold

onto him, like a child. Granted, he was interested in completing his education, but much later, when the war had ended. Enjoying a safe and easy life studying medicine or how to create good policies for Sudan was a coward's way out. Nyok stiffened as he marched with the other four soldiers. Yes, now he would perform his military duty for his country. Colonel Alier would applaud his decision. How many times had the colonel told him what a good soldier he would make?

Dr. Kerr had said that the United Nations banned child soldiers, and Nyok understood their mandate. But regardless of his age, he was a warrior-protector, and he had an obligation and a responsibility to carry out those duties. He refused to think how God might view the decision. The memory of fighting the lion dropped itself into the middle of his thoughts, forcing him to relive the fear all over again. Undoubtedly, God gave him strength and went before him to fight. Would He do so again? Would God protect him as He had done so many times in the past?

God doesn't run out of grace. That's what Bishop Malou said. Nyok squinted his eyes in an effort to concentrate on what the bishop had claimed in his last sermon. God always gives His children what they need, but not always what they want. Saving Sudan was a need. Protecting his fellow soldiers was also a need. Wants were new clothes and plenty of food.

*So many SPLA soldiers have died—like James.*

Nyok swore away the frightful remembrance. He dared not think of death, only of fulfilling his vow to avenge his family. God would not forsake him. This opportunity to become a part of the soldiers fighting for freedom and justice was not just luck. It had to be God's will. The circumstances leading up to it were odd, as though prearranged. While he was talking with the soldiers, four of them had received orders to head southeast into Warab Province. There they were to meet up with another battalion.

"Are you ready to fight for southern Sudan?" a soldier had asked him.

"Yes, I'm ready," Nyok had replied. Without a doubt, he knew his future.

Larson hugged Marty close. She bit back the tears and squeezed her eyes shut.

"We'll keep in touch." Marty sniffed. "Next time we'll meet under better skies than ... than this one."

Larson pulled back and wiped the dampness from her friend's cheek. "Hey, chocolate and girlfriends. What could be better? The next time will be wonderful."

Marty smiled through her tears. "How do you do it? How do you manage to keep your sanity day after day? I have God, and still I'm a puddle of emotion. I'd hate to think where I might be without Him."

Larson didn't know how to respond. "I just live one day at a time. When things get bad, I stuff it back, then move on."

"So you don't deal with the pain?"

"I try to ignore it, try not to get involved." Larson realized that her words conflicted with Marty's view of Christianity. She took her friend's hand. "You have to choose how much to absorb in order to survive what is being done to these people. I love them, but I do all I can to avoid emotional attachment."

*Lies. You're lying to her, My child.*

Marty clamped down on her lip. "I think you know God more than you care to admit."

Larson refused to answer. She would not upset her precious friend. The trauma of the past few days had been enough. "We all have our ways of dealing with life's pressures."

"I know you don't want to hear this, but I will continue to pray for you."

*And I hope you see how to eliminate the crutch you call Christianity.*

She heard Paul call her name. "I need to go." She scanned the area one more time in hopes of seeing Nyok.

"You'll find him," Marty said.

"I hope so." Larson knew he had left with the soldiers. He had been determined to fight; nothing could persuade him otherwise. "Have a good trip home." She turned to walk toward Paul. His face looked worse today than when the soldier had hit him two days ago. At least Ben had told her the truth, but she felt certain he could have stopped the beating.

The SPLA had left about an hour earlier. Ben was cordial, assuring her that if Nyok had accompanied the soldiers, he would soon know it.

"Will you send him back to me?" she had asked.

She had recognized the rigid lines across his forehead. How many times had they discussed this issue? During those times she had Nyok with her. Now Ben and Nyok held the advantage.

"He has the right to choose, Larson."

"He's a child."

Ben's gaze soared over her head. "Arguing won't solve a thing."

She wanted to slap him. "You're right. I'm not asking, I'm begging you to think about it." Larson lifted her chin. "I'll do anything you want to bring Nyok back."

Ben paused. His gaze swung back to her, and he softened. "I understand."

As she replayed her conversation with Ben, she understood the sacrifice of a mother's love. Whatever Ben wanted from her, she would comply. She would sleep with the whole royal family of Khartoum, if it meant getting Nyok or Rachel back.

An hour later, the truck jostled Paul and Larson along the road. Again mud slapped against the side of the vehicle. Once she stopped to allow a ten-foot crocodile to crawl across the path. A small group of red colobus monkeys screeched and scurried from one branch to another, reminding Paul of squirrels back in the States. A vibrant green sunbird and a raven crisscrossed in front of the truck.

"Beautiful, huh?" Larson's hushed voice whispered above the rustling of the thick-leafed plants and towering trees.

"Yes, it is. Gives a whole new meaning to paradise," Paul said. "How about taking up residence here? We can be Tarzan and Jane."

"I'll have to work on my Jane call." Larson laughed, the first time since she had left Warkou. It felt good, really good.

"And we'll have to make a trip to New York for a new wardrobe," Paul added.

Larson leaned her head back. "Thanks," she said. "You have a way of making me forget about reality."

"At your service, ma'am."

She needed to bring up their relationship—get it out in the open and settled, then forgotten. Taking a deep breath, she searched for the words.

Paul's cell phone rang, sending the wildlife into another tizzy. He jerked it out of his backpack. "Hey, Tom." He grinned at her.

She offered a queenly wave and watched a mother monkey yank on the arm of her little one. Tuning out Paul's conversation, she thought of Nyok. The boy may have seen fighting, but he knew nothing of the life of a soldier. *Keep him safe*, her thoughts pleaded before she realized a prayer had formed in her heart. She would gladly turn to God if He returned Rachel and Nyok unharmed.

"Now that's a twist of events." Paul dropped the phone back into his backpack and interrupted her tormented thoughts.

"What's that?"

"FTW offered me a directorship for all of Africa. I'd work in California and fly here occasionally."

"Sounds like a great opportunity." She forced optimism into her reply.

He pressed his lips together and tilted his head. "Possibly, but I don't feel God's in it."

"What do you mean? Oh, I know. You have to pray about it first."

"Exactly, and I don't feel the least bit inclined to accept."

Irritation snaked up Larson's back. "You're going to pass this up, aren't you?"

"Yes, unless God sends a banner across the sky telling me otherwise."

"What about the brain He gave you?"

Paul drummed his fingers on the cracked, split dashboard. "The brain *He* gave me is to be used for *His* purpose."

"I seem to remember that God wants the best for His children. Dying of disease or at the hands of the GOS or SPLA is not the best for an intelligent man. Do you have a martyr complex?"

Paul chuckled. "No one sets out to be a martyr, Larson. It happens when a follower loves Christ more than his own life."

"Right." She knew he spoke the truth. Deep down she envied his faith, but not enough to embrace it. She dared not.

"Seriously. I'm scared to remain in Sudan, but I made a commitment to help find Rachel, and I'm sticking it out."

"Of that, I'm glad," she said. "And now Nyok is missing," he added.

"But we know where he is." Larson's stomach twisted and threatened to unload its contents.

Paul turned and placed his hand on her shoulder. "I'm here until both of your charges are returned. If God wants me directing the African lines for FTW, then the job will still be there."

"You are the best friend I've ever had." There, she said it.

"Do we need to talk about it?"

"I'm not in the mood." And she wasn't.

"Neither am I. Basically I'm a little embarrassed. I apologize for taking advantage of you."

Battling the twister inside her, she concentrated on the road. "I apologize too. So it's settled. We're friends."

"Until Nyok comes back, I'll stay with Sarah. No need in having anyone gossip."

Larson chose not to reply. They would both placate Ben. She would endure the inconceivable, and Paul would suffer through his bruises.

# 27

Paul finished unloading the truck while Larson prepared a maize mixture resembling mush for them to eat. Not exactly a five-star menu, but it provided the necessary nutrients and filled the ache in the stomach. Most of Africa had survived on it for a long time. Paul craved rest, and surely Larson felt worse. He stepped into the clinic where she sat waiting for him. A lantern rested on the table. If he had felt jovial, he would have said something about a romantic dinner. Two cracked bowls and two tarnished spoons rested on the small table. She looked exhausted, but she usually did.

"Sorry about the cuisine," she said.

"I'm not complaining." Paul took a seat opposite her. "I'd like to pray." She said nothing but bowed her head. "Thank You, Lord, for getting us back safely. We appreciate the food before us. Take care of Rachel and Nyok, and bring them home safely. And, Lord, bless this country and all those who are struggling to make it free. Amen."

"What kind of government best suits Sudan?" She cupped her chin in her hand and leaned on the table.

"For the entire country or a separate north and south?"

"That's part of the question." She stirred her spoon through the thick mush while steam rose from the bowl.

"I'm sure Ben has given you his viewpoint."

"Of course. He's for a totally independent southern Sudan. I wondered about your thoughts."

Paul took a spoonful of the mush. She had thrown in a little butter substitute and some salt, which helped tremendously. "And what is your opinion?"

Her eyelids looked as though they were weighed down with lead. "I asked you first. Besides, I'm not sure yet."

"I believe Ben's right. I don't see how the GOS would ever allow other non-Muslim religions to practice freely. Their beliefs encompass government and people control."

"So you're saying that independence is the only way to establish democracy?"

He shrugged. "Third-world countries don't comprehend democracy. The one who wins is the one with the power. I think the same people would be voted back into office." He stared into her face, the tired lines more evident than usual. "The key is education for the south."

She nodded and closed her eyes. "So who governs the country while the people obtain an education? You're talking years."

"And we're back at ground zero." He took a long drink of water. Weariness settled on his neck and shoulders.

Larson rubbed her face. "I'm too tired to discuss politics. I simply want to see an end to this mess. I know it's a complicated war, all of the fighting over religion, politics, and oil. Both sides agree to peace talks, while the GOS bombs the civilians and takes slaves. Then the SPLA fights back."

"I know." Paul didn't try to muffle his impatience. "Little boys carry guns and are exposed to atrocities that most adults hope never to encounter. The way I see things, the SPLA is the only hope for southern Sudan. I think the leadership there is good, but who am I to say? A public policy expert is the best person to answer your questions, Larson." He glanced at her, wondering what settled so heavily on her mind. "Why did you bring this up tonight?"

She pushed back the half-eaten bowl of mush. "Rachel, Nyok, and the air raid at the Red Cross station. And that's just for openers."

"Why don't we talk in the morning when you're rested?"

"You're right. Tonight is one of those nights when I'd like to give up." She forced a laugh. "Trouble is, I don't know where I'd go."

*Only one road leads home, Larson.*

"I'm envious of you," she continued.

He met her gaze. Curiosity moved him to ask more, but they were too tired.

"You are so confident of everything." She waved her hand in front of his face. "Don't tell me it's God. With you it has to be more. Nothing shakes you. You're always in control."

He leaned back in his chair. Kissing her hadn't been in control, but that subject wasn't to be brought up. "If I appear that way, it's the Lord shining through me."

Larson stood. "Great. You and Marty should get together."

Paul watched her head out of the clinic toward the hut where she slept. "See you in the morning," he called after her. "I'll spend the night in the truck until I make arrangements with Sarah."

"Suit yourself." She kept right on walking.

Had he heard sobbing in her words? The past four months were etched on her face. First Rachel, and now Nyok. *Oh, Lord, show Larson Your love for her.*

If the emotion was her inner struggle with the Father, perhaps she had been reached.

Larson woke, groggy and achy. She had dreamed of the farm

again. Twice she had told Paul about her childhood. Maybe if she closed her eyes, she could venture back there again. At least she would be assured of more sleep. Soon, someday soon, she would take a morning off and sleep until she was rested.

She pulled herself from the cot and spread back the netting. *A new day,* she told herself, *more rain.* Blinking to force her eyes to focus, Larson remembered the bits and pieces of conversation with Paul the previous night. He had made her angry again with his talk about God. She held her breath and crossed her arms. *He didn't make me angry. I made myself angry.* The subject of God always infuriated her. She had left those lies behind, hadn't she? If she didn't believe in a Supreme Being, then why did her heart pound at the mention of His name?

Massaging her shoulder, Larson bent to straighten the cot and gather up her clean clothes. As she tucked in the thin coverlet at the bottom, she remembered a topic she did want to discuss with Paul. Ben said the problems in Sudan had existed for centuries, but she wondered if his words were accurate. In her effort to treat all of these people, she hadn't taken the time to learn how all the problems in their country had come about.

*I'm embarrassed. I don't know Sudan's history, and I desperately want to learn why the north has spent the last twenty years trying to kill the southern people.*

After a quiet bath in the river, Larson found Paul in the front seat of the truck, all scrunched up with his head under the steering wheel and his knees at a ninety-degree angle. Staring at him through the window, she elected to let him sleep, but right then Paul opened his eyes.

"Let me out of here." He reached over his head to the door handle. "This metal cocoon has got to go."

"It's your own fault." She laughed. "You had a perfectly good bed in a snug hut."

He climbed out, his hair tousled and the imprint of the worn seat on the left side of his face. Combined with the bruises and black eye on the opposite side, he looked like a candidate for plastic surgery.

"First thing I'm going to do this morning is down a pot of coffee," he said. "Then I'm going to jump into the river for a bath."

She wiggled her nose. "I'll make your coffee while you bathe."

"Thanks a lot. Have any other requests?"

Her earlier questions resurfaced. "Seriously, I do, but they can wait till breakfast." She staged a wide grin. "Not much today but oatmeal. Marty gave me some instant packets with bits of apple and cinnamon."

"Wonderful."

"I expect you to sound more enthusiastic come breakfast."

Paul pulled his backpack from a hole in the front floorboard. He scowled and sauntered toward the river. He waved to Larson without turning around. The sounds of the village broke through her thoughts. Children chattered, and the rustle of movement felt strangely comforting.

*This is home. The farm is gone. Granddaddy and Grandma are resting beneath a huge maple tree near the old place. And Mom and Dad, they are still praying for me to find my way back.*

Larson crossed her arms over her chest and fought back the tears. Too many regrets. All these emotions she could deny while Rachel and Nyok shared her days. But they were gone, and she hated the loneliness, the lack of purpose.

Paul stepped into the clinic soon after the coffee finished brewing and hot water awaited the oatmeal.

"I'm ready for the day." He smoothed his wrinkled clothes. Leaning his backpack against the mud wall, he settled his gaze on the coffeepot.

"It's done." She handed him a cup. "I had some of the oatmeal yesterday morning, and it's quite good. No more mangos until the dry season."

He took a sip of the coffee, its steam rising above his nose. "I appreciate your sharing Marty's gift."

Once they sat at the table and began breakfast, she brought up her questions.

"This is humiliating for me, but I want to understand a few things." When Paul didn't respond, she braved forward. "How in the world did the Sudanese get to the point of killing each other? I know it's the Muslim north wanting to control the south—the oil, the people's religion, the black slavery. But has it always been this way?"

Paul raised a brow. "You want hundreds of years of history summed up in a few moments of conversation?"

"Yes, exactly."

"All right." He sighed and appeared to contemplate his words. "I'll do the best I can. In my opinion it's all about religion. Always has been. Somewhere around the sixth century, Christianity came to northern Sudan and thrived among the Nubians. They had strong Christian kings who were successful in keeping out the Arab invaders. Muslim followers slowly infiltrated the people through intermarriage and eventually turned the people toward Allah. Meanwhile, in southern Sudan, Christian missionaries worked at converting black Africans. Also during this time, the north found a lucrative trade in black slaves. So right there you have two reasons for the south to despise the north."

"Religion and slavery? Things have never changed. They've always been the same?"

"Basically. Great Britain and Egypt ruled Sudan in the latter part of the nineteenth century and up until 1956 when Sudan became an independent nation. During that time, Britain outlawed slavery and established schools for the south. They encouraged the north and south to keep their autonomy, as though encouraging the separation."

"I'm not so sure all that was good," Larson said. "It seems to me those measures further divided the country."

"Some blame the British." He shrugged. "I think they saw the extreme differences in the country and also saw how easily the north could overrun the south. I've read that the Brits wanted to eventually incorporate southern Sudan into the British colonies that then surrounded Sudan. In any event, hundreds of years of culture and values can't be wiped away with legislation, which is exactly what the north has tried to do since 1956. To date the death toll in this war is about two million, while around five million more are displaced either in government-controlled camps or in refugee centers outside of Sudan."

"And the civil war continues," Larson said. "Ben has said some of the same things, but I didn't know if his words were spoken out of anger or fact."

"Ben has a respected position because the leaders of the south realize his intelligence. No doubt once this conflict is over, he will be rewarded."

"Odd how you can commend him, considering."

"We have our differences of opinion, but he is definitely an asset for this country." A bird sang outside the hut, and they both smiled. "There are volumes of Sudanese history and politics." Paul rose from the table and poured another cup of coffee. "Larson, what I just told you is a poor skim off the top. I can give you past wars, key political figures and their stands, the current-day officials, whatever."

"And I do need to know those things. When you're back in the States and have the time, would you search out a good history book for me? I've thought about it for a long while, because I should have had a thorough knowledge of the situation before I came."

"I'd be glad to." He leaned against the back of the medicine cabinet.

"All these people have ever known is war," Larson said, "and the likelihood of things getting better depends on other nations urging peace."

"Probably forcing peace."

"Trade sanctions would do it, along with pressure from humanitarian organizations." Larson turned her attention to the sound of voices outside the clinic. The Dinka tongue and its rhythmic clip had become a part of her. "I'm ashamed of myself for keeping my nose stuck in medical journals and ignoring the rest of the world. That's ended. If anything of value has come out of Rachel and Nyok's disappearance, it's an awareness of how much work it will take to put this country back together."

Paul stared at her, saying nothing but sipping on his coffee. She wondered about his thoughts. Did he think she was stupid? Not that it mattered. Two women and their toddlers walked into the clinic. Wrinkled Sarah trailed after them. She hugged Larson and chatted away. The old woman's face was a permanent smile. How could Sarah face each day with such happiness and joy? How could any of them find peace and contentment? Where was their hope?

Larson inwardly shuddered. Her precious Sudanese people clung to Jesus. She didn't understand how they thought He could help. If God was sovereign, and He ruled the universe, why hadn't He stopped the genocide?

# 28

*L*arson endured another sleepless night. The nightmares were increasing, more so since Rachel's and Nyok's disappearances. She swung on a pendulum between the past and the present. She had no purpose, no focus, no meaning in life, except to continue what seemed to be a futile existence. Everything had become so complicated. A constant lump in her throat and a cramp in her stomach revealed the truth. She had to get rid of this poison. But how? God was not the answer. He had tricked her, and she would not fall prey to that deception again.

Rising from her cot, Larson realized that she had a friend who would listen without pretense or judgment, someone who would keep her confidence and possibly even understand a little. That friend was Paul. She would talk to him this morning—bare her soul to him. Perhaps then the nightmares would stop, and she would have some peace.

Paul had started coffee by the time she stepped into the clinic. He had the patients' charts ready, and everything was neat and orderly.

"Good morning," he said, then frowned. "Nothing personal

here, but you didn't sleep well, did you?"

She avoided his gaze. "Not really."

"Worrying about those two won't bring them back a moment sooner." Paul's words were gentle, as though coaxing her to tell him everything.

"I know." She slid onto a chair and tilted her head back. "I need to talk."

Paul handed her a cup of hot sweetened karkaday tea, made from a variety of crushed hibiscus, and sat in the chair opposite her. "I'm a great listener."

"Can you keep dark secrets to yourself?"

"I'm a master at it." He smiled, and she braved forward.

"I need to talk about the real reason I came to Sudan. The part you know about the missionary's child dying merely sealed my decision. There's more, and if I don't tell someone soon, I'm going to explode." She stood with her cup and walked to the doorway. She blinked at the sunshine streaming its light and warmth. Larson shivered.

"When I was in medical school, I met a man—a wonderful man. We were both active in church, did all the Christian things. I soon learned to love Nathan very much. In fact, I took him for granted. He was strength, patience, and love—all of the things my grandfather and my dad were. I expected those special qualities, and Nathan gave them without question." Larson took a sip of her tea. It burned all the way down.

"I was spoiled by his lavish attention. I'm not so sure I gave much back. I prepared myself for life as a pediatrician and a wife. He was in law school at the time, and I knew we were not headed for any financial worries. I even found plans for my dream house. We set a date for the wedding. I selected a dress and picked out the china and silver for the bridal registry." She turned to face Paul. When she saw no condemnation, she took a deep breath and continued.

"One afternoon he came to see me, all excited. He said God

wanted him to practice law among the poor. You know, the kind of lawyer who takes the cases for those who can't afford legal fees. I couldn't believe it. I reminded him of our plans for our future together, and I told him that I didn't feel I deserved to have to support both of us for the rest of our lives. He was firm, and I was livid. We got into a horrible argument, or rather, I did all the screaming. I asked him to leave my apartment."

The silence seemed deafening before Paul spoke. "I'm sorry, Larson."

"Oh, that's not all. I called my parents and told them what an unfair decision Nathan had made and how he had jeopardized our future. They fueled my anger, by commending his decision." She took a deep breath. "Anyway, on his way home, he was killed."

"Oh no."

She nodded and wrapped her arms around her stomach. "A drug addict mistook my Nathan for someone else and shot him."

Paul stared into her face; his brown eyes radiated sympathy. "Is that when you walked away from God?"

"Wouldn't you? He killed a good man, a man who loved Him and obeyed Him without question." The old familiar throb in her head began to swell. She had thought that stating the truth might bring peace, but it hadn't.

"God didn't kill Nathan," said Paul. "The man who shot him made a choice to pull the trigger. Sin killed the man you loved."

"God is sovereign. At least that's what I was taught as a kid."

"You're right. We don't know why God allowed Nathan's death. This is just one piece of a huge puzzle. We don't have the whole picture, but we know that Nathan is in heaven."

"Well, whatever the reason for his death, it was wrong, and I blame God for it."

Paul started to say something, but she waved her hand in his face. "Don't preach at me, Paul. I thought you were the one person who'd understand my feelings."

"I do. I understand perfectly, and I want to help, but I can't take away your burden. I can only encourage you to trust in God."

Anger tore through her like wildfire. "How would you know about my burden? I sent a good man to his grave. Every day I face the same guilt—the same horrible shame. Every day I see the look on Nathan's face when I told him I hated him. I even told him he could rot in hell. Every day I hear his father's voice telling me that Nathan had been murdered. Every day I see the car with his blood all over the front seat. I never had a chance to say I was sorry."

Paul moistened his lips and stood. His face paled, startling her. If she hadn't been so irate, she would have asked him what was wrong.

"Where are you going?" Larson asked, her heart hammering against her chest.

Paul brushed past her. "Anywhere but here."

Ben tramped through the narrow pathway into Warab Province. Four of his men had left a day earlier to scout out a report of the GOS controlling a previously held SPLA village. The familiar sounds of birds and chattering monkeys normally soothed him, but not this time.

His mind turned to Larson. She had finally agreed to his way of thinking, but it didn't bring the satisfaction he had always believed it would. This wasn't the way he wanted to have her—as an exchange for Nyok. She would concede if Ben brought the boy back to her. Nothing of the emotions tearing through him for years had persuaded her, only her concern for the boy. Truth be known, she would sleep with the entire GOS for Rachel's return. No, that's not how he wanted Larson. His pride—or rather his love—demanded more. He had cared for her for a long time. She had taught him patience in a world where few possessed such a trait.

Right now, he didn't know whether he would yank Nyok from the men or allow him to stay. The boy had more hate and revenge than most, a trait Ben needed in his soldiers, and Nyok had intelligence and cunning. His excellent vision and the expedient manner in which he had learned how to use a rifle made him an asset to any army.

Ben watched a snake wiggle across the path in front of him. The SPLA searched for those of that caliber, but not a twelve-year-old boy. So what was really best for Nyok?

The noble part of Ben said he would retrieve Nyok, return him to Larson, and never ask for a single thing. The base, more significant part of him, said he should take what he could get. After all, he deserved a diversion from this war. A few passionate nights with Larson would help make up for all those sleepless nights when he had lain awake thinking about her. But what good was forcing her into his arms? Ben needed Larson to want him as much as he wanted her. Without those mutual feelings, he wondered if it all was worth it.

His father's warnings bolted across his mind. *Remember your calling, your duty, and your responsibilities to southern Sudan. Anything else will cause you to lose your focus. Anything you put above God will destroy your purpose.*

Ben pressed his lips together. Must all of life be a test or a temptation? A few weeks ago, the GOS had sent word of a lucrative offer if Ben would switch his allegiance from the south to the north. At the time, he had thought Farid had something to do with it. After all, Ben's disappearance had left Larson open to Farid's attention and the South minus one more colonel. Then the two men had spent time in Khartoum, and Ben's prejudice had begun to wane. He had seen another side of the Arab, a man who carefully planned every maneuver, a man who walked with respect and honor, a man who had a profound faith. Unless Farid had desired Ben to note those attributes in order to deceive him.

The forest sounds increased. More monkeys screamed and scampered about. Ben halted his men and listened. A larger animal might be disrupting the smaller ones. A cleared area to the left of them normally held elephants, giraffes, rhinos, zebras, and a variety of deer and gazelles. A lion or jackal might be on the prowl, or the GOS might be waiting behind the thick-leafed foliage and trees.

Nyok heard the sharp pop of rifles without warning. How many years had it been since he had sensed fear and loneliness without the comfort of Dr. Kerr? The memories of a young boy fleeing his village jarred his mind, but this time was different. This time he had a weapon. He wanted this, didn't he, a confrontation with the enemy? An opportunity to take revenge? Why did he suddenly wish he had stayed with her? *After this time it will be easier*, he told himself.

His right hand wrapped around the rife, and his left fingers were poised and ready. Ahead of him were soldiers. They crouched low and sought cover. Nyok did the same. Colonel Aier had instructed him well in the art of guerilla warfare. Nyok could remain motionless for as long as necessary. He could do this. He could do this well.

*Life is but a breath before eternity, Bishop Malou had said. This isn't our home, but a door into forever.*

Was death painful? Would he feel his lifeblood flow from his body? Would Jesus hold his hand and make it easier? Nyok fought hard not to tremble. Tribal beliefs of a wonderful hereafter mixed with his knowledge of God whirled inside him. He knew he should have faith in one, not many. God had taken care of him before. He had little choice but to place his trust in Him now.

A rifle cracked behind him. Nyok held his breath. They must be trapped. He wondered how many GOS surrounded them. Of course, it really didn't matter. It only took one bullet to pierce his flesh and end his young life.

Dr. Kerr had wanted him to study medicine, to become a doctor. Although he had refused to admit his interest, now he wished he had agreed. The many times he had been rude to her brought guilt upon his conscience. Now, he feared he would never be able to make things right between them.

*God, help me. I don't want to die. I refuse to make You promises I can't keep, but can I please have another chance?*

Larson grabbed Paul's backpack by the shoulder straps. He would soon remember he had left it, when he regained his senses after leaving the clinic. When she lifted the backpack, his thick journal fell to the floor with a dull thud. Bending to retrieve it, her fingers brushed across the soft brown suede. Many times she had wondered what he wrote in the book. Some days he wrote endlessly, and other days nothing. Without thinking, her fingers slipped between the pages, and she opened it.

Her gaze trailed down the page. He wrote in small distinct letters, and she squinted to read. The book was nearly full. It must hold years of journaling.

*So much I have left behind, but I consider it nothing except for the race before me.*

Larson knew where that line came from, one of the apostle Paul's letters to the early Christians. She flipped back several pages.

*I can't live in this fear any longer. I have true freedom in Christ. He has set me free, and this desire to hide does not come from my Lord.*

Curiosity moved her to turn to the first page. She sat on a chair, with the thought of reading only a bit. She knew so little about Paul. He avoided her questions, and she had so many.

*I've been a Christian for six months. Now that I'm on my way to the United States, I feel that my story must be written. Someday these words may help an unbeliever find the way Home.*

*My Christian name is Paul. I chose it because of my life before knowing Jesus Christ. The apostle Paul and I have much in common. My Sudanese name is Abdullah Farid. I am the eldest son of the first wife of the royal family of Sudan.*

Larson gasped. Her gaze darted about the clinic. She had heard something about this some years ago, but her mind wasn't clear on the details. She knew the last name. She should have asked questions. No wonder Ben hated him. She turned back to the tiny letters and strained to read every word.

*When I consider the wasted days in Khartoum and how I wanted for nothing, I am ashamed. I believed in the religion of my family; I questioned nothing. My abominable practices and my agreement to the persecution of non-Muslims were and are detestable.*

*Praise God, I have been made holy through the blood of the Lamb. The man who brought me to the Light was a southern Sudanese prisoner named Abraham. He had been tortured for his Christian faith; even his hand had been chopped off because he raised it to God in praise. I went to see this man because my father felt I should be a part of the infidel's punishment. Curiosity had fallen on me for why these Christians refused to renounce their faith. I was told to order his death, and I was prepared to do so.*

*The first time I saw Abraham, I was immediately taken aback by a certain light in his eyes. I shivered. I turned away, but the hypnotic gaze drew me back. The light held both love and compassion, as though I were the prisoner and he the free man. Abraham frightened me, but when he spoke, his words were gentle, reminding me of soft music. I ordered the guards to leave me alone with him. Then I noticed his age. Years had weathered his skin. Lack of food had left his body a mass of bones. His severed wrist, covered with a dirty cloth, needed medical attention. All that could have been taken care of by a single word—embracing Islam.*

*"Listen to your jailers," I said. "I promise you that food will be given you and a doctor will tend to you if you only turn to Allah." His unwashed body and the smell of raw sewage offended me.*

*The old man smiled. "I cannot turn my back on the one and only God—who is Father, Son, and Holy Spirit. He loves me—and He also loves you." The strange light glistened in his eyes. Indeed I feared the dying man.*

*"Me?" I was irate, yet I shook. "I serve Allah."*

*"And I serve the true God who gave His only Son to die for my sins. This Son, Jesus Christ, bled and died in my place so that I might one day live in heaven with God. This Jesus rose from the dead on the third day and sits at the right hand of God the Father. His Spirit lives inside me. I am a child of the King. I am of the royal family of God."*

*"Do you know to whom you are talking? I am of the royal family!"*

*Abraham smiled again. "I dreamed you would be sent here to see me. You are my purpose for being held captive. God wants you to know Him. He wants you to know He loves you and has a purpose for your life."*

*My heart pounded. I should have struck him down, but I was paralyzed by the words of an old man who was lower than the insects that ran about the floor and crawled on his body. I couldn't stop myself. I felt as though I wrestled with two worlds, as if a war waged in my spirit. At last I managed to speak. "Tell me about your Jesus."*

Larson read on. Her heart turned to Paul's words. She read how he became a Christian and helped Abraham escape. A suspicion rose in her mind, engulfing her senses. Tears streamed down her face at the realization. On she continued, learning how he transferred his wealth out of the country and fled Sudan at the threat of death. She discovered his love for the southern Sudanese and his country, his devotion to FTW. He yearned to find Abraham's family and prayed that God would one day reveal them. Paul thought the man must be dead by now, and it grieved him. Above all, he loved God and would never cease telling others about Him and what He had done for Abdullah Farid.

She couldn't stop the flow of tears. Repeatedly she swallowed, and still they poured from her very soul. So much she understood: the confusing conversations between Paul and Ben, Paul's heroic commitment to find Rachel, the reason he had blamed himself for his friend's death, and why he had flown from California to help her persuade Nyok.

"I know why you are here," she whispered.

"What are you doing?"

Larson's attention flew to the door of the clinic where Paul stood, his face stiff, his eyes cold.

"I … I wasn't snooping. It fell from your backpack, and—"

"You thought you'd do a little reading?" His tone was flat, angry. She had never seen him like this.

"Please, Paul. Don't be angry. I just …" She captured his attention. "Why didn't you tell me who you are? What you've done with your life is noble, outstanding. I'm humbled to know you." She bit back the emotion. "To think you've given of your time to help find Rachel, do trivial chores for me—"

"Larson, stop. I'm nothing. Didn't you read my beginnings?"

"Yes. Your story is what fills the rest of us with inspiration and hope for the future."

"Why?" His voice lowered, and the lines around his eyes softened. "I am a murderer. I persecuted the innocent. Only by the grace of God am I able to do anything at all for the Lord."

She nodded. A part of her, the old Larson, understood exactly what he said. A myriad of voices from the past—Granddaddy, Grandma, Daddy, Mama, Nathan—all echoed with the miracles of God. She had believed back then.

"Paul, there is something I have to tell you. I think it may be the reason you are here in this part of Sudan." Her voice quivered.

"What, Larson? You're pale, as though you're ill."

She took a deep breath and stood from the chair. Slipping the journal back into his backpack, she turned to him. "I know where to find Abraham."

# 29

---

Nyok huddled in the thick brush. He had no idea where the other three soldiers had positioned themselves. Rifle shots split the air. He wanted to fire but feared revealing his position to the enemy or shooting one of his comrades. Instead he prayed for guidance. From the depths of his memory came the Scripture he had learned as a child. The words washed over him like cleansing rain. Peace swelled and filled his very being. Death would only usher him into the presence of God. Nyok would thank Him for sending Jesus. He would be reunited with his mother, father, and dear brothers and sisters in a place where there would be no more persecution, no more tears.

The cry of a wounded man focused his attention on the present. Nyok didn't know whether the man was friend or enemy, but he prayed for him nevertheless. The moans of thousands of persecuted Sudanese sounded in his mind, all begging for justice and release. The voices became a deafening roar, thundering about him and crying for deliverance.

*Your will be done, O Lord. Do with me as You desire. My life, no matter how long or short, is Yours.*

The mystical cries stopped. In their place were the sounds of the forest. A spider scampered across his bare foot. The raindrops filtering through the treetops trickled on his head and shoulders. Nyok realized that God had shown Himself faithful, just as He had done when he was facing the lion. If he lived another second or until age wrinkled his skin and weakened his body, he would never forget this moment.

A rifle barrel touched the back of his neck.

"You know Abraham?" Paul asked, stepping closer to Larson. His utterance came more as a prayer than a question. His heart hammered against his chest. His ears tuned out everything but expectation.

"It has to be him. I can think of no other reason for all of this than your purpose to find the old man, Abraham." Her eyes pooled. Paul didn't understand her unveiled emotions, unless she spoke the truth.

"Tell me. Where is he?"

"He is Bishop Malou's father. He lives about two and a half hours from here." She swallowed hard.

"Slow down, Larson. It's all right. I've waited almost eleven years. I can wait a while longer."

"Abraham spent time in a Khartoum jail—in a ghost house. His right hand was severed for praising God. Everyone thought he had died, until he returned to his village with the miraculous story about the man who rescued him, a member of the royal family named Abdullah."

Heat consumed Paul, rising from his inner being to his face. His knees weakened. His mind raced. *Praise the Lord!* His prayers had been answered.

"Take my truck," she said. "I'll tell you how to get there. Better yet, I'll send someone to show you the way." She grasped his shoulders. "Abraham is alive."

He felt a smile spread over his face, and he began to laugh. "I can't believe it, after all these years. And you are lending me your truck?"

She laughed too. "Absolutely. That alone is a miracle."

*Perhaps this is another step in your return to God.*

Within an hour Paul headed toward a village the name of which he had forgotten to ask. He had been in too big a hurry to remember, even if Larson had told him. Sweet, sweet Larson. He would be forever indebted to her. Sarah rode beside him. She had a daughter who lived there, and she welcomed the opportunity to see her again.

He felt as though he had consumed a gallon of coffee, for excitement tingled in every nerve. In his mind he wanted to be cautious in case Abraham was not the right man, but in his heart he knew better. God had led him to Warkou for this purpose. Paul sobered. If he had chosen to stay in California to help Jackie or even taken FTW's offer to head up the African directorship, he would have missed this blessing. His heart soared, and in his next breath he began to sing "Amazing Grace." Sarah joined him. Somehow in his jumbled words, he had relayed to her his mission.

"God is so very good," she laughed. "He remembers us with His special acts of love."

"I want to tell you the story of how I came to know Jesus," he said, "and how I acquired my Christian name of Paul ..." When he had finished, he waited for Sarah to respond.

"I don't understand why Bishop Malou never offered the information," she said, laying a veined hand on his shoulder. "After all, you two were together for those weeks."

Paul shrugged. "We never discussed it. My story is not one that I readily offer here in Sudan."

"Oh, my brother. Those of us who love you would have seen how God worked in your life. None of us is without sin."

He stole a glance her way and viewed the compassion in her round face. "Thank you, Sarah. I should have had more faith in God's family."

"Now I see why Colonel Alier does not trust you," she said. "He must know the truth."

Paul nodded. Regret and guilt tried to seize control, but he shoved the accusations away. When God forgave him, He cast his past and his sins into a sea of forgetfulness. Satan would not triumph over this moment.

"I can't blame the colonel. He has a responsibility to the people of southern Sudan. I can only hope and pray that someday he will see me as a new man in Christ."

Sarah's hand remained on his shoulder. "He may never call you friend, but we can pray that he chooses to see Paul Farid as an ambassador for Christ."

"That's one reason I refuse to leave Sudan until Rachel is found. I would gladly trade my life for hers."

"And I'll pray it does not come to that."

They rode awhile in silence until Paul sought answers to the questions welling inside him. "What can you tell me about Abraham? What has he done these years?"

Sarah laughed and lifted her thin arms to the roof of the truck. "He is still raising his arms to God and telling everyone about Jesus. He has never stopped. Your acceptance of the Savior moved him to tell more and more people. Many have come to know the love of God. His faith is what moved his son to preach."

The miles could not pass fast enough for Paul.

The day swept by into afternoon like a cool breeze on a balmy day. The patients straggled in, and their problems didn't devastate Larson. She found herself laughing and dwelling on the conversations with Paul. How peculiar that she had confessed her past and uncovered Paul's in one early morning. How amazing that she had been a part of assisting him in locating Abraham.

Granddaddy would have said that she had been an instrument of God.

Did she believe after all? Had her life not been a series of heartbreaking events after all, but rather a carefully planned story with a purpose? If Nathan had lived, where would they be? She envisioned a thriving pediatric practice and Nathan ... who was to say what path he would have chosen? Would he have dared to please God, or settled to please her? Larson shuddered. She had been incredibly domineering, selfish, unkind, and prideful. Had things changed?

Larson saw her arms crossed over her chest. She allowed them to drop to her side. She was still domineering, selfish, unkind, and prideful. What good had she done with her years?

*You've cared for My children.*

But had she truly served the Lord? Larson sucked in a breath. Bitterness had eaten at her soul for so long that she didn't know if there could be release—except that every fiber of her being craved deliverance from this pit of doom. She had spanned an ocean and a continent to escape God, and He had found her. God had crowned her a princess, and His love still reigned. Her role as a doctor to the Sudanese was orchestrated long before she drew her first breath, as well as Nathan's early departure Home. Suddenly the years and the happenings held crystal-clear meaning. She had been blind, but now she could see.

Was it too late to grab the hand of Jesus once again and step forward in the faith of her parents and grandparents? Larson wrung her hands and stared into the steadily pouring rain. Had she run too far?

*No, My daughter, come home.*

If Paul had found forgiveness and peace—and yes, purpose— with his dedication to the Lord, how could she do any less? "Sin is sin," Granddaddy always said. "No matter how big or small, if what you're doing is against God's laws, then you've offended Him. The longer you wait to confess and repent, the longer the walk Home."

Larson knew what she needed to do. Her heart and soul longed to be clean. She stepped out into the rain and let the water pour over her head. It soaked her hair, and she swept it back from her forehead. Lifting her hands to the gray sky, she felt the trickles rolling down her fingers, over her hands, and soaking her arms. She closed her eyes and raised her face to the heavens, allowing the pure, perfect water to caress her skin and cleanse her soul. She laughed; she cried. Ten years had passed since she had worshiped God.

*Father, forgive me for running from You, for denying You, and for seeking false answers to the questions of life. Thank You for Your faithfulness when I was rebellious. Thank You for loving me and never leaving me. Thank You for placing people in my life who serve You. Thank You for seeing me through the eyes of Jesus, for I am unworthy of Your presence or Your love and forgiveness. I commit my life to You. May Your purpose flow through me like this cleansing rain forever.*

Paul waved and grinned at the villagers surrounding the truck. No doubt they recognized Larson's truck and expected her to be there, but he didn't care. His smile originated deep inside and seemed to burst forth from the very pores of his skin. He searched the crowd, looking for the man who walked across his most peaceful dreams. Selfishly he wanted to see Abraham alone for the first time—to drink in the sight of him and embrace his frail shoulders. Sarah knew of the man and had told Paul countless stories of his unwavering faith.

*Who would have ever thought ...* Paul shook his head. Bishop Malou had touched him like a brother. Now Paul understood why.

"Can you tell me where to find Abraham, the old man who is missing a hand?" Paul asked in Arabic to no one in particular. He tried to control his excitement, but he heard the half-trembling enthusiasm in his voice.

A young man pointed to a hut on the far right of the crowd. "There. He is probably resting."

Paul thanked him and hurried from the crowd, snaking his way through the welcoming throng of people. His pulse sounded in his head. His hands trembled. His step quickened, and he would have run if not for all the playing children around him.

When he reached the darkened entrance of Abraham's hut, he stopped. This was a sacred moment, and he thanked God for the gift he was about to receive.

"Abraham." The words uttered aloud sounded like the sweetest of music. He heard the shuffle of feet and waited.

Abraham stepped into the light. The lines had deepened in his face, and his eyes were more clouded. A scar creased down the left side of his face, and Paul remembered the guard who had struck him.

"Praise God," Abraham said. He didn't move a muscle. "Have my eyes betrayed me, or do I see Abdullah?"

"It's me, sir." Paul choked back the emotion. "My Christian name is Paul. At last ... at last my search for you is over. My prayers are answered."

Paul reached for Abraham and drew him close as though he were a child instead of an old man. Memories of those days when Paul visited him in the Khartoum jail floated in his mind, vivid and fresh: the agony of a suffering people, the stench of humans treated worse than animals, the plight of those cast into prison.

"I am blessed." Abraham's words were muffled with his weeping. "Because of you, because God used you to set me free, many more have come to know Jesus."

Paul laughed through watery eyes. "Because of you, because you showed me how I could be free from sin, I've been able to help many of the Sudanese."

Abraham pulled back and peered into Paul's face. "Do you have time to tell me all about your life since our last meeting in Khartoum?"

"You are the reason I've come." The afternoon rain began to fall. "I have much to tell and even more to ask."

Moments later, the two sat on the floor of Abraham's hut. Sentiments had been spoken, and Paul was eager to hear what had happened over the past ten years.

"I want to know everything," Paul said. "The last time I saw you, I'd entrusted your care to some fishermen who were sailing south."

Abraham nodded. "So many years ago, and still I remember it like yesterday. The fishermen were good to me. They brought me safely to the river's edge and helped me get to my old village." He breathed in and out, and a sad hush consumed him. "Everything was gone, and I feared that my family had all been killed. Later, I learned that my wife had died, but my son had escaped. He's a fine minister now with many churches in southern Sudan."

"I know your son," Paul said. "But he doesn't know about you and me."

"Why?"

"I've told few of my identity." He shrugged. "I wouldn't want anyone killed. Khartoum does not give up."

"No, they don't, but Christ is victorious. He has already won the war."

"Someday they will understand. Abraham, tell me more."

"I settled into a village and began to tell others about Jesus—what He'd done for me and how He'd rescued me by sending you. I'd done preaching before, but now God put a strong message in my heart. I've never stopped preaching. As long as I have breath, I will tell others about the Lord."

Paul struggled whether to ask about Abraham's remaining

family members. Since he hadn't mentioned them, they must not have survived. "What can I do for you? How can I pray?"

The old man smiled, his wrinkles deepening. "I lack for nothing, but please pray for southern Sudan. The SPLA needs prayers as well as the struggling church and all those who face persecution from the government."

"I will continue to do so."

"Now, please, I want to hear what has happened in your life over the past ten years."

Paul took the time to explain every detail of his journey from those days following Abraham's departure from Khartoum to Paul's flight from the country to freedom. He told how God used him in the United States and how he chose the name of Paul. He spoke about his work with FTW and why he remained in Sudan.

"I will pray that Rachel and Nyok are soon found," Abraham said. "I hear in your voice and I see in your face how much they mean to you."

"Thank you. I will do my best to visit you again very soon."

Abraham reached for Paul's hand. The old man's eyes were red, and he fought to keep them open. "God be with you, my son. I can now die in peace knowing I have lived to thank you for your brave deed."

Paul embraced him. "We'll always be together in spirit."

All the way back to Warkou, Paul reflected on the time he had spent with Abraham. The few days they had grown to know each other in Khartoum had sealed their friendship forever. God had orchestrated their meeting then and now. Larson had played a significant role in today's meeting, and he hoped she would be open to hear about the old man's faith.

Many prayers had been answered in Paul's life, and he appreciated every one, but the reunion with Abraham had brought such unexpected joy. Now, if only Rachel and Nyok were returned— safely.

# 30

"It's safe," Ben said, bending down beside Nyok. "We have the GOS on the run."

"What happened to the soldiers who were with me?" Nyok asked.

"One was killed." Ben studied the boy's face. Sorrow etched his smooth features beyond his years. Compassion swept through Ben. Until this moment, he hadn't realized how much Nyok meant to him. He was the son Ben never had. The boy had seen enough blood and killing. It must stop with the children. This was a man's war; it was not for innocent children who fought for revenge instead of a country's freedom.

"Thank you, Colonel. I'm ready to take my training. That's why I was with your men."

"I know." Ben stood at the sound of men moving through the forest. He avoided looking at the boy. His mind warred with what he should do.

"I'm ready to die for southern Sudan." Nyok's voice quivered with his words. They lacked conviction. "You've shown me how to use a rifle. The rest will be easy, and God will be with me."

Still Ben wondered what he should do with him. The decision had nothing to do with Larson's offer. It was a struggle with his conscience, a struggle between right and wrong.

"You're a brave man, Nyok," Ben said. "I saw you fight the lion. The SPLA would be proud to have you in its ranks."

Nyok raised himself from the earth floor, his shoulders arched back.

"But I believe you'd best serve your country in another way."

The boy's brows narrowed. "How, sir? What is nobler than a soldier's life?"

"An education." Ben scarcely believed his own words. "Soon southern Sudan will have freedom. Did you see how we overpowered the GOS just now? The country will need leaders—medical personnel, engineers, ministers, teachers, those who know how to run our country. You can be one of them, Nyok."

Nyok tilted his head. "But, sir, for the past four years you have told me that education could wait."

Ben stiffened. "I've changed my mind. You are among the brightest of our people. You need to leave the country and seek an education. Then your knowledge can be used to help others."

The boy glanced about. Confusion settled on his features. "Are you taking me back to Dr. Kerr?"

Ben nodded and shifted his rifle. He took Nyok's weapon and cleared his throat. "I'm ordering you to fight this war with your mind. Discipline and training will serve you well."

"Yes, sir. I'll not disappoint you. God has delivered me many times, and possibly it is for this purpose."

"Excellent. Tomorrow you and I will head to Warkou. I believe Larson and Farid have researched schools for you."

Ben turned and made his way through the narrow path where most of his men waited. They had captured eight of the enemy. He would give them the opportunity to fight for the south, and another soldier would explain Christianity to them. Tonight he would bury a good soldier. Tomorrow he would stop at the man's village and inform his wife and children of his death. When would it ever end? Relief flowed through Nyok's veins. He didn't understand why, but he did know that once he had made his peace with God and resigned himself to die that he had been delivered. All along he believed in his joining the SPLA, but Colonel Alier's new orders changed everything. He now had a future and a purpose, and oddly enough, he felt good.

Nyok smiled. He could almost hear Dr. Kerr's musical laughter. She would be happy, and he would have the satisfaction of knowing that he had caused her to forget her troubles. He cringed at the thought of the cruel words he had thrown her way. She had wanted the best for him, and he had been too caught up in revenge and pride to see it. Perhaps his apology would mend the ugly rift between them.

Dr. Kerr had been a mother to him—nothing like his own mother, but a good one nevertheless. She had loved him and encouraged him to use his mind rather than a rifle. Nyok remembered Ben's words: *The country will need leaders—medical personnel, engineers, ministers, teachers, those who know how to run our country. You can be one of them, Nyok.*

Paul Farid was another matter. Perhaps he had judged the pilot unfairly. If God had given him another chance at life, then he could do the same with Paul.

Nyok sighed. Yes, being a doctor like Dr. Kerr sounded good. A deep sense of satisfaction flowed through him when he helped others, and he was interested in finding cures for so many diseases plaguing his people. He could hear Dr. Kerr's happiness with his choice. Sudan would be pleased, and most important, God would be pleased.

Ben and Nyok tramped for two days up from the Warab Province toward Warkou. Ben had broken the sad news to the fallen soldier's family and told the familiar story of the man's bravery. The family had cried together. For Ben, it never got easier.

The closer the two ventured toward their destination, the more relieved Ben felt about his decision to return Nyok. He didn't want Larson to feel pressured to do anything, especially giving in to him. That should be voluntary, not forced, and Ben had enough pride—and love—for the woman to step back. He wanted to talk to her about his feelings, if she would listen.

The Arab still provoked an intense distrust in Ben. He knew the man's story and his conversion to Christianity. Ben also knew the danger the man faced every day he walked Sudanese soil. Could he be such a fearless soldier of Christ that his life did not matter? That's what the media claimed, but Ben had his doubts. He remembered Farid's offer to provide global phones and computer data to aid in the war. Still, trusting the man went against everything Ben believed.

A few hours from Warkou, Ben elected to check on Quadir. By some chance the slave trader might have new information about Rachel. Twice Ben had nearly killed him when the man had failed to find out anything about his sister.

Ben and Nyok took a westerly turn and located Quadir in a small village on the border of Warab and Bahr Al Ghazal provinces. The people there tolerated the slave trader only because of his ability to return Sudanese to their families and friends. Ben found him hiding in an old couple's hut. Quadir spoke through a quivering voice.

"Colonel Alier. So good to see you. I do have news about your sister, but I hesitate to tell all in view of ..."

Ben despised the Arab. His high-pitched, whiny voice reminded Ben of a woman—and a weak one at that. "I know what you're saying. What news do you have?"

"My sources say they have found her."

"Unharmed?"

Quadir offered a faint smile. "Yes, Colonel. I have made arrangements to purchase her. I wanted to make sure I had the right young woman first."

"When?"

"Four days hence."

"Where?"

"Here." Quadir swallowed hard. He pressed his fingertips together. "You will bring the money?"

Rage flashed across Ben's mind, but he maintained control. "Yes, I will have the money."

The slave trader lifted his chin. "We have a deal, Colonel. Do not come with soldiers. Those who bring the young woman insist on it."

Shortly afterward Ben and Nyok moved on. Ben wanted to believe that the search for Rachel had finally ended, but he feared disappointment. He also cringed at the thought of finding out what the GOS had done to her. He remembered all the horrible tales of past slaves. His precious sister could have physical and mental scars. She could be pregnant or never able to conceive children. Whatever her condition, Ben loved her, and he would take care of her forever. He dragged his tongue across dry lips. Rachel must get out of Sudan too.

"Colonel, I'm afraid to believe this is true," Nyok said. "Can you trust Quadir?"

"He knows I will kill him if he lies."

Nyok nodded. "I'd help you."

Ben nodded in return. "Larson would help. Farid would pray for the man's soul."

Nyok laughed, and Ben joined him. Releasing all the pent-up emotions felt good. *Four days from now.* His men needed to trail him on the way to meet with Quadir. He understood the slave trader's fear, but Ben wasn't about to get caught in an ambush either.

Paul called for Larson before reaching the clinic. The exhaustion that normally accompanied him had fled in the wake of finding Abraham. Larson deserved to hear every word of their conversation.

"Larson," he called again.

"Come in, Paul. I'm anxious to talk to you." Her voice had a special lilt to it, and he grinned at the thought of her having a pleasant day.

He found her seated at the small table where they shared meals. She was writing, and from the looks of things, whatever it was covered several pages.

"You sound great."

"I am." She held up the sheets of paper. "I'm writing my parents a letter." She laughed. "It may be a book before I'm finished."

In the shadows, he met her warm smile. "What brought this on? I thought you didn't have contact with them."

"I don't, or rather I didn't," she said. "Sit down. I'm almost at a stopping point."

Paul eased in across from her and studied her face. The worried lines had vanished. She smiled as she wrote. If he didn't know better, he would believe—

"That'll do for now." Larson laid her pen aside. She peered into his face. Her eyes held a radiance he hadn't seen before.

"You must have had a great day," he said.

She nodded slowly. "Started off strange but got better as it went on."

"I apologize for jumping all over you about the journal. I should have told you the truth a long time ago."

"No problem. You found Abraham?"

He grinned. "It was wonderful, Larson. We talked for a long

time. Seeing him lifted my spirits, and I've been soaring ever since."

"I can see. I thought you might spend the night there." She folded her hands on the table.

"I didn't want to take advantage of your generosity. I was afraid if I didn't get back with your truck you'd send someone after me."

"I might have." She neatly stacked the sheets of paper. "Seriously, you should have taken advantage of the opportunity."

"I will soon. He's pretty frail, and I think I wore him out. I can visit him another time. It still amazes me that he is Bishop Malou's father." Paul hesitated. "What about your day?"

"Full of honesty."

He lifted a brow. "How's that?"

"When I was a little girl, Granddaddy used to have this saying—"

"Is this another Larson story?"

"Absolutely. Anyway, before I was interrupted, when Granddaddy discovered something that needed to come out in the open, he'd call a 'come to Jesus meeting.'"

"Spill-your-guts time?"

"You're catching on. Seriously," she took a deep breath, "I realized I couldn't outrun God and didn't want to anymore. He'd chased me across the world, and I needed to get caught."

Paul rubbed his arms. "I've got chill bumps with that one. Wow, that is incredible. Congratulations."

She shrugged. "I figured you were one of many who have prayed for me, so thanks."

"You're welcome. Tell me what happened. What brought all this about?"

Larson blinked back the wetness pooling her eyes. "Your journal, your life, and your commitment to Jesus. I no longer had a purpose to go on living. Guess you'd say I'd sunk as low as I could go."

"And what is your purpose?" Paul whispered the words, not wanting to miss any of Larson's reply.

"To serve the Lord by using the skill He gave me to treat these people I've grown to love—not just physically but spiritually too."

Paul couldn't stop grinning. "You are going to be the most dynamic woman Sudan has ever seen. Look what you've accomplished to this date; then think about the future."

She swiped at a tear. "My mouth can talk about Jesus while He guides my hands. And think of the power of prayer." She held her breath for a moment. "Sarah will be elated. I must tell her."

"Go." Paul rose from his chair and shooed her toward the door. "I'll clean and disinfect while you tell the good news."

"Are you sure you don't mind?"

"Outta here, lady. Don't come back until you have spoken with every Christian in the village."

"I might not be back for a week."

"No problem. I'll handle things as long as no one gets sick."

Larson hurried from the clinic, reminding Paul of a little girl skipping off to play with friends. He stood and watched her disappear in the direction of Sarah's hut.

God was good. Indeed, He was very good. Two answered prayers in one day. Paul turned toward the table and Larson's unfinished letter. He needed to write Jackie and the boys. They had been praying for Larson too. Paul glanced at his backpack on the floor near the doorway. He had much to journal today.

# 31

Sarah's round face fairly glistened. She pulled Larson to her and hugged her time and time again.

"Praise God. Our prayers are answered," the old woman said. "What a day this has been. I will remember it whenever times are hard."

Larson snuffed back the sobs. She hadn't laughed and cried this much in a long time. "Paul and I both found answers. Oh, Sarah, I'll bet my grandfather is dancing across heaven."

"He will need an African to show him how to do it. I've seen how you people dance."

They laughed again.

"I've started a letter to my parents. It's a little hard to put ten years into a few sheets of paper."

Sarah took her hand. "From what you just told me, they are good people."

"More than good. They've sent letters, but I never replied. They've never written anything condemning or asked uncomfortable questions." Larson tilted her head. "Maybe they should have confronted me with my rebellion. Then again, I'd probably have run farther."

"They will treasure your letter." Sarah nodded her head. "Let's walk. Many of the villagers will want to know you are now truly Christian."

"I feel like a little girl again—happy and excited. I know there are tough days ahead, but this time I won't give up on God." Larson covered her mouth. "My goodness, Sarah. God didn't send me any patients today. He knew. He actually knew."

Sarah slipped her arms around Larson's waist, and they walked toward the nearest hut where children were laughing and playing chase. Their giggles rose like sweet music, drowning out all the sad realities of a land torn with upheaval.

*Lord, I will need You to remind me of this day, especially if Rachel and Nyok never return. Don't give up on me.*

Hours later amid the singing and storytelling, Larson swatted at the mosquitoes, a habit formed from dealing with them for so long. In the last few minutes, she had begun to feel exhaustion take over her body. The time had come to head back to the clinic and see what Paul had been doing in her absence. She wanted to finish her letter to Mom and Dad. Everyone shared in her joy. She had seen the jubilation before when villagers accepted what Jesus had done for them, but she had kept her distance. Now, she was a part of a special community of God.

Ben's words echoed in her mind. *You don't even have a country to call home.* He had been right. She didn't belong in the States anymore, and she had never really fit into Sudan, but she did have a home within a fellowship of believers.

Larson stood from her position on the ground. "Thank you all very much for everything you've done. I hope I will not disappoint you in the coming days." She glanced about. "I'm going back to the clinic now. I'm very tired."

Once she stepped inside the clinic, she saw exactly what Paul had been doing. He had cleaned and disinfected every inch—a job she had considered but hadn't accomplished.

"This is great." She whirled around. Even in the dim lighting, she saw the sparkle and neatness.

"I didn't want you to come home to work." He sat at the table, writing in his journal.

*Home. What a pleasant sound.* She yawned.

Paul pointed his pen at her. "See, I was right. All that celebrating has worn you out."

"You should have been there."

He shook his head. "I felt this should be your special celebration."

"Thanks." Larson slid into her chair. "I wanted to finish this letter, but I might go on to bed. My mind is a bit muddy."

"Have you considered a furlough home?"

She hesitated. "In fact, I have. Thought about it all afternoon. I know I need a break, and reconciliation with my parents sounds really good." Larson yawned again.

"If you don't get some sleep, you won't have the energy to get up in the morning."

Rubbing sore neck muscles, she agreed. "I want to savor the day, but I may have to do it in my dreams." A thought occurred to her. "I don't own a Bible anymore. Bishop Malou may have to lend me one in Arabic."

"Do you read Arabic?"

"A little." She laughed and yawned again. "I'm going to bed."

Paul laughed. "Wise decision—among those other wise ones you've made today."

"Thanks." Larson stood and moved toward the doorway, too tired to do anything but wave good night. Once inside her hut, she peeled off her clothes and slipped into pajamas. She crawled onto the cot, pulling the netting over her head. Her thoughts rambled for a moment, but she soon gave in to sleep.

"Dr. Kerr," a voice said.

Larson stirred. In her dreams, she heard Nyok call her name.

"Dr. Kerr."

What a beautiful dream to hear Nyok speak without the harshness from days gone by. She loved the sound of his voice, the cracking of a syllable indicating one more venture into manhood. Oh, how she wanted to be a part of his life, if only he would come back to the village.

She felt a hand on her shoulder, a gentle shaking. "Dr. Kerr. Wake up."

Larson stirred, and in the darkness she opened her eyes. Confusion settled upon her. She sensed someone kneeling by her cot. Perhaps this person needed medical attention.

"How can I help you?" she asked.

"It's me, Nyok."

She caught her breath. "Nyok. Am I dreaming, or are you here?"

He lifted the netting and touched her face. "I have come back to you."

Tears trickled from her eyes, and she reached up to embrace him. This was the boy she remembered, the one who looked to her for strength when he feared the world. "I was so afraid for you."

"Colonel Alier found me and brought me here."

She kissed his cheek. "I know we've had problems, but we can talk them through."

"The problem's been me," Nyok said. "I was wrong to say and do the things I did. God has shown me how wrong I've been."

Later she would tell him about her decision. "We've both made mistakes. Nyok, I love you so much."

"I want to go to school—wherever you think is best. I need an education to best serve my country. I think I may become a doctor like you."

Now fully awake, she didn't want to release Nyok for fear she was dreaming. "I'm so very, very, happy."

"I want to thank you for all you've done for me. I think I was too full of hate to understand that," he said. "While I was with the soldiers, I realized that you have been my mother since my parents died."

Larson listened, sealing each word in her heart. "And you have been the son I never had."

"We have much to talk about tomorrow, but Colonel Alier is here. He has news too."

Larson wondered if it could be news of Rachel, but she dared not believe it.

"Dr. Kerr, you might want to dress and meet with him."

"Is it Rachel?" Larson's pulse raced.

"I will let him tell you. He's in the clinic talking to Paul."

In the next instant, she grabbed a robe and wiggled into it, grateful for the darkness concealing her tattered pajamas. Hurrying from the hut to the clinic with Nyok beside her, she tried to prepare herself in case the news was not what she wanted to hear.

Ben stood next to Paul, and her gaze flew to the colonel. He didn't look grieved.

"Thank you for bringing Nyok back," she said. "I'm very grateful." Later she would talk to him about his price. With her rededication to the Lord, she couldn't go through with her commitment to give in to Ben's desires, but could she explain it to him in a manner he would understand?

"On our way here, I stopped to see a slave trader."

She trembled. "What did he say?"

Ben hesitated just long enough for her to wonder if the news was bad.

"Tell me, Ben."

"He says they've found Rachel. I'm to meet him in four days."

Larson covered her mouth. Gratitude washed over her. "Ben, oh, Ben." She rushed into his arms, laughing and crying at the same time. Never before had she hugged him, never before had she felt his seasoned muscles beneath her fingertips. In the next moment, she sensed a deep awkwardness. Instantly she drew away. Guilt assaulted her with how he must have interpreted the embrace. "Did he say she was all right?"

"He doesn't know anything, only that she is alive."

"I see." Larson said. "You will let me go with you, won't you?"

A rare look of tenderness passed over Ben. "It could be dangerous."

"I'd like to go," Paul said. "Waiting here would be hard."

"Me too," Nyok said.

Ben shook his head. "I don't think it's a good idea. The GOS may have gotten wind of her identity and be there waiting."

"I'll take the chance," Paul said. "Accompanying you couldn't be much worse than dodging the GOS in Khartoum."

Ben whirled around to face him. "Capturing the pair of us would make their day."

"As I said, I'll take that chance." Paul's face showed no trace of fear, and Larson admired him for his courage. Now that she knew the truth about his past, her respect for Paul knew no bounds.

"Well, I think all of us would make a prize catch, but I'm not afraid, and I want to go," she said.

"And I'm Dr. Kerr's protector," Nyok added.

"This is a bad idea. We may be walking into a trap." Ben's forehead creased. "I can't risk any of you. Who would take care of the villagers? And Paul, who'd bring food and supplies into the war zone area? And Nyok, you're a young man who needs an education."

Larson couldn't believe Ben had shown concern for the three of them. "I don't think you can dissuade any of us. We've waited too long for Rachel's return."

Ben raked his fingers through his short hair. "I can't permit it."

"Then I will follow you," Paul stated. "But I agree that Larson and Nyok should stay here."

"Absolutely not!" Larson said. How dare he exclude her! She didn't need protection.

Ben shook his head. "I know I will regret this, but as long as you understand what might happen ..."

"Nothing can stop me from going after Rachel," Larson said stiffly. "I believe God will be with us."

"God?" He swung a startled gaze at her.

"Yes, God. He and I have gotten back to where I should have been all along."

Ben headed toward the door of the clinic. "Then you'd better spend the rest of the night in prayer, because I'm a fool to permit any of you to go. In fact, I hope you see better of this whole thing in the daylight."

Larson watched him leave. She caught Paul's attention. "This day has been filled with blessings. I refuse to back down just because Ben suspects there might be trouble." She lifted her chin. "I'm going after my daughter."

# 32

*P*aul woke before Larson and Nyok. He had no idea where Ben slept, because he hadn't returned after voicing his reservations about the three of them accompanying him to get Rachel. He had spent the past two days with his men, obviously hoping Larson, Paul, and Nyok had changed their minds.

Paul's mind had spun most of the night with the myriad of happenings since he had first landed his plane near the village. One unfortunate thing after another had occurred until he wondered if he had been cursed. Now, in the course of one day, they all had reasons to rejoice. As wonderful as it sounded, he felt a bit skeptical about redeeming Rachel. It seemed too easy, or had he merely grown accustomed to the hardships of Sudan?

*I've become a cynic instead of praising God for all His gifts.*

He hated to think about Rachel tortured and her mind forever scarred by the abductors. All manner of horrible things could have happened to her. She could be pregnant or have endured sexual abuse and never be able to enjoy her womanhood … or worse. Paul went about making coffee and praying for Rachel instead of worrying about her.

"You're up early," Larson said from the doorway of the clinic.

"So are you. I couldn't sleep thinking about Rachel and bringing her home today."

Larson offered a half smile. "I tossed and turned. Finally gave up thinking about the what-ifs and prayed instead. I need to be grateful for Nyok—" A strange, almost fearful look swept over her face. She shook her head. "Nyok's back, and I have to believe everything is all right with Rachel."

"Smart girl." Paul glanced beyond the doorway and saw Ben heading their way. "Here comes the colonel. I still can't believe he's letting all of us go."

"I'm not surprised. Both Nyok and I know the way to the village. This way he can keep an eye on us."

Ben sauntered inside. He looked like he had been awake most of the night too. "I smell coffee."

"You sound like an angry lion," Paul said. "I'll pour us a cup, and we can talk about today."

"Don't remind me." Ben turned to Larson. "I wish the three of you would reconsider."

"Not a chance," she said.

"Let me remind you. Have you considered the damage inflicted to our cause if all of us are killed or captured today? Besides, I work faster and better alone."

Paul handed him a mug of coffee, but Ben's gaze never left Larson's tranquil face. Paul saw the look of concern—and yes, love—in the colonel's eyes. Larson couldn't be blind to those obvious emotions, but she acted as though she was.

"I'm going, and there is no point in discussing it any further," Larson said. "When do we leave?"

Ben turned to Paul. "Together again?" When Paul nodded, he took a long drink of the hot coffee. "We leave within the hour."

Ben drove Larson's truck, despite her objections. This morning was not a day to argue with him. Nyok chose to bump along in the back, which still left the three of them crowded in the cab. Ben was certain Larson and Farid felt like he did—hot, cramped, and edgy. He would rather be in the heat of battle than stepping into new territory.

He wrestled with the question of Rachel's condition. He didn't want to be a fool and hope she had been treated well. On the other hand, he didn't want to learn what the GOS had done to her. He had seen too much, and the memories haunted him. The best he could hope for focused on Rachel's strong faith and God's helping her endure the brutality.

Ben glanced down at his clothes. He had chosen to wear a plain shirt and cotton pants. No point in advertising his identity to the GOS.

"Do you have the money?" Larson asked.

"Yes, that and more, in case he has other slaves to redeem."

A long silence followed, and Ben wished she hadn't said anything. The sound of her voice drove him to distraction.

"Shall we talk?" Larson asked. "This silence is deafening."

"I don't have anything to say," Ben said.

"Well, I'm a little scared." She glanced at Nyok through the rearview mirror. "Later I want to discuss your role in bringing Nyok back."

Ben glanced at Farid, who stared at the tall grass to the right of them. "There's nothing to talk about. You can relax."

She managed a faint gasp. "Thank you."

"Wars are won by force, anything else is barbaric." His words were soft, nearly whispered, but he had spoken them. Ben wasn't going to admit to love, even if Farid hadn't been with them. Some things were better left unsaid.

Larson saw the village ahead, the one where the slave trader lived. She shifted in the truck, her backside sore from the worn seat. Admittedly, her anxiousness had nothing to do with the uncomfortable ride. She could barely wait to wrap her arms around Rachel. No matter what evil had befallen the girl, the future must be better than the past. Larson could only imagine Rachel's heartache over her capture and the sight of the soldier gunning down James. She had had no one to turn to these past months for comfort, no one but God. But now all that was about to change. Now she would have those who loved her and would encourage her spiritual growth.

The thatched-roof huts grew closer. The village looked typical, nothing out of the ordinary. Children rushed to meet them, and curious adults stopped their work, no doubt recognizing Larson's truck. The Sudanese called it "medicine wheels."

Ben pulled the vehicle to a stop. "I'll check with Quadir and be right back."

"I'd like to go with you." Paul's words were firm. Larson wondered how he and Ben had kept from killing each other when they journeyed to Khartoum. Each one wanted to be in charge.

"No. Quadir is suspicious of strangers. I'll explain to him why you're with me. Be ready in case he refuses."

After Ben disappeared, Larson and Paul stepped from the truck and stretched. Nyok climbed over the back. The rainy season had left the ground soggy and the plants a brilliant shade of green.

"I hate waiting." Larson paced the length of the truck. "I've prayed until there isn't another word inside me."

Paul stared at the direction in which Ben had disappeared. "I'm trying to imagine how he feels. This must be killing him."

Larson studied the path Ben had taken. "He's a lonely man. Despite his combative personality, he has a heart for those things that count."

"I've seen his heart," Nyok said. "When I was with the soldiers, he acted like a father to me."

"You can't blame the colonel for the things he does," Paul said. "His every action stems from his commitment to the south. I admit that at times I've found it hard to forgive him, but that's been when my pride stepped in the way. None of us would want his responsibilities."

"You're right," Larson whispered. She wrapped her arms around Nyok's waist. "He sets out to do what is right, even if his methods are not always the best."

The colonel headed their way. A short Arab walked with him. How surprising that a villager hadn't slit the slave trader's throat. Larson braced herself. She studied Ben's face as he approached, looking for anger, grief, anything.

"You can go," Ben said. "We have about a kilometer walk."

"You have no weapons?" the man asked.

"Quadir, I told you these people have no need to bring guns. They are merely concerned for the girl's welfare."

Quadir stepped toward Paul. "You are a peculiar one." He patted Paul's pockets and down the side of his pants. "If any of you show any signs of hostility, the deal is off. Agreed?"

Larson nodded, as well as the others. Without another word they followed Ben and Quadir beyond the outskirts of the village through a narrow path among the tall grass. Larson's heart thumped against her chest. Her stomach churned, and her fingertips tingled.

*Lord, she has to be all right. I beg of You, let her be all right.*

Paul didn't trust the slave trader any farther than he could throw him, and he didn't think Ben did either. Something about the greasy-looking man reeked of deceit. Paul remembered Ben referring to him as a jackal—the term fit the man.

The grass cleared. In the distance a large baobab tree, with branches that sprouted upward like roots, seemed to touch the sky. Some tribes used the wide trunks of the trees as jails or pens for animals. An eerie sensation spiraled up Paul's spine. Why, he didn't know. God had answered their prayers for Rachel's return. Paul had no need to fear, but apprehension still needled him.

"There." Quadir pointed. "We will make the exchange near the tree."

Paul studied the area, as he well realized Ben did the same. The tall, thick grass could serve as a perfect hiding spot for the GOS. The tree was wide enough to conceal at least a half-dozen more.

Within ten feet of the tree, Quadir held out his hand to stop the small party. "Bring the girl," he called.

From behind the tree, three Arab men emerged with Rachel. She looked thinner, but Paul couldn't tell anything else. Rachel wasn't close enough to reveal her eyes, for in them would lie the truth—and the pain.

"Is this the young woman you're looking for?" Quadir asked as though he addressed thousands of people.

Ben clenched his fists. Not a muscle moved. "Yes." His reply echoed around them.

"Now that you've seen her, do you have the dinars?"

Ben held out one hand and reached inside his pants pocket with the other. He pulled out the redemption price.

Quadir motioned to the men behind him, and one gave Rachel a slight shove. She walked up alongside Quadir. Not a trace of emotion crossed her lovely face. "Do you know this man?"

Rachel lifted her chin. "He is my brother."

Paul caught his breath.

"And what is your brother's name?"

"Colonel Ben Alier of the SPLA." Rachel glared at her brother.

Paul heard Larson gasp behind him, but he dared not move.

Quadir grinned. "Speak louder, please."

"Colonel Ben Alier of the SPLA."

"What is this?" Ben started to reach inside his shirt just as Quadir whipped out a pistol.

"I would not advise that, Colonel."

From behind the baobab tree, five GOS soldiers stepped forward, their rifles ready.

Quadir laughed. "I did not believe you when you gave me your name before, but the truth is here." He pointed to Rachel. "Whom do you serve?"

Rachel stiffened. "Allah. There is no god but Allah."

"Rachel!" Fury flew from Ben's mouth. "What have you done to my sister?"

"Nothing that she didn't choose for herself," Quadir said. "My sources told me she willingly embraced Islam and offered to betray her brother."

"Is this true, Rachel?"

"My name is no longer Rachel, it is—"

"I don't want to hear it."

A soldier waved a gun in Ben's face. "I have an order to execute you, Colonel." He spat the title as though it sickened him to say it. "Although, we thought you'd be a fool to fall for this. You're getting old." He waved the gun at Paul and the others. "None of you will live to see another day. Move up beside the colonel."

Nyok moved to Ben's left while Larson and Paul stood at his right. Paul could see Rachel clearly. She moistened her lips. Did he see regret? Did she remember the love Ben, Larson, and Nyok held for her? More important, did she remember what Jesus had done for her on the cross?

Paul stepped forward. "I believe your men would rather have me than the colonel."

"Why? Who are you?"

"I'm Abdullah Farid, the eldest son of President Farid."

"You lie," the soldier replied. "I'm smarter than that."

"I have no reason to lie. Contact Khartoum. They will tell you the truth."

"Shut up. You're wasting our time," the soldier said.

"Let the others go," Ben said. "It's me you want."

The soldier laughed and raised his rifle.

Rachel screamed, "No, don't shoot!"

Paul watched Rachel break from Quadir's side. She stepped between the soldier and her brother. Paul threw himself into Ben and Rachel's path, knocking them both to the muddy ground and protecting Rachel's slender body. Rifle fire split the air. Paul heard Larson scream, and more shots whizzed around him. He realized that mere seconds more and one of the bullets would find him.

*Jesus, take us home with You. I pray for Sudan and all of its people.*

Silence.

*What had happened?* Rachel lay beneath him quivering, sobbing. He couldn't tell whether the colonel still lived. *What of Larson and Nyok?*

"It's all right, Farid," Ben said. "The GOS soldiers are dead and so is Quadir."

Paul turned to look around him. Several SPLA surrounded the area. Larson slowly rose to her feet along with Nyok. Paul rolled from Rachel, her tears soaking his shirt.

"Ben, I'm so sorry. I don't know what came over me. I thought my faith was strong until they did things …" She buried her face in her hands. "Please, forgive me. I'm so weak. I thought I could endure the torture, but I gave in. It wasn't until I saw you and Larson and Nyok that I realized how wrong I'd been. I'm so sorry. I should have died for Jesus."

Ben knelt by Rachel's side and gathered her into his arms. He held her like a small child, rocking her, kissing away the tears.

"It's all right now. You're safe. I'm here with you."

Paul saw that Larson was crumbling. He pulled her to him. "It's all over," he said to her. "Rachel is back, and she's unharmed."

"I know. I just never expected—"

"It doesn't matter."

"You're right." She swallowed hard and leaned her head on his chest.

Ben peered up at Paul. "Thank you. I owe you for this. I've been wrong." He paused. "I'd be honored if you'd call me friend."

With Ben's arms wrapped around Rachel, Paul grasped the colonel's shoulder. "Friend it is."

Ben nodded and smiled, a rarity for the big man. "As my friend, I'm entrusting you to help me get Rachel and Nyok out of Sudan until the country is safe."

"I can do that," Paul said. For a moment he thought the big man would break down.

"Larson," Ben began, "would you allow my new friend to take care of you too?"

Paul whipped his gaze to her, hoping and wondering if she felt any of the magnitude of feelings that he held for her.

"I wonder if he could use my help." Her voice trembled.

In her eyes, Paul saw the light of love. He reached for her hand and squeezed it lightly. "I think we'd make a great team, as long as she is willing to stay in Sudan."

"For as long as it takes."

# Author's Note

As of the writing of this book, the southern Sudanese have been ravaged by civil war for two decades. An estimated two million people have been killed and four to five million more displaced from their homes. The people are in desperate need of food, medical provisions, proper education, and the tools necessary to help them rebuild their lives. They also need prayers and support. If you would like to contribute time or money to assist these people, please contact:

Aid Sudan Foundation
Frank Blackwood
P.O. Box 924176
Houston, TX 77292-4176
www.aidsudan.org

South Sudanese Friends, Intl. Inc. (SSFI)
Isabel Hogue
P.O. Box 8582
Bloomington, IN 47407-8582
www.southsudanfriends.org

World Vision International
800 West Chestnut Avenue
Monrovia, CA 91016-3198
www.wvi.org

International Mission Board
Southern Baptist Convention
P.O. Box 6767
Richmond, VA 23230-0767
www.imb.org

May God bless you,
DiAnn Mills

# Readers' Guide

*For Personal Reflection
or Group Discussion*

# When the Lion Roars

The daily life experiences of the characters in *When the Lion Roars* are much different from those we face in the United States; yet the spiritual struggles Paul, Larson, Ben, Nyok, and Rachel experience are like those faced by people everywhere.

Each of us is called by God to serve Him in his own particular life circumstances, but some people feel called to enter the battle between good and evil in other countries or circumstances. Paul could have donated money to the Feed the World organization and let others do the actual work. Ben and his sister, Rachel, paid a heavy price for his assuming leadership in the SPLA. Larson could have served a short term of medical service in Sudan and then returned to a comfortable practice in the United States. Do you think the kind of passion the characters demonstrate on behalf of the situation in Sudan is acceptable to God? Is it expected by God?

Perhaps you have performed volunteer service for a local, national, or international organization that is meeting the needs of people. If you have volunteered, what did that feel like? Do you believe that people can make a difference? How about just one person—can one person make a difference?

Think about these questions not only in light of the story in *When the Lion Roars*, but also in terms of what you know is happening in the world around you. Does the story of these people, imaginary though they may be, give you a better understanding of the struggles going on in other places in the world? Is your faith strengthened by their individual acts of courage?

1. How do you feel about those from foreign countries entering your neighborhood?

2. Have you ever gone hungry, couldn't afford medical care, or were persecuted for your faith? What brought you through that experience?

3. How does the Bible address slavery?

4. How do you feel about slavery in today's world?

5. When does the Bible say it is correct not to follow the mandates of a government?

6. Do you feel wealth is a sin? The Bible states that it is easier for a camel to pass through the eye of a needle than for a rich man to enter heaven. Does this mean that the wealthy are destined to live apart from God?

7. If the apostle Paul were living today, what do you think he would recommend about the situation in Sudan?

8. Who did you feel was responsible for Rachel's abduction? Why?

9. Do you ever feel war is justified? Under what circumstances?

10. What does the Bible say about selecting friends?

11. When Nyok fought the lion, a miraculous experience occurred. He gave the credit to God. How do you explain it? Why?

12. Think about Nyok's experience when enemy soldiers killed his family. What would you say to him regarding hope?

13. The Sudanese people refused to renounce their Christian faith in favor of Islam as mandated by their country's government. Is your faith this strong? Are you willing to die for Jesus Christ?

14. The SPLA is the Sudanese People's Liberation Army, the rebel movement fighting for the rights of the southern Sudanese. For Ben, Larson, Paul, and Nyok, the rebel army represented different principles according to their personal beliefs. What do you think God would say about the SPLA? How does John 3:16 affect how you consider this question?

15. Paul had a driving need to find Abraham. Why do you think it was important?

16. Paul denied his earthly heritage and claimed his new birth in Christ. What about the crimes he'd committed against people in the name of Allah? Must Paul spend the rest of his life doing good works and risking his life in order to prove his love for Christ?

17. When Hank died, Paul blamed himself. In looking at Paul's past, that is understandable. What does God say about the past?

18. Ben worked with Arab slave traders in an effort to recover Rachel. He found it difficult to pray for his sister's safe return. Why do you think he couldn't bring himself to ask for God's help?

19. Paul stopped at Kakuma, Kenya to view the refugee camp for so many displaced Africans. God has specific things for us to do in regard to the poor and needy. What are they?

20. What part do you think education plays in the future of third-world countries?

21. Ben had strong feelings for Larson. Considering their spirituality and temperaments, do you think a marriage between the two would have worked for good?

22. Why do you think Larson allowed the past to comfort her at some times and condemn her at other times?

23. Bishop Malou said to Paul, "He who began a good work in you will carry it on to completion until the day of Christ Jesus." What was the bishop referring to?

24. While in Khartoum, Paul and Ben shared danger. The issue separating the two was trust. What does God say about trusting man? What does God say about trusting Him?

25. What do you think was the biggest reason why Paul didn't want Larson to know the truth about him?

26. The bombing at the Red Cross center led to Nyok joining the SPLA. Did this particular incident move the boy to take up arms, or was he motivated by something else?

27. Larson blamed God for the suffering Sudanese. Who do you blame? Why?

28. Paul offered himself as a sacrifice when it looked as though Ben would be hurt. What was Ben's reason for saving the man's life? What does the Bible say about this matter?